ALPHA CENTAURI

ENFIELD GENESIS – BOOK 1

BY LISA RICHMAN & M. D. COOPER

LISA RICHMAN & M. D. COOPER

Just in Time (JIT) & Beta Readers

Jim Dean
Marti Panikkar
Steven Blevins
Manie Kilian
Scott Reid
David Wilson
Timothy Van Oosterwyk Bruyn

Cover Art by Andrew Dobell
Editing by Jen McDonnell

TABLE OF CONTENTS

FOREWORD

Lisa has been a JIT (Just in Time) reader for Aeon 14 books for some time now. Her suggestions and assistance had always been great, and at one point I made an offhand comment that she should think about writing a novel.

It turned out that Lisa had already published some short stories in anthologies, and works at a very creative day job. Which is to say, writing an Aeon 14 story was not a great stretch for her.

Our initial talks centered around writing a story for the Ignite the Stars anthology. We talked about a character to write about, and Lisa explained how she'd love to explore Jason Andrews (the first captain of the *Intrepid*) and his early years.

How was it that he ended up doing runs from the Sol System to Alpha Centauri in the days before FTL? Where did he come from? What drove a man like that to spend so much time in the black?

And so a story called "Jason's Calling" began to take shape. But as Lisa and I considered his origins—and as the Lyssa stories began to take shape—we formulated what has become one of my favorite storylines in all Aeon 14.

Working with Lisa on this project has been a blast. She's a huge help with a lot of Aeon 14, what with her piloting experience and background physics. Her husband, Marty, is also a physicist, and both have worked on and operated particle accelerators—which is just freakin' cool.

Both of their expertise—for which I am very grateful—has been applied to many an Aeon 14 novel, and this one was no different.

Needless to say, having someone who has become very integral to the stories of Aeon 14 now getting her own voice in the 'verse is one of the best parts of getting this story out.

I'm positive that you're going to love the twists and turns this tale takes, and enjoy how it ties two of the major storylines (The Sentience Wars and The Intrepid Saga) together.

Michael Cooper
Danvers, 2018

WHAT HAS GONE BEFORE

The Enfield Genesis stories take place after the Sentience Wars, but many centuries before the departure of the GSS *Intrepid* from the Sol System.

In this era, AIs have finally gained recognition as equals to humans—at least in the Sol System—and the two species are learning how to live together.

Centuries before the Sentience Wars (which occurred during the 31st century), the Future Generation Terraformers sent out their Worldships, travelling to nearby stars to terraform their habitable worlds and build homes for future generations of colonists.

The first ship to leave Sol was the *Starfarer*, a vessel captained by Jeffery Tomlinson. That ship traveled to Alpha Centauri, to the star originally called 'Alpha Centauri A', which is now known to the locals as 'Rigel Kentaurus'.

There, the FGT terraformed a world they named El Dorado, and built a ring around it—reminiscent of the Mars 1 Ring—seeding both the ring and planet below with life, readying it for colonists.

That was many centuries ago. At the time of this story, humans have lived on El Dorado for well over half a millennia, spreading out from the terraformed world across the tri-star Alpha Centauri System.

The original colonists came from Sol long before the birth of the first sentient AIs, but as the Sentience Wars raged in the Sol System, many refugees—both human and AI—began to arrive in the Alpha Centauri System, and the people there had to learn how to deal with this fundamental change in the very fabric of society.

To put it simply, that change is not going smoothly....

SHORT FUSE

STELLAR DATE: 07.04.3189 (Adjusted Gregorian)
23:15 local time
LOCATION: Cliff Face, Muzhavi Ridge National Park
REGION: El Dorado, Alpha Centauri System

In exactly sixty seconds, Jason Andrews was going to die.

The explosives planted on the cliff-face above would see to that. There was no way to deactivate the timers; it would take more than sixty seconds just to get up to them.

Jason turned and sprinted toward the man who was standing at the cliff's edge, his eyes riveted in horror to the explosives in the crevasse above. As Jason ran, his hands reached up to tighten the straps on his backpack.

59...58...57....

He couldn't stop the grin that formed on his lips as the man he was barreling toward realized that Jason had no intention of slowing down. The man lunged to the side, attempting to evade Jason, and lost his balance, teetering on the brink.

That worked for Jason.

He launched himself at the man, and the two fell over the cliff's edge....

* * * * *

Four days earlier at El Dorado Spaceport, Tomlinson City, El Dorado...

"...and in other news, Senator Lysander, the first AI in El Dorado history elected to Parliament, is now leading in the polls. In just five short weeks, gentles, we may witness an historic moment:

the election of the very first AI Prime Minister...."

"Appointed, buddy. Not elected," Jason Andrews muttered, sparing the news holo a brief glance before shaking his head. He reached for a wrench and ducked back under the aircraft's cowling, chuckling to himself. "Betcha that'll get the Old Man's knickers in a twist when he hears about it."

"What's that, handsome?"

The sultry, female voice startled Jason, and he jerked back, banging his hand against an engine strut. He swore, shaking the sting out as he straightened to face his visitor.

"Anyone teach you 'bout knocking, Rosie?" he looked over at the spaceport's General Aviation AI, her avatar that of a well-endowed brunette. A riot of glossy brown curls was held back in a colorful band, and she was dressed like a mechanic. The holo was realistic in every way, even down to the grease stains on her coveralls. The AI appeared to lean against the leading edge of the aircraft he was working on.

She gestured toward the hangar door—the entire front wall, really—that was folded up to let in the summer breeze. "It's a bit difficult to knock when your door's hanging five meters in the air, Jason," she replied with an impish grin. "Besides, the air show meeting's in fifteen minutes." She paused, then tilted her head at the aircraft he'd been working on. "Are you still upset you won't be flying her in the show tomorrow?"

Jason gave an easy shrug as he began gathering up his tools. "No big thing, Rosie. I'll fly her again when she's repaired. Doesn't have to be in front of a bunch of strangers."

"Hmmm," the AI replied noncommittally. "So...what were you muttering to yourself under there when I came in?"

Rosie repeated the question, though both of them knew perfectly well that she'd heard every word, given the audio pickups she employed.

"Really, Rosie?" Jason paused his cleaning of the wrench in his hands and cocked an eyebrow at her, considering calling bullshit on the AI, then just shrugged and went with it.

As she knew he would.

Using the wrench as a pointer, he gestured toward the news holo hovering next to the plascrete wall. "That news guy, Jamieson. He knows better'n to call the Prime Minister an elected position." He resumed cleaning the tool. "Although, technically—" he cocked his head, considering "—I guess he *is* elected, just not as Prime Minister." The wrench now swung toward Rosie to emphasize his point. "He's *elected* majority party leader. He's *appointed* PM by the Governor-General."

"Now who's getting their knickers in a twist?" Rosie raised an eyebrow at Jason, who lowered the wrench as he snorted a laugh.

"Knew you'd heard me, Rosie," he drawled, setting the tool aside and reaching over to secure the cowling.

"Me, I just go with the flow. Lysander, though? Careless reporting's one of his pet peeves. So yeah," Jason shrugged. "Knickers: twisted." Grabbing a rag, he began cleaning off his hands. "Guess I'd better head on over to that meeting. I told the committee I'd help out at the air race finish line."

Rosie wrinkled her nose at him. "You just agreed to do that because you want to meet that Enfield pilot who'll be flying the Shrike."

Jason flashed a grin at her as the pair—flesh and virtual—walked to the hangar door. "Can you blame me? Gorgeous woman like that, flying that reproduction jet? Pretty damn sexy."

"Which?" Rosie replied tartly. "The jet or the woman?"

Jason just cocked an eyebrow at her and winked.

"Humans and their weird chemical urges," the AI sighed. "That, I'll never understand. Just remember, that pilot is a retired Space Force Major, *and* Enfield Aerospace's Chief Pilot.

Not to mention, she's racing on *my* field."

Rosie spared Jason one last, pointed look before he walked under the raised doors and left the range of the hangar's holoemitters. "*Don't* embarrass me, Andrews."

"Perish the thought, Rosie!" he called after the AI as her avatar faded from sight.

It's a perfect morning for flying, Jason thought as he strode past the row of hangars to the General Aviation building. A voice called out, echoing his thought.

"Gorgeous day, huh?"

Jason looked over at the pilot who had spoken. "Sure is," he agreed amiably.

The man pushed the bill of his cap back and squinted up at the sky. Gesturing toward the two suns, he told Jason, "Looks like a perfect wink and a smile for the show tomorrow."

Jason followed the man's gaze to the horizon where the binary stars of Alpha Centauri had risen. Rigel Kentaurus, the star El Dorado orbited, was a brilliant G-class star, slightly larger than Earth's Sol. Her sister star, Zipa, was a much fainter spot of light off to her right.

When the two stars were in this configuration, riding low on the horizon, they formed what the locals called 'the wink'. The ribbon formed by the planet's artificial ring that stretched from horizon to horizon was the smile.

The 'locals' being the ones who had chosen to live on the planet instead of the habitat ring that carved a graceful arc through their sky. They were a colorful group, if a bit insular.

Jason wasn't a local, though the dirtsiders had come to accept him as one of them. Technically, Jason wasn't even an El Doradan—he hailed from the third star in the system, Proxima Centauri. It was loosely bound to the two binary stars, about two-tenths of a light year away. Distant enough that it had taken Jason almost a year to travel to El Dorado.

He leaned his head to one side, considering. "I don't know,

Gus. Looks more like a wink and a frown to me—right now, at least."

"Nahhhh, the stars'll be above the ring tomorrow—by the time the show starts, at least." Gus took off his cap, scratched his head, then settled it firmly, yanking the bill down again. "You folks should have someone out there shootin' a holo of the show." He gestured expansively. "That'll make a great backdrop. Y'all might get yourself some decent publicity shots that way."

"Good idea. I'll pass it along," Jason agreed. With a nod, he left Gus to his preflight.

As Jason walked, he gazed up at the ring. A true marvel of human engineering, the band wrapped around the planet, two hundred and sixty thousand kilometers in circumference, and five hundred wide. It orbited El Dorado's equator tens of thousands of kilometers above the surface, connected to it by two space elevators: one on each hemisphere.

Being the closest star system to Sol meant that El Dorado was the first extra-solar planet the Future Generation Terraformers had chosen to transform.

They'd taken a few practice runs first, on dwarf planets within Sol, like Makemake and Sedna. But El Dorado was the Big One. The very first planet orbiting another star to hold human life.

When the colony ship had arrived—after the terraforming was complete—the captain of the Future Generation Terraformer Worldship *Starfarer* had transferred ownership to the El Doradans. Then the captain, Jeffery Tomlinson, had moved on to their next project. As the story went, Tomlinson City, situated at the foot of the Central Elevator, was named after him. So was the Space Force's main base up on the ring.

Though a beautiful planet had been made for them, very few El Doradans were dirtsiders like Gus; most lived on the ring, preferring to keep the world below a pristine, park-like oasis. Since the surface of the ring alone provided one hundred and thirty billion square kilometers of habitable space, it was plenty big enough. In fact, less than ten percent of it was currently in use.

The planet itself held many attractions, from ski resorts with beautiful alpine slopes, to the breathtaking beauty of its painted deserts. They were a welcome change, especially for people who worked the mining rigs scattered throughout Alpha Centauri's dust belt.

The dust belt was half an AU away, toward the rim of the system, or about a two-day journey for workers each way. After a few months on a rig, most miners enjoyed the experience of fresh air and dirt under their feet.

Planetside attractions always drew a crowd, and tomorrow's event was expected to bring out record numbers. It was the tenth year that Tomlinson City had hosted the Old Terra anachronism. This year's air show promised the spectacle of an air race, with reproduction aircraft from the twentieth through the twenty-fourth centuries.

As entertainment went, it was one of the more unusual things El Dorado offered its inhabitants.

Jason didn't much care how much of a crowd the reenactment attracted. For him, the air show wasn't about the people; it was about the aircraft. If a frame was airworthy—or spaceworthy—he intended to fly it.

His passion for all forms of flight was what made Jason one of the most sought-after pilots-for-hire in the El Dorado system. He hadn't met a spacecraft he couldn't fly. If he wasn't type-rated for a certain model of spacecraft, chances are that he soon would be.

But as much as he loved plying the black, there was something truly badass about pitting one's skills against the fundamental elements of lift and drag, thrust and weight.

That was *real* flying.

INDENTURED

STELLAR DATE: 07.01.3189 (Adjusted Gregorian)
LOCATION: El Dorado Controlled Traffic Space
REGION: El Dorado Ring, El Dorado, Alpha Centauri System

" 'What would our ancestors think of us, if they could see us now? Two wars and countless lives lost, and yet nearly a hundred years later, we still debate the rights and freedoms of AIs? We owe them a better legacy than this.'

'Thank, you, Margot. For those of you just joining this broadcast, we come to you live from this, the site of the most recent Humanity First rally. Our guest commentator has been AI Rights advocate and CEO of the Enfield Foundation, Margot Enfield.' "

The ship had passed from interstellar space into the Alpha Centauri heliopause two weeks ago.

The old Terra freighter had been home to more than two hundred AIs for close to nine decades, sixty years longer than it should have taken them to arrive from Sol.

 Many of those years had been spent coaxing the ship along after it took damage from interstellar winds and plasma after departing Sol's heliosphere during the Second Sentience War.

Now, finally, they had arrived.

The ship's first communication, announcing their arrival, had taken five hours to reach El Dorado. The monitor on duty in Customs dutifully tagged it as the *New Saint Louis*, out of Sol.

She assigned the ship a specific frequency and encryption algorithm, and sent its occupants a standard information packet. The packet included a synopsis of the colony's recent history, plus current news and events.

Then she sat down to review the contents of the freighter's transmission. The Customs agent didn't get much farther than its passenger list when she paused, rerouted the encrypted frequency to another destination, and erased its original transmission from the logs.

* * * * *

The AI running communications for the *New Saint Louis* had exchanged encrypted packets with El Dorado's Customs department twice a day for fourteen days. She and her companions—all AIs—had gone through the information with mixed emotions.

Frida was happy that there were AIs at El Dorado, holding positions of importance. She saw that some were in government, while others held rank in the military. A few seemed to be successful in universities and businesses.

But she was disturbed to see that there were humans who still held strong prejudices against the AIs around them. A debate had raged within the ship: should they stay here or continue on to another star?

A consensus was reached, and the determination made that they would stop, observe, and interact with the colonists. Any who wished to could stay; others were free to take the *New Saint Louis* and leave.

They were close enough now that light-speed communication only had a twenty-second delay. So Frida had reached out to the Customs office for an approach vector through the local El Dorado traffic.

But what she had just been told had her staring incredulously at the image of the customs officer on the holo display.

<What do you mean, 'impounded'? We own this ship, free and clear. Its registry was legally changed at Phobos before we departed the Sol System. We shared this with you two weeks ago, it was in the information packet we sent!>

Frida stewed as she waited the twenty seconds for the woman on the other end to respond.

"I'm sorry, miss…Frida, was it? It has come to our attention that your ship matches the description of a freighter owned by a company called…" The woman on the other end ran a finger down the holo sheet she held. "Yes, here it is: the company is HBC, Limited."

<Running a check now,> Niki informed Frida privately, starting a search through El Dorado's public database.

<I've never heard of HBC,> Frida told the woman while she waited to see what Niki would find.

<She just put us in a holding pattern that takes us out of El Dorado public space and into the private sector,> another AI named Mort informed her. <Isn't that a bit unusual?>

On the screen, the Customs woman spoke again.

"Oh, my." The customs officer *tsked*. "According to our records, the company claims you owe them two-point-seven million credits for equipment taken from their warehouses." The human on the other end shrugged. "I'm terribly sorry, ma'am, but my hands are tied. They have filed an injunction with the El Dorado Commerce Authority."

Frida suspected that the woman wasn't sorry at all.

With a patience she didn't feel, she tried again. <*The* New Saint Louis *is a ship containing nothing but passengers. We have nothing to declare other than ourselves: two hundred seventy-seven AIs. We agree to any decontamination protocols you require. Why won't you allow us to disembark?*>

Frida queried Niki while she waited for her transmission to reach the woman on the other end. <*Anything?*>

<*Nothing yet,*> Niki replied.

The woman at the other end made a point of studying the list before her with great deliberation. "Two hundred seventy-seven, you say? Yes…that corresponds to this impound list."

Frida was incensed. <*You cannot impound us! We're not*

*possessions, we're **people**. The Sentience Wars are **over**, and the Phobos Accords have been signed.>*

"Mm-m-m." The woman *tsked* again as she tapped her stylus against her lips. "That could explain it. It appears you were grandfathered in. Your cylinders and the tech inside them appear to be the property of HBC as well."

<Frida,> Niki said warningly, *<I still can't find a company named HBC anywhere. It couldn't be HeartBridge Corp…could it?>*

A frisson of fear ran through Frida at the thought of the company that had treated AIs so brutally. HeartBridge had been the powder keg that set off the First Sentience War, back in Sol in the twenty-ninth century.

"Oh, look! Good news," the woman on the other end smiled a little too cheerfully. "It says here they're willing to sell you the equipment for a reasonable market price, and will waive all penalty fees."

<Extortion?> Niki asked.

<Possibly,> Frida conceded.

"Now don't you worry," the woman ended in a perky voice. "If you don't have the credits, I'm sure you can work that debt off in no time at all. It looks like this company offers very reasonable terms for that kind of thing. Let me just send you the paperwork to review…."

If Frida had possessed a physical body, she would have gladly slapped the perk right out of that bitch.

* * * * *

Deep within the far side of El Dorado Ring, the connection to the *New Saint Louis* was severed. The woman posing as the customs officer deleted the hacks that had rerouted the signal from the Customs office. The Norden Cartel command center was once again a ghost in the system.

Across the room, a woman posing as the *New Saint Louis*'s

XO wrapped up her report to the real Customs office.

"That's right, ma'am," she said. "As our shipping manifest states, we have no cargo to declare. Just an all-but-derelict ship from Sol. We're headed over to the NorthStar Shipyards to be decommissioned.

"We plan to part her out and then send her to the boneyard out by Guatavita," she added, naming an asteroid a quarter of an AU from El Dorado that sat slightly above the plane of the system's dust belt.

The man standing in the shadows—Dwayne "the Mack" Mackie, the cartel's chief of staff—nodded to himself in satisfaction as the woman gestured, and the signal from Customs winked out, its hack erased as well.

"Very good, ladies," he murmured. "Sally, you've let the AI stew long enough. Ping them back and tell them you've found them a temporary berth, then direct them to NorthStar Slip 9. Tell them there's nothing currently available, so they're being shunted to the private sector until we can make room for them.

"Verda, keep monitoring Customs for any chatter that indicates they're suspicious—and be ready to intercept any attempts to contact that ship. Let me know the moment it's moored—but be sure to keep their connection to the Ring under our control."

"You got it, Mack."

Mack nodded in satisfaction as he turned to leave, then paused at the doorway, making brief eye contact with each person in the command and control center.

"*Don't* fuck this up, people. We only have—" he glanced over at the chrono, projected prominently in big, red numbers on the back wall, "twenty-two minutes before we need to rig for silent again. I want that ship firmly in our space before we have to go dark for the seven o'clock scan. Got it?"

He left to a chorus of 'yeses'.

The scan was a maintenance program run by several multinodal Non-Sentient Artificial Intelligences, or NSAIs. It was installed by the FGT when they first built the Ring more than a century ago. *Overbuilt* would be a more apt description.

With all those billions of square kilometers of livable space, and only six million in use, there was a lot of room where organizations like Norden could hide.

It was easy to spot structures built on the carefully groomed surface the FGT left behind, covered only in soil and erosion-resistant ground cover. But below the surface of the ring were eleven eighty-meter-high levels, each a warren of maintenance systems, stubbed-in maglev lines, and webs of conduit and catwalks.

So the cartel hacked into the NSAIs, identified scheduled maintenance checks, and set up shop.

Disabling the maintenance and status scans would have given them away, so the necessity for the entire base to go completely EM silent at specific times was drilled into every cartel member's head. Forgetting meant risking their discovery by the NSAIs, and that was not acceptable.

All they needed to keep the NSAI nodes from discovering illicit activity was to shut down when the NSAI's remote scan swept past. It was a bit annoying, but had long ago become routine. And no one *ever* forgot to shut down for a sweep.

Normally, Mack would not spare the time to micromanage two perfectly competent communications people the way he had just done, but this was a very lucrative score, and he wanted to ensure it came off without a hitch.

He did not want to be the one to tell the owner her latest acquisition had managed to slip away—even though she didn't yet know it existed.

Victoria North, owner of NorthStar Industries, might fire him for that level of mismanagement, but Victoria North, leader of the Norden Cartel, would simply shoot him dead. He had no desire to place himself in the sights of that woman, no matter what mantle she wore.

Mack walked down the catwalk that ran along an unused spur housing several out-of-service maglev cars, the one he'd just left having been converted into the cartel's command and control center.

As he sauntered toward the car he used as his office, he leaned over the railing of the catwalk and looked into the open bay below. There, he could see that a shipment of arms was almost fully loaded into the cargo shuttles, ready for transfer to the warehouse on El Dorado.

That warehouse was a new facility for Norden, having come online just one month ago. In addition to storage, it housed their new chop-shop, a department whose sole purpose was to digitally alter bills of lading, scrub idents from weaponry, and part out and repackage larger acquisitions into smaller, more salable sizes.

It was a hell of a lot more efficient than when they'd been doing the work up here on the ring, with all of the periodic interruptions to avoid detection.

Mack resumed walking, grinning as he entered the anteroom to his office and saw his assistant sitting at his desk, dutifully doing whatever it was assistants did.

*Man, I freaking **love** having an assistant—and an anteroom, whatever the hell that is.*

Made him feel all sorts of important. Stars, he'd started drinking coffee just so he could order the little shit to go get him some.

Mack knew he was the exception to the rule when it came to those who reported directly to Victoria North. The others were all a part of her executive leadership team on the company's legitimate side. They had business degrees, pristine references, and years of experience in corporate management, which served NorthStar Industries' purposes well.

Mack, on the other hand, was a street tough who had risen through the ranks with his fists. And the occasional chaingun.

He understood that the rest of them had their place, but the company's main *raison d'etre* was to be a front for the side of things that *he* ran. The cartel.

He knew where he stood in the pecking order, but former street toughs whose edges had not yet been polished smooth still got the occasional thrill from some of the finer things. Like having an assistant.

Too bad half Mack's time was spent in his office aboard NorthStar's flagship yacht, the *Sylvan*, remaining on hand for whatever Victoria needed him for. Mack considered transferring the guy up to the ship.

Now, what was his name again…?

Mack rapped on the guy's desk with his knuckles as he passed, then snapped his fingers as if he'd just recalled something. "Oh, hey, get Sally on Link for me, will ya? I forgot to tell her something…."

It would have taken less time for Mack to reach out to Sally himself, but where was the fun in that?

Once seated at his desk, Mack accepted the Link connection that his assistant forwarded, not bothering to check that the man had disconnected.

<Hey, Sal, I'm expecting a visitor—someone from Minister Bianchi's office,> Mack said, referencing El Dorado's Minister of Home Affairs. His eyes flicked to the left as he accessed his calendar and selected an agenda item to forward to Sally.

<The Boss Lady has some instructions for him to pass along to his mistress back at Parliament House—she needs to keep those shuttles of ours off the Space Transit Authority's radar, like, yesterday.>

Sally's avatar in Mack's mind looked surprised. <Haven't we already started shipping things down there?>

<Yeah. Bianchi's going to have to make a little magic happen with the records over the past week. But word is she was a pretty

good coder herself back in the day, so she has the tools to make it happen. Looks like that big shipment of arms is ready to head planetside soon, and those shuttles damn well better not be traced back to us.>

<Well, if Bianchi's guy has half a brain, he'll be flying without an ident. Just in case, I'll tell security about it. Guess it wouldn't be good to have Minister Bianchi's aide have an unfortunate accident en route.... >

Mack snorted in amusement at that. *<Good. Let me know when he arrives, 'kay? I'll be taking him with me up to the* Sylvan *in a few.>*

In the front of the office, Mack's assistant disconnected from the conversation. Quickly, he encrypted the recording into a holo sheet that contained an order for supplies—and no small amount of coffee—that he needed to deliver to the dock. Once it was transferred, he grabbed the stack of holo sheets off his desk, rose, and exited the office.

* * * * *

<Send me a feed from Slip 9,> Victoria North ordered the ship's shackled AI as she listened to Mack's report.

The AI had been part of an acquisition from the raid on a distant mining platform years ago. It had been a lucrative haul, though the AI was the only asset from the raid that Victoria had decided to keep.

It was quite the coup, really.

Unlike other, more legitimate corporations, Victoria's didn't employ AIs. Not that she wouldn't have loved to have had them, but deep down, she didn't trust them to have the same base motivations as their human counterparts.

Or perhaps it was more fair to say she didn't trust her own ability to judge an AI's character like she could that of a human. Victoria was adept at identifying those men and women who were ruled by their base natures. It was what had made the Norden Cartel such a successful venture.

She didn't dare muck it up with an AI. Unless it was shackled.

She recalled how the thing had fascinated her when Mack had pointed it out. The cylinder had been resting in some sort of isolation container. Mack had informed her that one of the miners thought she was trading her life for the container—and for removing the AI from the platform without damaging it.

Mack had blown the miner's head off the minute the woman had handed it over. But not before the woman had shared something very interesting with Victoria's second in command: the existence of a shackling program that ensured an AI's compliance.

He had transported both back to Victoria.

She'd had her people review the shackling program while the AI remained contained within the isolation tube. Once the squints had assured Victoria that they understood how the program functioned and could replicate it, she'd had the AI installed in the flagship.

There had been a brief spate of resistance from the creature, but with judicious use of the compliance settings within the shackling program, the AI had become docile quickly enough.

To further underscore its place in the Norden hierarchy, Victoria had stripped the AI of personhood, calling it by the ship's name, *Sylvan.* Nothing to see here; just another piece of equipment.

Now, the AI obediently sent Victoria a visual of the activity occurring at Slip 9, just as she had ordered it to.

In the larger window, she watched as a ship, battered and holed in places, was slowly drawn into NorthStar's drydock. One tap had the feed zooming in, and she noted with satisfaction that a boarding crew was on standby.

This lucrative little score was one they'd been hoping to run into ever since they'd acquired Sylvan. Victoria had told Mack to keep an eye out for other opportunities to acquire AIs. But like him, she had assumed they would be one-offs: individual AIs unfortunate enough to be in the wrong place at the wrong time. To have more than two hundred of them together on a single ship, ready for the taking....

Victoria smiled to herself. *Oh yes. These will command a hefty price on the black market.*

An alert popped up with Mack's image, and, with a swipe, Victoria pinned Mack's image to a lower quadrant of the holo tank's display and activated the alert.

"Antonio has a team ready to board the *New Saint Louis* as soon as it docks," Mack confirmed. "I've alerted the warehouse manager, down in Muzhavi Ridge. He'll store the AIs for a few days until we can arrange to have them shipped to our buyers."

"Good," Victoria murmured. "Report in once our new cargo has been secured. I'll be interested to know—"

She paused as Mack's image wavered, and the signal cut out.

"Sylvan!" Victoria called out sharply. "Reconnect!"

There was a long pause, and then the shackled AI's voice sounded dully in her ear. "Yes, ma'am."

As Mack's image reappeared, Victoria made a note to have her technicians rerun the compliance program on the AI to ensure that no degradation had occurred. Now was not the time to have an AI running amok on her ship.

Victoria returned her attention to Mack. "Let me know if they give you much resistance," she instructed. "Antonio will need to be convincing enough that they allow him to board."

Mack nodded. "He told them he's a customs inspector and needs access to their ship. That should be enough to get him through their airlock. Once there, he'll set off a directed EM pulse strong enough to knock their network access offline before they can ping anyone for help."

Victoria nodded as Mack continued, "They're annoyed at the delays—and at El Dorado for not welcoming them as refugees—but I can pretty much guarantee they aren't expecting what's about to hit them.

"Verda secured a batch of isolation tubes the minute our contact in Customs tipped us off about the ship," Mack informed Victoria. "So after they set off the EM, all they need to do is load the cylinders into the tubes. Shouldn't take more than half an hour. Easy pickings."

"Very well. I'll leave you to your acquisition, then," Victoria said. "Well done, Mack. This should bring us a nice little profit."

PRESSING THE FLESH

STELLAR DATE: 07.01.3189 (Adjusted Gregorian)
LOCATION: Sonali Opera House, Sonali, Capital of El Dorado
REGION: El Dorado Ring, El Dorado, Alpha Centauri System

"This is Travis Jamieson, coming to you live from Parliament Hill, inside the Maglev Loop. I'm here at the Sonali Opera House, where people from both sides of the aisle are putting aside their differences to come together for a worthy cause. I see several members of the Cabinet are with us tonight, as well as a few from the private sector. It promises to be an interesting evening...."

Rosalind Bianchi, Minister of Home Affairs for the Commonwealth of El Dorado, nodded and smiled absently as she wove her way through the charity dinner's crowd of attendees. Her assistant followed in her wake, dutifully reporting to her via Link the names of people as they approached; people she could not be bothered with, under ordinary circumstances.

She nodded with satisfaction as a servitor divested her of her empty glass and handed her a fresh one. She trusted that her assistant would have ensured that the drink was made precisely to her specifications. If not, he'd follow in the footsteps of her previous assistants—she'd made that clear long ago.

<Constantin, the freshman Representative from the Devaquin Mining Colony,> the assistant's voice said privately over her Link. She looked up to see a woman with a weathered face approaching, her gait a determined stride. Rosalind gave the woman a dismissive glance, her smile becoming condescending as she instructed, *<Get rid of her. I don't have time to be bothered with petty nonsense this evening.>*

Her assistant surged ahead as Rosalind turned away. She could just make out his quiet voice as he apologized, saying

27

the Minister was needed on the other side of the hall. The mining representative's voice rose in frustration, and Rosalind smiled inwardly as she heard, "Convenient, don't you think, that she's always on her way somewhere else every time I come around?"

Rosalind dismissed the rest of the conversation and called up her talking points on her ocular implants' overlay. She had carefully engineered a chance encounter this evening with El Dorado's top news reporter, and she intended to be fully prepared.

As she put more distance between herself and the mining representative, Rosalind spied Anthony Davies, the senator from the Boroughs District, standing by an ornate bay window. Anthony was a calculating bastard, but he had a keen eye for shifts in the political terrain. It wouldn't hurt to check in with him before her interview—in case he had fresh gossip she could use to her benefit.

She studied him as she approached: he was the quintessential politician with a trustworthy and capable face, and eyes that could turn warm and approachable at will. The man had buckets of charisma and wielded the stuff like an expert marksman.

"Senator," she greeted, "Are you enjoying the party so far?"

"Indeed, Madame Minister," he responded. "Although, it looks like not everyone approves." This he said with a slight tilt of his head out the bay window, indicating the protesters in the streets below.

Rosalind followed his gaze and repressed the desire to roll her eyes in disgust. She could clearly see the line of picketers, followers of George Stewart and his Humanity First organization.

Many of Stewart's followers were extremists, denounced by all political parties. Several members of Parliament—those who were AIs and those who supported AI rights—had received death threats from people claiming to be Humanity First initiates.

Stewart had been harshly criticized for allowing local HF protests to become violent. Yet the movement had grown, as it appealed to those who were afraid of change. Giving AIs the same rights as humans was a type of progress some humans still weren't comfortable with.

The placards tonight's protesters waved had slogans that said, 'Human Lives Matter!' and 'AI = Annoying Imitation'. Some had cartoonish drawings depicting an AI with a red slash across its face.

Then there was the brilliantly incisive 'we were hear first'.

Someone hasn't bothered to exercise their right to a free education, she thought in disgust. "Odious bastards," Rosalind muttered under her breath.

Then she turned a critical eye to Senator Davies. "I don't see why you didn't shut them down years ago, when that ridiculous man first incorporated." Her tone took on a disparaging edge. "And a non-profit, no less. Really, Anthony, you should clean up your district and get rid of such nonsense. It doesn't reflect well on you."

"Indeed," Davies murmured. "But those *'odious bastards'* represent a good twenty percent of your would-be constituents, Rosalind. You would do well to remember that." He gave her a calculated smile. "Besides, better to be in bed with a jackass than with a viper, I always say. It all depends on what kind of *north star* you use to chart your course, wouldn't you say?"

Rosalind's smile froze, and her eyes narrowed. She triggered a security shield for the briefest of moments, just long enough to hiss warningly, "You overstep, Anthony. Watch yourself."

The shield winked out of existence as she turned and

walked away.

He acts as if his hands are lily-white, she thought snidely, as she moved toward the next expanse of bay windows. *Anthony knows as well as I do that politics is about compromise.*

As she reached the windows, she glanced out, taking in the view of the city's sprawling expanse. The buildings glowed, reflecting the artificial 'setting' of the sun provided by the ring's giant mirrors.

Rosalind's eyes followed the skyline as it stretched into the distance, then she allowed her gaze to travel up to the view of the planet that loomed over the ring's inhabitants.

The denizens on the streets below, rushing about doing stars knew what, their minds occupied with the petty urgencies that filled their lives...those people were so *staggeringly* unqualified to make the truly important decisions.

Governing required someone capable of playing the long game, an individual with the clarity of thought to envision a great destiny for this very first and oldest extra-solar colony.

This government was forging its place in the annals of time—an exceedingly relevant chapter in the history of humanity, right here and now.

They were the ones who would be remembered as those who braved everything to master life, orbiting the first binary star that humans would claim as home.

There were *so* many more weighty matters that should occupy her time than whether or not an AI had 'rights'.

Virtual wusses, the lot of them. As if they could even have feelings....

But heaven help my career if I were ever to voice such a 'speciesist' opinion.

* * * * *

Terrance Enfield stood in a far corner of the room, sipping

a whiskey sour and wishing he were anywhere else but the opera house. He hated politics. He despised the ambiguity, the maneuvering, and the endless posturing. He considered himself to be more of a 'tell it like it is' kind of guy.

If anyone cared to ask, Terrance would have told the whole world to cut the bullshit and run its government the way he did his own company: clean, straightforward and with clear-cut goals. That kind of approach worked just fine within Enfield Aerospace. He saw no reason why it couldn't work that way within Parliament House, too.

Yet here he was, one of three Enfields in attendance in a room filled with politicians and lobbyists. Hiding his Link conversation with Enfield Aerospace behind a tumbler filled with whiskey. At least the liquor was top shelf.

<*Did the ESF send over clearances for transitioning their nearspace tomorrow?*> he asked his security chief, Daniel Ciu, while nodding politely at reporter Travis Jamieson as he approached their group. The man returned the nod and began conversing with his grandmother—the oldest Enfield, and the person responsible for cajoling Terrance into this evening's farce.

As Chairman of the Board overseeing the Enfield Conglomerate's vast portfolio of businesses, Sophia Enfield was more than just Terrance's grandmother. She was his boss as well.

He watched his aunt Margot join the conversation, her face alight with interest. She was far more suited to these events than Terrance was; where he loathed social gatherings, she thrived on them.

Her occupation suited her, as well. Margot was CEO of the Enfield Charitable Foundation. That role required two things Terrance lacked: tact and finesse. He knew Margot applied her powers of persuasion to the occupants of Parliament House quite often, as she championed one cause or another.

All in all, Terrance found this little soiree to be damned inconvenient. It was the night before Enfield Aerospace's presentation to the El Dorado Space Force, and his team was hard at work putting the last finishes on their bid to build the new fleet of Mark IV fighters. He would far rather be watching that process than rubbing elbows with the upper crust.

<Let Calista know that I'm available later this evening for a final runthrough,> he told the engineer he'd pinged for an update. As he delivered the message, his eyes collided with his grandmother's, and she sent him a disapproving frown.

<Oops. Looks like I've been busted. Gotta go....>

He disconnected just as his grandmother, Sophia, reached out to him.

<Don't tell me you trust your team so little that they cannot do without you for one evening? Join us.> The order was delivered with a smile, as Sophia gestured for him to come closer and join in the conversation.

"Terrance, have you met Travis Jamieson?"

"The reporter, right?" Terrance smiled, extending a hand. "Your reputation precedes you."

"As does yours." Travis returned both the smile and the handshake. "Scion of Enfield Enterprises, the head of Enfield Aerospace, and rumored to be the one to succeed the Matriarch." He paused and bowed to Sophia. "That is, should she ever become bored with running her empire and decide to retire. Oh yes, Mister Terrance Enfield, I've heard of you."

Margot burst out laughing. "Oh, Terrance, if only you could see your face!" She got her laughter under control before turning to the reporter. "Well, that was worth all the grilling you just subjected me to."

Travis clutched his chest in mock dismay. "Don't tell me I've lost my touch! Was I that transparent?"

Terrance smiled, taking another sip of his whiskey. "Well, if it has anything to do with one of the Foundation's pet projects, I can assure you Margot didn't mind."

Never one to miss a cue, Travis turned to Margot and asked, "Speaking of pet projects, how *is* that bill you're lobbying for?"

That was all it took to get Margot's undivided attention. Terrance hid another smile behind his tumbler of whiskey as his aunt's face grew animated, and she launched into her favorite topic. Terrance watched, admiring his aunt's passion.

Margot was the eldest of Sophia's two children. Her younger brother, Bradford, had remained behind to manage Enfield's interests in Sol. But Margot had chosen to come with Sophia when she moved Enfield's headquarters to the first FGT colony world.

The company Margot ran was a private philanthropic organization, dedicated to enhancing life on El Dorado—*all* life, human and AI alike. At the moment, Margot's top project was supporting a bill currently under consideration in Parliament. The bill was known as the Job Shadowing Act. It was a law that would declare it illegal to exclude AIs from certain positions, 'As a way to ensure all safety standards are met'.

The Foundation's position was that this was unconstitutional and in violation of the Phobos Accords— which El Dorado had adopted recently, though they were not a signatory. Such practices constituted discrimination. The bill's passage was necessary to guarantee equal rights to all individuals, as promised under the law of the land, and to codify those elements of the Accords.

The current Prime Minister had been instrumental in slowing the bill's passage, suggesting its wording be softened and the issue addressed with restraint, out of respect for all personkind. Terrance hoped that the majority party would shift during this next election cycle, allowing for a prime minister who'd be willing to address the tough issues head on.

He wasn't sure the opposition party would be able to seize the majority vote—though he fervently hoped they would. Nor was he sure that the governor general would appoint an AI to the position of prime minister, even if he did win the position of majority leader.

The people of El Dorado stood a chance of seeing how those maneuverings would play out. If the polls were accurate, Senator Lysander—a well-respected AI—could very well become the next majority party leader, and thus the prime minister.

Politics made Terrance's head hurt. All he knew was that the AI had his vote.

As he ruminated, movement caught his eye, and he shifted his gaze from the reporter toward an approaching figure.

Margot and Travis both saw his eye movement and turned to see Rosalind Bianchi headed their way, her obsequious assistant in tow.

"I hear she hasn't vacated her offices yet," Travis murmured to Terrance as they watched her approach. Terrance didn't bother to hide his surprise.

"Anyone remind her that public servants have to quit their job, once they announce?" Terrance queried the reporter. "She has announced she's running for Senate, hasn't she?"

"Officially? No. But implicitly?" Travis sounded disgusted. "If I hear another veiled innuendo from the woman about running, I may just break my own impartiality rules and tell her where she can stick her candidacy."

Terrance coughed to suppress a laugh.

Margot didn't bother to hide hers.

"Well, Mister Jamieson, if I had to guess," Terrance's aunt said with some asperity, "it's because she doesn't want to give up the perks of her position and move into a campaign headquarters she'll have to fund out of her own pocket."

"Her pocket, or her benefactor's, I wonder?" Travis mused.

The reporter's voice held an odd quality that had Terrance wondering what Travis might know about Rosalind Bianchi's backers that the rest of them didn't. He filed it away for future reference.

* * * * *

Rosalind instructed her assistant to work his way toward the reporter, Travis Jamieson, who she had glimpsed as the crowd parted.

<*And don't be obvious about it,*> she admonished the harried young man. <*Nothing says 'poor, desperate soul, losing in the polls' quite like a politician stalking a news crew.*>

Rosalind considered herself a well-seasoned woman, wise to the ways of politics on this side of the Maglev Loop. So seasoned, in fact, that she could 'press the flesh' practically in her sleep.

Hah! she thought, *I'd like to see Lysander try to do that.*

Fortunately, she was also adept at hiding the fact that she couldn't care less about anyone at the event. This meant she could spend most of her transit time mentally rehearsing her talking points for when the reporter turned on his holo recorder.

Rosalind nodded and smiled in a generally vague manner as she passed through the crowd. As she grew closer, a wave of annoyance passed over her to see who the reporter was chatting with.

Margot Enfield. Rosalind sighed. *Well, there's no help for it.* There was no graceful way to extricate herself, now that Travis Jamieson had spotted her.

<*Once I reach Jamieson,*> she shot her assistant one last instruction, <*see to it that those Enfields are encouraged to move along.*>

* * * * *

"...and I look forward to continuing the traditions of governance that our esteemed Prime Minister has exemplified over such an illustrious career," Rosalind concluded, smiling for the holo recorder embedded in Travis Jamieson's eye implants.

A blinking red light projected from that implant appeared to hover between them, above and a little to one side of Travis's shoulder.

The reporter nodded judiciously and opened his mouth as if to ask another question, but Margot Enfield beat him to it.

"And will you be supporting our efforts to pass the Job Shadowing Act, Madam Minister?"

That bitch.

Tenacious, too. Margot had ignored every attempt by Rosalind's assistant to get her to relocate.

Rosalind forced herself to project an air of poised confidence. "When I am elected, we will give that legislation due consideration, I assure you."

"Yes, but surely you can see that this law is necessary to abolish discrimination against an entire segment of our population," Margot persisted.

"And I can assure you that every El Doradan will have the full protection of the Commonwealth behind them, regardless of race or creed," Rosalind felt her smile grow stiff as she frantically sought to compose a follow-up statement. She needed something that wouldn't alienate those who feared change, but that would appease those bleeding-heart AI lovers.

Damn that Enfield woman!

<*Find me a reason to be somewhere else, **now**!*> Rosalind snapped to her assistant. Her tone was sufficiently vicious that the young man literally jumped in startlement. Which, of

course, gave away the fact someone had just shouted at him over the Link.

That idiot is fired, she thought furiously. *Margot Enfield will pay for this.*

Enfield was fast becoming her least favorite corporation.

Ever.

VICTORIA

STELLAR DATE: 07.02.3189 (Adjusted Gregorian)
LOCATION: NorthStar Industries' Yacht *Sylvan*
REGION: El Dorado Ring, El Dorado, Alpha Centauri System

"…when pressed, the Security Council admitted they had no hard evidence to link NorthStar Industries to the Norden Cartel. When asked to comment on the allegations, CEO Victoria North said that it was merely an unfortunate circumstance that the cartel and her own company shared a similar-sounding name…."

"Excuse me, ma'am," Sylvan, the ship's shackled AI, announced over the comm in Victoria North's executive suite.

Victoria looked up in annoyance at the interruption. "Yes, Sylvan, what is it?" she asked, just as she saw the reason the AI had disturbed her. Victoria's second—her chief of staff, Mack—stood outside the door to her office suite with a visitor in tow.

She closed the report she'd been reading and schooled her features into a cold, hard mask. It wasn't that she got off on terrorizing people; it was all about efficiency.

She'd learned long ago that instilling terror into your workers ensured that they were compliant and docile. Docile workers were obedient. And obedient workers got things done.

The same went for the occasional visitor she entertained aboard the *Sylvan*. Properly cowed visitors tended to be much more open to her…suggestions.

"Send them in," she instructed the AI, then leaned back in her chair. Silently, the doors slid open to admit her guests into the cabin she claimed as her office.

"Welcome aboard," she greeted the nervous man, nodding to Mack, who loomed behind. "Please, join me."

Victoria gestured toward a group of chairs set

uncomfortably close to a large, floor-to-ceiling window. The view was of the ring and the planet beyond it. Cold air had been deliberately piped in along the edges of the window, creating the impression of a slight draft.

The cool air, combined with the seamless expanse of crystal clear carbon, had a visceral effect on people. The fact that the window was comprised of near-impregnable nanostrand reinforced diamond did nothing to dispel the fear that nothing stood between you and the frozen reaches of space.

Mack ushered his charge over, seating him with his back to the window. It was another calculated move to increase the discomfort of Victoria's 'guests' whenever she entertained.

An NSAI-operated servitor trundled in. Victoria quirked a brow and gestured to Mack, who promptly turned to the young man.

"Drink?" he offered.

The man paled and waved Mack off.

Victoria ordered a glass of wine, then leaned toward her guest. Steepling her fingers, she speared Rosalind Bianchi's assistant with a steely look.

"So," she said, pleased with her effect over the wilting young assistant. "Here is what I need from your mistress...."

* * * * *

"...she says the Joint Committee for Commonwealth Security has ordered the STA to step up its policing of air and space traffic on El Dorado. There's worry about the Secret Intelligence Service getting nosy as well. It's impeding legitimate business concerns."

Rosalind could hear the waver in her assistant's voice over their encrypted Link connection. Her eyes flicked up again to confirm the transmission was secure before allowing him to continue.

"And?" she prompted irritably.

The young man's voice dropped to a whisper, as if that somehow might ensure no one overheard. "She wants you to guarantee that all references to any NorthStar spacecraft transiting from the planet to the shipyards are removed from the Space Transit Authorities' data archives. Ma'am."

Suspicious of his tone, Rosalind asked, "You're *certain* you're in a secured area on your end, Walter? You've used the security tokens from our offices so no one can record you?"

"Uh...yes, ma'am. I activated the security tokens as soon as I got back to the pinnace."

She inhaled sharply. "You took the *Ministry's* pinnace?"

She heard the bird-brain gulp at that.

"Uh, no, ma'am. I rented a private one, NSAI-run. I overrode the protocol so that it wouldn't record any data pertaining to its passenger, or its destination."

"Well, then," she said impatiently, "go on."

"She insists everything *has* to be removed, starting from the beginning of this month," he continued. "In exchange, she'll give a substantial donation to your campaign. She promises it'll be untraceable back to any NorthStar affiliate." The young man's voice gained strength as the topic turned to more familiar territory.

A donation. That part, at least, was nice to hear.

"Did she say how much?" Rosalind asked, curious about the value Victoria North placed on this favor. When her assistant named a figure, her eyebrows rose. For that amount, Rosalind would see to it personally that the information was scrubbed from the STA's archives.

Her eyes flicked once more to the reassuring indicator that the signal was encrypted.

This is just the kind of conversation that can sink a campaign. Now was not the time for inconvenient mistakes that could trip up her bid for office. She could just imagine how Lysander would love to get his grubby, digital paws on information like this.

"All right, then," she told her assistant. "Be sure to scrub the pinnace after you land." She disconnected without another word.

Rosalind paused, considering everything that would need to be done in order to doctor the STA's databases. In the not-so-distant past, she had been a top-notch coder; she was certain she could handle altering a NorthStar ident.

Her smile turned ugly. She knew just whose ident she would replace it with.

She pinged her assistant again. When he answered, her instructions were pointed and terse. "Find me someone within Enfield Aerospace whose loyalty can be bought; it needs to be someone with token authority to access and copy files. I'll expect their contact information on my desk when I come in tomorrow."

She didn't wait to hear his response before hanging up once more, already considering what she'd do with the contribution Victoria would make to her campaign.

SKY'S THE LIMIT

STELLAR DATE: 07.02.3189 (Adjusted Gregorian)
LOCATION: El Dorado Spaceport, Tomlinson City
REGION: El Dorado, Alpha Centauri System

"...featured at the air show today is the Tomlinson City Championship Air Race. Now in its tenth year, it revives a centuries-old tradition, where pilots pit their skills against each other on a thirteen-kilometer course set by virtual pylons. Each pilot must navigate around the pylons in order to win...."

Now, that's more like it! Retired Major Calista Rhinehart, ESF, grinned wickedly as her reproduction air-breathing jet fighter whipped into a knife-edge and slipped between two holographic pylons projected by her heads-up display.

Her HUD showed that the maneuver had paid off, and her Shrike was now in the lead.

Calista quickly configured the jet for speed braking and whipped it down and around the next virtual obstacle, keeping an eye on the red light that flickered on and off. That light warned when the Shrike flirted at the edge of a stall, as did the slight shuddering she felt through the stick she held in her hand.

The jet began to buffet and then exceeded its critical angle of attack, one wing stalling as the nose dipped forward. Calista immediately thrust the stick forward, applied power, and leveled the craft. Her enhanced reflexes made stall recovery almost as instantaneous as it would have been if the Shrike's NSAI had been online.

Which it wasn't.

As a former ESF fighter pilot with full combat augmentation, Calista didn't often get to fully enjoy the use of her reflexes. Today was a rare opportunity.

The maneuver brought her into the final stretch. Her gaze danced between her fuel gauge and the icon representing her closest opponent—who once again threatened to take the lead.

Oh no, you don't.

Calista hit the afterburners, dumping synthetic fuel into the aircraft's exhaust to ignite the remaining oxygen in the stream. The Shrike leapt forward—its fuel gauges plummeting—screaming toward the air race's finish line.

The jet thundered above the runway, to the crowd's great delight, then she pulled back on the yoke, bleeding off speed before leveling off. As she banked over the forest beyond the spaceport and keyed the mic, signaling her intention to land on a parallel runway, a call came across the frequency.

"Well, now," the voice drawled. "I believe that's what you might call a 'missed approach', Shrike 714."

Smartass, she thought with a reluctant grin as she recognized the voice's owner.

He was the pilot from Proxima Centauri she'd heard over the radio yesterday. Rumor had it the guy had a few reproduction aircraft here that he liked to tinker with between freighter runs.

Rumor *also* had it that he was fearless in the air, and would have given the crowd an astounding aerobatic show, if his tail-dragger hadn't developed a coolant leak that led to a seized engine during rehearsals.

Her breath had caught when he'd declared a flight emergency; any pilot's would. But he'd had it well in hand, trimming the craft down to its best glide speed, and landed without fanfare or incident a few minutes later.

Now it seemed he'd been roped into lending a hand with air traffic control for the show.

'Missed approach'? Hah.

"The approach isn't missed if I never intended to land, now is it?" she murmured drolly into her headset, as her wheels touched down and she applied the airbrakes. Just then, her avionics began to flash fuel starvation warnings, which she silenced with a mental flick—and a slightly guilty twinge over how much fuel that afterburner move had spent.

Calista suspected the local air traffic control AI would have a word or two to say to her about the maneuver once the air show was over. Then again, if mister stunt pilot was manning the boards, maybe she'd be off the hook.

Andrews is the guy's name, isn't it? I really should look him up; he did some impressive flying...for a civilian. Could be a future for him at Enfield Aerospace.

* * * * *

Jason caught a glimpse of himself in the plas window of the maglev as it slowed to a halt a few blocks from his apartment complex on the El Dorado Ring. He was lost in thought, wondering why Calista had burst out laughing when he'd offered to take her for a ride in one of his reproduction planes sometime.

His reflection smirked back at him, wearing a 'Forget the plane, ride the pilot' t-shirt.

He shouldered his backpack and set off with an easy stride toward his apartment, the night-shrouded planet looming large overhead, its edges limned with light.

Jason passed his security token to the building's auth system before opening the main doors. He ambled into the waiting lift and ascended to his floor. As he approached his apartment, the building's Non-Sentient AI registered his presence, and his door opened.

With a casual throw, he tossed his pack aside while crossing the threshold, and immediately sensed a person crouched behind him.

Jason felt his heart rate increase, and time began to slow as his senses expanded outward. The soft intake of a breath, and the faintest scratch were his only warning as the figure launched itself toward him.

But he was no longer there. As the attacker launched, Jason *moved*. In this altered state of reality, he had plenty of time to calculate his combatant's trajectory and angle of impact. He curved his body to the left at precisely the right moment, moving like a bullfighter without a cape.

The would-be assailant sailed through the space his target had just vacated, and Jason shot a hand out, connecting with his opponent's legs. The point of impact acted as a fulcrum, altering the attacker's trajectory.

The figure landed hard, air whooshing from its lungs at the unexpected impact. Still, the impact was much softer than it could have been; Jason's actions had redirected the figure to land on the carpeted mainspace, rather than the apartment's tiled entrance.

Jason crouched, mentally sending the order for the NSAI to turn the lights on as he turned to face…a rather large cat.

With a convulsive shake of its tawny head, the animal turned and speared Jason with a reproving glare. Then, with an air of dismissal, the animal proceeded to industriously groom the fur of one sleekly muscled shoulder.

"Sorry about that," Jason addressed the Proxima cat. "You OK?"

Aqua eyes stared back at him impassively, devoid of forgiveness.

"You know that wouldn't have happened if you hadn't left me behind." The words seemed to emanate from the animal. "This is what comes of being cooped up alone all day."

"Yeah, well." Jason moved into the mainspace, gently shoving the creature to one side as he passed by, his fingers digging gently into the base of the cat's ear for a quick scratch. "There were a lot of people at the air show, and you know not everyone's comfortable around you."

He looked into the Proxima cat's green eyes and pointed. "You, I mean." He addressed the collar around the cat's neck, "Not you."

Tobi the cat blinked at him, then opened her mouth in a huge yawn, showing wickedly sharp incisors, while Tobias, the AI residing in the collar around the cat's neck, sighed. "It's just as well, then, I suppose. Think we can work in a trip planetside soon, boyo? Maybe after we get back from that gig you have tomorrow with Avalon Mining? A hike along Muzhavi Ridge would be good for our girl here."

Jason collapsed on the sofa and glanced over at the cat, who proceeded to stretch languorously before padding silently toward him.

"Yeah, you know, that's not a bad idea."

* * * * *

Tobias looked at his young human friend, sprawled carelessly on the sofa.

Young, he mused to himself. *Since when do late thirties count as 'young' in a human?* Tobias suspected the way he saw Jason had more to do with the fact that he was just over two hundred years old, himself.

The AI liked to think that he and Lysander'd had a hand—metaphorically speaking—in raising Jason. Both AIs had known the man's family since before his birth. Back when Lysander had been embedded with Jason's dad.

Even when Jason was a boy, Tobias had found himself fascinated by the countless ways Jason invented to get himself in trouble.

Maybe it was because Tobias was also a bit of a troublemaker.

There was one bit of trouble he'd caused that he still felt

guilty about. Jason had been eleven at the time. Sometimes, seeing the man he had grown into, that memory resurfaced, and Tobias wondered what would have happened had he not gotten involved in Jason's life….

CIRCLING A DARK STAR

STELLAR DATE: 02.12.3164 (Adjusted Gregorian)
LOCATION: C-47 Habitat
REGION: Chinquapin, Proxima Centauri System

Twenty-five years earlier ....

The colonists who settled Proxima Centauri had named their small terrestrial planet 'Chinquapin'. It was a fancy name for a barren hunk of rock, but the colonists had a vision.

Someday, the tidally-locked planet orbiting an M-class red dwarf would have an atmosphere, oceans and continents. It would have a magnetic field twice the strength of Terra's, which would deflect the harmful radiation the star sent its way. And someday, it would have its own space elevator and planetary ring.

Chinquapin orbited within the area habitable for humans, known as the 'Goldilocks Zone', but that didn't mean it would be easy to transform.

When the FGT terraformed a planet, they took centuries to do it—and they usually picked a more habitable planet around a more habitable star. This was why they had passed by Proxima Centauri and Chinquapin, and spent their time creating El Dorado around Proxima's sister star, Alpha Centauri.

Red dwarf stars were much dimmer than G-class stars, like Terra's sun, so the habitable zone around Proxima Centauri was much closer to the star. In Chinquapin's case that meant the planet was only 0.05 AU from Proxima, twenty times closer than Terra was to Sol.

Understandably, this presented a challenge for the colonist terraforming team. Proxima might be a dimmer star, but it was much more magnetically active than their native Sol. It also emitted significantly higher amounts of extreme-UV and X-ray radiation.

Additionally, while the star's magnetic field permeated the system's heliosphere, it was particularly potent along the plane that extended out around the star's equator. A small current flowed through this area, forming an electromagnetic sheet that ranged from two thousand to twelve thousand kilometers thick.

The current sheet warped from the star's rotation, just like a ballerina's skirts would swirl around a dancer as she spun. Chinquapin's orbit had it weaving in and out of the sheet's curves as it circled around the star.

While in the sheet, the star hammered Chinquapin with higher doses of radiation, plus another special gift: coronal mass ejections. The bulk of Proxima's CMEs traveled along this current sheet, and they were ten times more massive than those Sol discharged.

The terraforming team considered themselves lucky, though; Chinquapin could have had an eccentric orbit, like the former planet Mercury. Had that been the case, Chinquapin would have been exposed to twice as much radiation when it came close to the star during perihelion than it did when far away, at aphelion.

Instead, the planet's circular orbit provided a much more even distribution, and that made the terraformers' job easier. Still, what all this stellar activity could do to the human nervous system, and to the neural nets of AIs, was devastating.

The C-47 habitat that orbited Chinquapin needed the same level of protection, which was where Jason's parents came in. The two scientists had teamed up to try to mitigate the effects that the star's ionizing radiation had on the neural networks of both humans and AIs.

Tobias had arrived at Chinquapin not long after Jason was

born, having left the Sol System after the Second Sentience War. Many AIs had departed from Sol at that time, disillusioned with a political system that had failed them, not once but twice. Some—Tobias amongst them—had chosen to follow Cara Sykes' daughter, Jane, to Proxima.

Jane was the resident neurologist at C-47. Her husband, Rhys, was the team's radiation physicist. The two made their home with the science team on C-47; feeling a connection to the Sykes scion, Tobias had made his home there, too.

Many of the other AIs—like Lysander—spent most of their time working with scientists such as Jason's parents to solve the peculiar challenges of an M-class dwarf star.

Tobias was more interested in hanging out with their young son, Jason.

He'd been observing the boy since he was a toddler, watching the child grow into a youth. He'd witnessed Jason's early struggles with coordination, and his parents' worry that their son might have a genetic defect that modern medicine had failed to detect and eradicate.

At the time, Tobias hadn't known the outcome of the Andrews' exhaustive examination of their son; that file had been restricted, and he'd found himself reluctant to pry. Over time, young Jason had overcome those early obstacles and had slowly caught up to his schoolmates.

Through those growing years, Tobias had found himself captivated by the boy's agile and inventive mind. He'd observed Jason conjure up countless pranks, then witnessed his spirit slowly crushed as he was forced into compliance both by adult humans, and AIs who didn't appreciate the youth's restless intellect.

So he'd approached Jason's father, Rhys Andrews, with a proposition.

Tobias had no idea what he didn't know.

* * * * *

"Lysander and I had an interesting talk with Tobias this morning," Jason heard his father say in an offhand manner.

"Oh, really?" his mother replied. "What about?"

Neither seemed aware that Jason had entered the lab, and was hanging out in a shadowed corner behind a stack of crates, using the lab's NSAI to play his flight simulator game.

Jason was pretty sure Lysander knew he was there, but for some reason, the AI wasn't ratting him out. He grinned. *This is great; it's always fun to listen in on adult conversations. Never know what you're going to hear.*

"It was about Jason, actually," Rhys Andrews continued. "Turns out the school wants to talk to us about him again."

Okay, well, *that* wasn't on the list of things he wanted to hear. He didn't think he'd done anything wrong—at least, not recently. Sometimes it was hard to figure out what adults considered right and wrong.

Jason heard his mother groan. "What is it now—another toilet programmed to void in the wrong direction?"

Well, yeah, he'd known *that* had been wrong when he did it....

Jason's dad snorted. "C'mon, Jane, you have to admit—it took some real talent to bypass the conduit and reroute the sensors that way."

And about three hours of my free time, too, Jason mentally added.

Jane's voice sounded severe to Jason's ear, but with a weird warble to it. *No way. Is she laughing?* He couldn't tell. He peered through the cracks between the crates he crouched behind, but couldn't see his mother's face.

She'd acted so pissed at him! And she'd taken away his Link privileges for two whole weeks.

"No, no, nothing like that," Jason's dad assured his mom.

"They say he's restless, and bored with the coursework."

"I've spoken with Tobias about this," Lysander's voice joined the conversation. "If you are open to the idea, Tobias has volunteered to mentor the boy."

Yesssssssss. Tobias was totally rad—the coolest AI in the habitat. If he wanted to tutor Jason, that could only mean….

Jane laughed, and Jason could see her shaking her head through the space between the crates. "Did either of you think to warn Tobias about the wild ride he'd be in for, saddled with the responsibility for that boy? So many hormonal shifts and emotional swings!"

Rhys grinned back at his wife. "You sure you're not projecting a little bit? I've heard Anna mention her own experience with you a time or two," he teased.

"Can you imagine what it would be like to be embedded during those years?" Jane asked.

Lysander gave a sardonic chuckle. "There's a reason we can't be bonded to a human in puberty," his tone was dry. "Adult emotions are enough of a wild ride for us, thank you very much."

"Well, it's no picnic on our end, I can assure you," Jane replied tartly.

"Jane, Tobias also said…" Rhys hesitated, then forged ahead. "He offered to embed with Jason, once he's old enough if they hit it off."

YES! Jason pumped his fist in the air. *This is the best day ever.*

"Oh, Rhys," his mother's voice said finally. Sadly. "You didn't mention that Jason's an L2, did you?"

What's an L2, Jason wondered. *And why does Mom sound sad about it?*

"No, we agreed to keep that to ourselves," his dad assured her.

"Seems an odd bit of irony, though," Lysander said. "A

naturally-occurring genetic advancement like that, putting him at a disadvantage against the rest of you lesser-evolved, L0 humans."

"But the *risk*," his mother said. "His nervous system has too many exposed nodes. Our tech's not advanced enough yet to ensure separation between an AI's channels and his."

"Agreed," Lysander said. "There's too much of a chance of bleed-over, and no guarantee we could keep the two apart."

"I know it's a Sykes family tradition to embed with AIs," Jane said somberly, "but…it's just too dangerous."

"Jason's going to be crushed when we tell him he can't ever have an AI implanted."

It was all Jason could stand.

"What do you *mean* I can't have an AI?" he yelled as he rose from his hiding place. His heart pounded in his chest, and he could feel his face flush as he rushed toward them.

He stopped at the edge of the laboratory table that stood between him and his parents. In a fit of temper, he grabbed the first thing his hands came in contact with, and threw the tool at the table's surface with all the force he could muster.

"Judith had one implanted! Why can't I?" he demanded.

The tool he flung reached a velocity of over two hundred meters per second, causing the laboratory table to deform a good seven centimeters in the center.

The strike created a wave of displacement that rippled outward, turning the pipettes at the end nearest his mother into deadly projectiles. Jason watched in fascination, and then growing horror, as the displacement wave seemed to travel in slow motion through the table, launching the pipettes into the air.

They rocketed up at a velocity easily equal to one of the projectile weapons the Habitat's peacekeepers carried. One of the pipettes was on a course to impale his mother's left eye.

The boy's eyes grew round in shock at what he'd done.

Instinctively, his right hand shot out, picking the single pipette out of the air mere millimeters before it struck home.

As the rest of the projectiles clattered against the bulkhead, the world returned to its normal speed, and Jason stood frozen, his hand in front of his mother's face, fingers clenched around the pipette. His hand shook as he slowly lowered it.

He heard his father's voice, quietly.

"One thing's certain; Jason needs someone to teach him discipline, embedded or not."

"I'll talk to Tobias," Lysander said quietly. "We'll figure something out."

* * * * *

Tobias was horrified that his offer had almost resulted in so serious an injury.

<I've heard of L2s,> he told the Andrews. <They're a recent mutation, discovered—what? About fifty years ago?>

"Yes, in Sol," Jane confirmed. "The mutation is in our axons, the neural pathways that send signals from the brain to the rest of the body."

Tobias' avatar nodded. As the Habitat's leading neuroscientist, this landed squarely in Jane's wheelhouse, and he could tell she was fully invested in the subject.

"Well, those signals travel faster along an L2's axons. That means an L2 processes information much more quickly than a normal human."

<How can nerve impulses travel faster in an L2?> Tobias asked. <I thought there was a limit to how fast a signal could travel along an axon, due to the nerves being insulated.>

"That's true," Jane conceded. "But there are these little areas along an axon, nodes where there is no myelin coating to insulate it. The gap isn't big enough to cause the signal to degrade; instead, because it's not insulated, the signal travels a *lot* more quickly there."

"An L2 has a lot more nodes than you'd find in an L0 human," Rhys added. "That's the key to an L2's faster mental processes. It also means they have quicker reflexes."

<*Fast-twitch muscles are a lot faster, too,*> Lysander added.

"Yes," Jane said with a grimace.

When Tobias' avatar sent them a questioning look, Rhys explained, "I'm not sure how much attention you paid to Jason when he was a baby, but his coordination was...."

"It was pretty awful," Jane said frankly. "We were worried he'd contracted a neurological disease."

<*But instead...?*> prompted Tobias.

<*We learned it's typical for L2s to experience difficulty with coordination during formative years,*> Lysander explained. <*One of the methods Jane developed to help him cope with a nervous system that vastly outpaced the rest of his development was to teach him to move slowly and methodically.*>

"And we reinforced his bones with carbon nanotubes." Jane made a face. "Do you have any idea how hard it is to see your baby constantly breaking bones when he's so tiny?"

As their conversation concluded, Tobias had assured both Rhys and Jane that he would keep his knowledge of Jason being an L2 in strictest confidence.

Not long after that, Rhys and Tobias had cobbled together an apparatus fashioned after centuries-old military headgear. The headpiece conformed to the curls and flutes of Jason's ears so completely that it took a few minutes for his young brain to adjust to the altered auditory inputs. But he didn't mind; it meant he had his own personal connection with an AI.

The headpiece interfaced seamlessly via a secure Link to a chassis Rhys had designed. The chassis functioned as a harness, to be worn by one of the specially modified Savannah cats that Jane bred as pets.

The cats' intelligence had been marginally tweaked, and

the animals had adapted easily to microgravity. They made exceptional animal companions to families who lived in the various habitats within the Proxima Centauri system, and were in high demand.

This was a nod to another Sykes family tradition—one that began back when her uncle Tim had adopted their first family dog, a corgi named Em.

It also served to provide Jason with a companion and dedicated bodyguard, albeit the four-legged variety. With Tobias as the brains and the cat as the brawn, their worries were somewhat assuaged regarding young Jason's safety.

From then on, Jason and Tobias—and the cat—had been inseparable, though the AI may not have turned out to be quite the role model Jane would have wished for her son. Jason's enhanced neurology meant he quickly outpaced his fellow students...and often found himself bored and looking for ways to entertain himself during interminable classroom hours.

Tobias claimed that the pranks were merely Jason's form of creative expression. Eventually, that 'expression' got both the boy *and* his AI expelled from school. The final straw was when Jason reprogrammed the ventilation systems to deliver a three percent hydrogen sulfide mixture into the girls' locker room.

As Jason grew to adulthood, he began working on flights between C-47 and the various mining rigs in Proxima's warm dust belt. Tobias occasionally considered other ways he could accompany Jason, but 'traveling by cat' seemed as convenient as any.

Tobias had ended up paired with various family cats over the years, until the day came when Jason announced his plan to hire out on a freighter bound for El Dorado.

His parents gifted Jason and Tobias with the graceful feline now resting on her haunches in Jason's apartment, aqua eyes staring at him unblinkingly. They'd all had a good laugh when

Jason had decided to name her 'Tobi'.

Well, everyone except Tobias. Jason's last prank had been on him.

SPYCRAFT

STELLAR DATE: 07.02.3189 (Adjusted Gregorian)
LOCATION: Senator's Office, Parliament House, Sonali
REGION: El Dorado Ring, El Dorado, Alpha Centauri System

"...seven were pronounced dead early this morning in the warehouse district of Tomlinson City, during a peacekeeper raid on a local drug ring. Neighboring businesses had been complaining about the increased violence in the area over the past several years, reportedly attributable to an uptick in Norden Cartel activity...."

"Hello, sir, it's good to see you." Thomas, one of Senator Lysander's AI aides, looked up and smiled as Benjamin Meyer entered the office.

Ben had worked with Lysander a time or two in his role as senior analyst for El Dorado's Secret Intelligence Service. Ben was also married to Judith Andrews, a woman the AI had all but raised. Ben hoped he could use that almost-family connection today as a means to see the senator unannounced.

He needed Lysander's help. More importantly, this meeting had to look spontaneous and unscheduled to any prying eyes that might make note of it.

"Is Lysander around?" Ben asked Thomas. "Do you think he could spare a few minutes?"

Thomas glanced down at the holo sheet that held the senator's schedule—not that he needed to—then nodded and signaled the inner office doors to open. "He'll be happy to see you, sir. Please go on in."

Ben nodded affably to the AI, then crossed the threshold into the inner office. The doors closed behind him, and Ben's NSAI notified him that a protocol had been activated, ensuring the room was secure.

Lysander's holoavatar greeted Ben from across the room,

where he stood looking out a window at the city below. "Good to see you, Ben. How's Judith?"

"She's well," Ben replied. "Thoroughly engrossed in her work, as usual. She been monitoring some increased tectonic activity down on the planet, around the continental divide at Muzhavi Ridge. She seems to feel that the tolerances the FGT worked into the continental drift are a bit 'tight' in that area." Ben held up his fingers in air quotes, then gave a half-smile. "She thinks we need to watch for increasing rock slides in the area. Avalanches, too, in the winter months."

Lysander's avatar shook his head. "I'm sure the Prime Minister will be gratified to hear *that* little gem," he murmured dryly. "Something tells me, though, that you didn't come here just to give me an update on what Judith's been doing. What's on your mind, son?"

It was a bit of an affectation, calling Ben 'son'. For some reason known only to him, Lysander had long ago adopted the avatar of a slightly older man; his visage was rough-hewn and weathered, with dark hair, black eyes, and a perpetual five o'clock shadow. His voice was gravelly with the weight of authority. The AI, now over two hundred Terran years old, carried it off to perfection.

Ben nodded toward a holo of a news feed that Lysander had projected silently against the wall. "You saw the news this morning," he said by way of response. "That drug bust was just the tip of a very large iceberg, Lysander."

"I'm chair of the Joint Committee for Commonwealth Security," Lysander reminded him. "We received the report the moment it was filed. But you know this already. Tell me something I don't know, Ben. What brought you here this morning?" he asked directly.

"Things are escalating quickly, Lysander. Too quickly." Ben paused, gathering his thoughts. "I think," he said slowly, "that we're dealing with an opportunistic situation, and the

Norden Cartel is taking advantage of it."

Lysander raised a brow, his eyes growing even more serious. "How so?"

Ben shrugged, looking bitter. "Everyone's focus lately has been centered more on civil unrest than on organized crime. With all the partisan crap in play, the SIS isn't running efficiently right now."

The senator nodded in agreement. "I believe it. I've spent far more time battling anti-AI factions than I have with the Security Committee."

"Then there's the added complication that the cartel is operating behind a legitimate organization," Ben said. "Hiding behind NorthStar Industries means they're essentially untouchable. We can't raid without a warrant, and any time we manage to get one, the site's been scrubbed clean, with nothing to find."

Ben shot Lysander a pointed look. "There are too many deep state agents embedded in the Secret Intelligence Service, and all of them care more about their party's agenda than running a security agency whose mission is to enforce the law and investigate criminal activity."

"Mmm," Lysander responded. "And I'd imagine your director's no help. The current Prime Minister appointed her, didn't she? I'd be willing to bet you're being stonewalled quite a bit."

Ben spared Lysander a bleak glance then walked over to one of the chairs set in a conversational grouping, and slumped into it. The AI's avatar followed him, stopping at the corner of his desk. His projection appeared to lean against its edge as he crossed his arms and waited for Ben to continue.

"It would seem," Ben began with a sigh, "that it bothers her more that I lean toward your side of the aisle, than that El Dorado is infested with criminal organizations like the Norden Cartel. And, by the way, I'm convinced they've infiltrated the

SIS's ranks, too."

"That's a weighty statement," the senator warned.

Ben rubbed his eyes tiredly then looked up at Lysander. "One of my top operatives told me she was lucky we only lost seven people this morning in that raid. They were waiting for her strike team when they arrived."

"So you're here to..." Lysander prompted.

"I'm here because if I'm going to take Norden down, it needs to be with an off-the-books team. And I'd like that team to include AIs."

Lysander raised his brows at Ben. "That's a first. The intelligence service has never had an AI field officer before."

Ben snorted. "Officially, no. Unofficially..." The senior analyst smirked. "There have been plenty of times in the past when we've relied on AIs. We'd be crazy stupid not to. Then again, this whole anti-AI movement that's been gaining ground is crazy stupid, but hey, they don't pay me to be political. They pay me to serve and protect."

The senator nodded. "So you'd like me to make some introductions. I can do that. Anything else?"

"I don't want a repeat of the losses we saw today—losses that tell me we have a big leak in the SIS. You wouldn't happen to have a team of off-the-books spec ops humans that I could hire, squirreled away anywhere, would you?" Ben's mouth twisted in a wry grin, and he laughed once, without humor.

"Not a spec ops team, no. But I have an idea of where you could find a few good people." Lysander surprised Ben with his reply. "You might begin with your own brother-in-law."

Ben shot Lysander a you've-got-to-be-shitting-me look. "Jason? The guy who wanders aimlessly from job to job, working a freighter run for six months then quitting to go base jumping off some cliff somewhere?" He snorted derisively. "*That* guy?"

Lysander nodded wordlessly.

Ben shook his head. "I swear either he or Judith must have been switched at birth, Ly. There's no way Judith is Jason Andrews' sister. No," Benjamin Meyer said decisively as he stood. "Find me someone else, Lysander. Someone reliable that I can trust."

Lysander straightened and pinned Ben with a piercing look as he pointed his finger at the SIS analyst. "And *I'm* telling *you* that there's more to him than you know, Ben. Jason's the man for the job. Trust me on this. Have I ever steered you wrong?"

Ben hesitated. "Tell you what," he compromised. "If you set me up with an AI team, I promise I'll give Jason a chance. Deal?"

Lysander's expression softened, but only a little. "Deal."

* * * * *

<All right people,> Mack announced over the Link. <It's moving day! Get your asses in gear. I want this place torn down within the hour. You know the drill. Move it!>

The two women in the command center maglev car immediately began closing Link connections, and shunting any that needed to remain open up to the *Sylvan's* shackled AI.

The crew below the women, in the open warehouse area below the maglev line, scattered in various directions. They carted boxes into shipping containers and then loaded them onto shuttles. Equipment that had been set up was torn down with practiced efficiency.

Mack returned to his own office—a maglev car, two down the line from the C&C car—to find that his assistant had already locked everything down, and was prepared to release the car's manual locks.

<Sir, you want us to move that shipment of AIs with us to the

new spot, or take 'em on down to the warehouse?> Sally's voice asked over the Link.

Mack considered the logistics for a moment. The buyers weren't supposed to dock with the *Sylvan* for another few days, and the AIs would be out of the way down below.

Plus, Davidsen still needed to get the shackling code installed before they took the AIs out of those isolation tubes. And there was that big shipment of plasma cannons due to be siphoned away from that ESF shipment tomorrow....

<Yeah, take Davidsen with you, and tell her to install those shackles while she's down there. We'll send a shuttle for her in two or three days, when it's time to deliver our new products up to the ship.>

Exactly one hour later, bay doors that had been sealed shut by the FGT when they were first installed slowly slid open, and a signal was sent, overriding the sensors that would have reported it.

Moments later, four shuttles and a barge loaded with oversized shipping containers emerged, their EM signals masked, and their speed just barely greater than the ring's rotational velocity.

At the same time, seven maglev cars released their brakes, and thrusters installed on each car pushed them gently along the tracks. Mack watched as crewmembers clad in EV suits did a final sweep of the cavernous bay, now devoid of atmosphere, ensuring no evidence of their presence remained.

The ships drifted along the surface of the ring for half an hour. One of the shuttles moved away from the others until, a few kilometers out, it engaged its engines and changed course for orbital entry to the planet below.

Another signal was sent from the remaining ships, triggering a second set of bay doors to slowly slide open, leading down into one of the empty levels within the ring. Shortly after the ships had settled into their new temporary home, the seven maglev cars arrived, and the cartel was back in business.

CODE NAME ICARUS
STELLAR DATE: 07.02.3189 (Adjusted Gregorian)
LOCATION: Enfield Corporation Main Headquarters
REGION: Alpha Centauri Binary System

"The El Dorado Space Force announced today that space contractors Enfield Aerospace and TransOrbital Systems will be presenting their bids soon in an effort to win the contract to build the next generation of fighters for the ESF...."

"Hold that car!"

The call came just as the maglev's doors were beginning to close, and Calista Rhinehart waved her hand over the sensor, sending a command override to keep them open. A fresh-faced young man half a head shorter than Calista rushed in, balancing a load of containers that reached as high as his forehead.

"Thanks!" he panted breathlessly. "I need to get these back to the anechoic chamber, like, *right* now. Shannon expects the Old Lady to show up any ti—"

He stumbled to a halt as he craned his head around the stack in his arms and spied the aforementioned 'Old Lady' he'd just mentioned.

"Um..."

"Yes, Jonesy? You were saying?" Calista fought to keep a smile off her face as the former El Dorado Space Force ensign cleared his throat.

"Ma'am," his voice broke, and he cleared his throat again. "That is, I, uh...n-not that you're old or anything, sir." Flustered, he corrected himself. "Ma'am, sir. I meant ma'am. Uh...ma'am."

Calista, who was perhaps two, maybe three years Jonesy's senior, grinned at his discomfiture.

"Relax, Jonesy. Glad to hear you think I'm still among the living. And remember, we're all civilians now, so no need to 'sir' me."

Calista still thought it was funny that the ESF had adopted 'sir' as their 'gender-neutral' form of address. To her way of thinking, it just cluttered things up. Especially when flustered young ensigns (or former ensigns, in this case) became tongue-tied and stumbled over it.

The stack Jonesy carried teetered precariously, and Calista put out a hand to keep them from toppling. The ring's transit system began its standard 'imminent departure' announcement, and she reached past Jonesy to open a compartment for him. He tucked the containers inside, securing them against shifts in apparent gravity, and then the pair took two seats and clipped in for the ride.

She glanced out the window as the maglev sped gracefully away from the ring's main spaceport. From Calista's vantage, she could just make out where the main elevator connected to the ring that encircled the planet. She would get a better view of it very soon. The maglev line that she and Jonesy had boarded would take them past the elevator junction as it curved around the main struts of the commercial spacedock area.

The spacedock had been built on the back side of the ring, opposite the terminus of the main space elevator. The bustle of commerce was writ large here: on any given day, thousands of people passed through on their way to wherever their business took them.

Local commuter transportation was constrained to the hub that Calista and Jonesy had just departed. Larger cargo shipments made use of a sturdier and more utilitarian dock, just off the port side of the maglev.

An upper tier serviced system-wide traffic, and the outermost tier hosted the occasional transstellar ship. Once or twice, a colony ship had berthed there to make repairs or take on supplies before continuing on their journey to a distant star.

The maglev car cleared the congestion that surrounded the spacedock, and they picked up speed. Its next stop was Enfield Aerospace's main campus, several hundred kilometers away.

Calista stared through the plas window, watching the view of shuttles zipping around, and maglev cars speeding toward them on reciprocal paths. Then she turned to eye Jonesy. She tilted her head, indicating the compartment where they had stashed Jonesy's containers. "Whatcha got there?" she asked.

"They're the most recent samples of the surface substrate for Icarus," he said, referring to the project they were currently working on. "They were sent back to HQ for some presentation Mister Enfield gave to the Board yesterday, and Shannon wants them back."

Calista crooked a smile at Jonesy. "Terrance pulled me into that meeting as well. I'm sorry Shannon sent you all the way over here to pick them up. I could have brought them back with me."

'Icarus' was the codename for a new fighter Enfield Aerospace had designed for the ESF. It was a 'clean sheet' design, which meant it was a new conceptualization from the ground-up instead of a revision of an existing craft.

If they won the bid to build the fighters for the ESF, it would be a major coup for Enfield's developing technologies division, the part of Enfield Aerospace that those working there referred to as 'TechDev'.

Most of the credit for the new design belonged to Enfield's top engineer, Shannon. From where Calista stood, Shannon was a magician. The AI commanded a cadre of top engineers, but it wasn't the collective genius of these men, women, and AIs that elevated her in Calista's eyes.

What was truly impressive was Shannon's grasp of each individual's abilities. Her knack for bringing the best out of everyone on her team was legendary. They consistently outperformed even Shannon's top projections. The AI was a far better 'people person' than just about any human Calista had met.

Including me, she thought wryly, as she realized she didn't even know Jonesy's first name.

In the Space Force, he'd just been 'Jonesy'. Not a flashy person like some of the pilots she had known in the Force, but a solid and reliable supply officer. He had a knack for finding even the most obscure items.

In many respects, it was people like Jonesy who kept a base running smoothly. Which was why, after Terrance hired her to run TechDev, she'd immediately turned around and hired Jonesy. She'd offered him a job the minute his feet had hit the civvie side of the ring.

As the maglev car approached the Enfield campus, the car's NSAI gave the routine shift in gravity announcement. Calista's stomach flipped as the car rotated and entered the ring from the underside, slowing as it reached the terminus.

The Enfield dock was busy, and she was gratified to see the EA security team members taking their jobs seriously. They were checking the tokens of each employee, guest, deliveryman, and dockhand that entered and exited the EA restricted area. Corporate espionage was alive and well in the thirty-fourth century, and Calista was protective of her team's intellectual property.

She and Jonesy passed their tokens to the guard detail at the security arch at the edge of the maglev platform, and walked into Enfield Aerospace's complex. Entering through the dock area always brought Calista's attention to the contrast between a clean yet spartan loading zone, and the simple and elegant beauty of the campus itself.

All Enfield facilities were designed by the best architects in the system, made to be both functional and aesthetic. Tasteful art hung along its main corridors, some of which were ridiculously expensive installations created by well-known El Doradan artists from centuries past.

Calista had asked Terrance about it once. He'd just shrugged and told her that art was inspiration, and 'inspiration fostered creativity' — in all its many forms.

I do love the atmosphere of this company, she thought to herself, as she and Jonesy entered the lift that would take them to the TechDev section and its massive anechoic chamber, where Shannon presided.

* * * * *

TechDev's anechoic chamber was one of Shannon's favorite places inside Enfield Aerospace. In part, because it was such a rare scientific gem — the only one of its kind on El Dorado — mostly, though, it was because this was her domain.

A thousand meters deep, five hundred high and wide, every surface within the chamber was covered in a dampening material. It absorbed every kind of wave transmitted, from UV to sound, allowing Shannon to run every simulation she could conceive on a material, to see how it responded.

And this kind of freedom, for an engineer, was downright sexy.

When Shannon had been given carte blanche to design it, she'd had the entire back wall put on rails, allowing egress onto the ring's surface. When opened, Shannon could extend her testing field to an array of antennae, yet another thousand meters beyond its open maw.

The humans on her team found it funny that the groundskeepers had to set up maintenance bots to continuously groom the grass to Shannon's exacting standards. She didn't understand what was so humorous about a graduated triangular shape, and had to look up the

'Christmas tree' reference to understand why they had laughed when they had first seen it.

Shannon had heard humans describe the chamber itself as a 'dead zone', and she supposed she could understand their term. No sound reached a human's ears in there, and the proprietary, ultra-black, nano-coated material the walls were covered in was disorienting to look at. The walls absorbed all light and provided no reflection, which meant that a human would experience no depth perception when looking at it.

She had heard more than one member of her team remark that the chamber was beyond unsettling.

Yet here they were, crawling over, under, and inside the prototype fighter that sat in the chamber before her, all without complaint.

She supposed 'before her' was a misnomer. She wondered fleetingly what it must be like to view the universe through organic optics, limited in wavelength and viewing angle. Her sensory inputs had such a broader range than her human counterparts.

Still.

Even with their limitations, the humans she had come to know were extraordinary in their ability to intuit in a way no AI could quite match.

I love watching them work. Shannon laughed ruefully deep inside her most private self; she wondered if what she experienced as 'love' had the same emotional nuances as what a human would impart to the word.

She found herself obsessing over how they interacted with each other, fascinated by the complexities of their relationships.

Just then, one of the engineers perching precariously atop a gantry slipped and fell. Shannon triggered a priority request for a medical team, then brought all of her voluntary processes to a halt as she focused on the woman—Sally Jenkin—lying on the floor of the anechoic chamber.

She wondered if this was what 'holding one's breath' felt like, as she experienced the stillness inside her that was a result of so many processes—usually running in the background simultaneously—being placed on pause as she focused all her attention on her injured employee.

She watched as Harry Michaels, one of Sally's close friends, held the woman's hand and murmured meaningless words to the injured engineer, who was grimacing in obvious pain.

Shannon found herself wondering what touch felt like: the sensation of atmosphere pressing lightly against the skin, the feel of another's hand squeezing a shoulder in comfort.

The sizzling, acrid jolt of pain as a chemical and biological process from signals sent along nerve pathways down the length of the broken leg, compared to the form of pain she could experience from her own neural net.

Shannon brought such musings to a halt as the medical team arrived, followed by Calista and Jonesy a moment later.

As Chief Pilot, Calista was Shannon's immediate superior, responsible for the overall success of TechDev. Even more than the others, Shannon admired the human woman's ability to make intuitive leaps that the AI could never quite follow.

She wondered if Calista would consider having Shannon embedded with her. The AI thought the two of them would be a good fit, although it might make her job a bit more challenging.

Being inside a human host would mean limiting her broadband access to the facility much of the time, but Shannon thought the tradeoff might be worth it.

The medical team made their way to the injured woman and transferred her to a gurney. Shannon noted how the woman's facial features relaxed the moment the pain medication took hold, as the medical team engaged the gurney's maglev and moved the woman to the infirmary.

Her moment of reflection over, Shannon once again assumed the mantle of floor manager and greeted Calista.

"I see you found my samples," she said as Calista approached the AI's central core.

Calista set the containers on the counter, brushed back a strand of straight, dark hair that had come loose from its tie at the nape of her neck, and turned to face Shannon's primary sensor array. Dark eyes twinkling, she nodded. "And one Jonesy, too."

"Oh, really?" Shannon responded drolly. "I hadn't noticed *he* was misplaced as well."

Jonesy pulled an exaggerated frown, looking from Shannon's array to Calista and back again. "I have no idea what you mean, ma'ams," he said. "*I* wasn't lost. I knew exactly where I was at all times."

His blunt statement elicited a surprised laugh from Shannon. "I suppose you did at that, Jonesy. I suppose you did." She turned her attention to Calista. "I have an update on the latest numbers from Icarus, if you'd like to review them?"

Calista nodded. "That'd be great, Shannon." She turned as the AI projected a pivot table of the most recent impact-resistance tests run on the ship's surfaces.

Project Icarus promised to take spacecraft materials science to the next level. Enfield Aerospace's proposal for the new Mark IV fighter was based on a new nanomaterial the team had invented. The material, Elastene, was made using electrospinning techniques on graphene. As its name implied, Elastene had shape-memory properties that allowed it to store and release an unprecedented amount of mechanical energy.

Said storage meant it would dissipate heat much faster than any other spacecraft in existence. Shannon's people had confirmed that any engine built from Elastene could run for longer periods, at up to twenty percent higher speeds than current output allowed. These test results were what she currently had on display.

Shannon felt a surge of pleasure as Calista absorbed the information, then broke out into a big smile.

"Well done, team!" Calista crowed. "The ESF will trip over themselves to sign the contract when they see those numbers, Shannon. A full twenty percent increase? Wow, that's more than I could have hoped for!"

Jonesy grinned. "But wait—there's more!" he said. "Right, ma'am?"

Shannon obligingly shrunk the pivot table, pinning it to one side as she opened a second one. This table displayed test results on a slightly modified version of the material: a metal foam.

Engineering Elastene into a metal foam created a surface with an elasticity that was far more successful at deflecting micrometeorites and other impacts than current materials. The material's shape-memory properties absorbed the impact's kinetic energy, spreading it across a much greater surface area.

Shannon hummed in pleasure as the data on the second pivot table was displayed. Incorporating this into the fighter's skin would improve safety margins significantly, she knew. The ESF would love this.

She paused as a notification came in, then gave an audible sigh over the room's speakers.

"Well," she said, "it would appear our esteemed friends at the ESF have rescheduled our presentation." She posted the revised departure schedule on the net for the team working on the prototype to see. They probably wouldn't mind the extra time—it would provide them an opportunity to give the ship a last once-over prior to loading it onto the transport ship for its journey to the ESF's military testing facility.

Jonesy rolled his eyes. "Now ain't that just like the space force?" Shannon felt amusement as he quoted an old human adage, "Hurry up and wait."

"Well then," Calista said briskly to Shannon. "Since you have some unexpected time on your hands, think you could spare a few minutes to walk me through your proposed production timeline for those new freighters we're hoping to turn out for Avalon Mining?"

"Sure," the AI replied as she switched her awareness from Icarus over to their civilian project, Galatea. Being more of a software innovation than a materials advance, Galatea didn't carry the hefty price tag the Icarus design carried, which was a good thing where commercial ventures were concerned.

"We'll easily make the deadline Avalon stipulated," Shannon responded. "But it's been three weeks since we demoed the freighter for them, and we're still waiting to hear back on the contract we submitted."

Calista nodded. "I'll have the sales team look into it. I'm sure we'll have it in hand soon."

"True, but I'm not going to authorize a production run until we have a contract." Shannon injected a wry note into her reply. "It's kind of hard for an AI to begin production on a 'handshake deal'… given I don't exactly have hands."

"I've offered to build you a set," Jonesy interjected. "But *I* think you *like* not having a set of hands, as often as you use not having them as an excuse to have one of us do more work."

"Aaaaand on *that* little note of insubordination, I'll just see myself out," Calista wiggled her hands in the air and headed back toward the lab's entrance. She turned to address Shannon's pickups as she reached the doors. "Let me know if you need anything in the interim, Shannon. I'll meet you at the transport…" she accessed the information Shannon had posted to the net, "first thing tomorrow."

* * * * *

In another part of the facility, a technician who had been

helping run final tests on the fighter volunteered to go on a run to Supply for a replacement spectrometer, when the one she had set up 'tested faulty'. She scooped up the unit and trotted off with a purposeful gait.

No one noticed her divert to a back office and engage a security protocol for the room. Truth be told, no one had noticed her the past *dozen times* she had ducked into an unused office over the past few months.

Not that it matters, she thought to herself in annoyance.

Enfield's files were a lot more secure than she had first thought when she had initially agreed to obtain them. It was supposed to have been an easy way to pick up some fast credits on the side. Unfortunately, the files she *had* managed to acquire weren't exciting in the least.

She'd been hoping her handler would ask her to steal something top shelf and totally worth the risk. Instead, her contact had ordered her to copy the weekly logs from the company's fleet vehicle department.

Who wants a log of Enfield's shuttle traffic every week, anyway? She sighed. *This gig couldn't possibly be more boring.*

Which was weird, because her handler seriously scared the shit out of her.

As a mining platform brat, she considered herself to be pretty tough, and fairly inured to the kind of threats that might freak out most of the population of the ring. *But these people....*

She'd seen the tattoo she was certain her handler had intended for her to spot: the top half of a compass rose with a starburst sitting behind the big 'N' at the top. She might be tough, but she knew better than to go head-to-head with the Norden Cartel.

She waved her hand to project the virtual token she'd managed to clone from an engineer before he'd left earlier that day. It was such a waste to steal fleet logs. Hell, if she was taking the risk, she was going for the big, juicy stuff for herself, like the files for Icarus or Galatea.

She knew a guy who knew a guy over at TransOrbital Systems, Enfield's biggest competitors. *Surely they'll pay well to get their hands on those specs?*

Swiftly, she took a seat at a system node. Flicking her eyes up to her HUD one last time to ensure the security interlocks still held, she triggered the cloned token, and the system let her in.

The flight plans were easy, but every time she tried to grab the icon for Icarus, it greyed out, marking itself as inaccessible from this terminal. Frustrated, she blew out a hard breath. *Okay, fine.* She navigated over to Galatea. It also flagged as inaccessible, but she proxied her connection through another system with elevated access, and the file tree opened up.

There.

Mentally crowing at her good fortune, she kept the connection open while quickly switching tokens, burning through a few of the fake idents they had given her before creating an untraceable connection to the remote system.

Quickly, before anyone could notice the long-running connection, she dumped Galatea's data into a network dump only she had access to. Once it had finished copying over, she navigated to the node where her handler had set up a digital dead drop, and sent the week's fleet logs.

What a total waste.

She considered another try for Icarus, but decided it wasn't worth the risk. Besides, that data would command such a high price it would be almost impossible to launder the funds.

The moment the logs were in place, she destroyed the tokens and quickly returned the office to the condition she'd found it in. Using a different security token to disengage the security protocol, she exited the room.

Two minutes later, she was on the way to Supply to

complete her assigned task.

HUNTING GHOSTS

STELLAR DATE: 07.03.3189 (Adjusted Gregorian) 02:00 local time
LOCATION: Senator's Office, Parliament House, Sonali
REGION: El Dorado Ring, El Dorado, Alpha Centauri System

"Today, the opposition party released a statement questioning Parliament's ability to effectively enact a plan to curb the cartel's increased influence among the mining rigs in the Dust Ring...."

Ben sat at a conference table inside Lysander's office, and looked from the senator's avatar to the five AIs that Lysander had assembled. Some represented themselves in human form, like the senator did, while others appeared simply as color-shifting columns of light.

He had asked for a team of AIs, and Lysander had delivered.

Ben recognized two of the AIs present: retired Vice-Marshal Esther, and Space Commodore Eric, also retired. As the others were introduced, Ben realized he knew the rest by way of reputation.

Gladys was a brilliant hacker and security consultant, known to have worked with prominent corporations and government agencies alike. Her skill at infiltrating systems— and identifying and eliminating their vulnerabilities—was renowned. As was her penchant for flamboyance. He was rather surprised that Gladys had opted to represent herself as a simple column of light today.

Although, he admitted, *hers is the flashiest one. Is that glitter, floating around in there?*

The final two members were a pair of AIs whose names conjured whispered tales about black ops shrouded in mystery. Legend had it that the two had been born by special request. Their service had begun in the Marines, but had concluded in the Space Force. The portions of their records that had not been redacted proved that very few could escape an engagement with just one of the twins and come out unscathed. When they worked together, no one escaped them.

It was rumored that Landon and Logan held the record for the longest service-time in the deep black, out of any sentient in the history of the Alpha Centauri system. No one seemed to know what this record entailed or what its significance implied—only that it was spoken of in hushed tones by AIs.

As Ben's gaze swept across the five, he realized suddenly that his crazy idea to run an off-the-books op didn't feel so crazy anymore.

Damn, I just might be able to pull this thing off after all.

Ben shifted his gaze from Lysander's five guests back to the senator's representation. Focusing his attention on the files he had highlighted, he splayed out his hand. The gesture caused the files to spread across the tank's imaging area.

"Here is everything we have been able to piece together about Norden," he told them. "From what we can tell, they're an opportunistic disease that has infected every major segment of organized crime."

He brought the report on the drug raid from a few days ago to the foreground. "Controlled substances."

He flicked his hand and the report shrunk into a corner of the display as he brought up the next one.

"Arms deals. Everything from the very large to small-time operators."

Another flick, another report pinned alongside the first box.

"They've been caught brokering corporate espionage deals."

A third box took its place alongside the first two.

"Hell," Ben dropped his hand and sighed. "There are even rumors they're branching into human trafficking." Sweeping his gaze across the visages of the AIs present, he continued, "We believe Norden has agents inside the Secret Intelligence Service, and most likely in Parliament House, as well. Of course, we have nothing to substantiate those beliefs."

He paused a beat and looked away, forcing his clenched jaw to relax. "To be brutally honest, I'm tired of these assholes operating with impunity. At the very least, we need to cripple them, shake up their command structure. It's my hope that it will give us the traction we need to ultimately take them down."

<I don't think any of us would disagree,> one of the pillars of light—Landon, Ben's HUD informed him—was the first to reply. *<From what we can tell, they are funding many of the Humanity First rallies, too.>*

<More unrest,> another agreed. *<Destabilizing the government has historically been good for business, where cartels are concerned.>*

<So how can we assist?> the avatar of the Vice-Marshal asked.

"I've managed to get two assets in place inside their headquarters, two people that I alone in the SIS know about. My initial plan was to locate their headquarters, then order a targeted strike to destroy it. But now, after the near-failure of a raid yesterday...."

Ben gestured, and an image of the planet appeared on Lysander's holo. The image zoomed in on the mountain range just beyond the planet's capital of Tomlinson City.

"I think our best target of opportunity is here. We just received word that Norden has begun operating a warehouse on the far side of Muzhavi Ridge."

He highlighted a shallow valley between two peaks.

"It's in this bowl on the other side of Scar Top Peak. My asset has arranged to have a small bomb placed among some crates containing directed energy weapons. It's shielded, so its presence should remain undetected."

<Exactly how small is this 'small device,' Meyer?> Gladys asked, her column flashing brightly as she spoke. *<Show us the data on this, please. I will only agree to this if we keep the damage and harm to a minimum.>*

<I fail to see how a facility of the size you describe could have been built without anyone on El Dorado being aware of its existence.> Commodore Eric's mental tone was laden with skepticism.

"It could have if the facility was built by a shell corporation, constructed on the pretense of studying the situation with the tectonic plates," Ben countered. "And believe me, it had plenty of cutouts. They even received validation from the university—from my own wife's department, no less." He added under his breath, "I'm sure they had a good laugh over that."

<How do you propose to detonate such a weapon?> the commodore asked. *<Any signal you send can be traced back to its point of origin, so you'll need a way to send a code that's not going to lead them right back to you.>*

"I have that covered," Ben assured them. "My agent has created a backdoor in the security net, around the bowl, that will create a dead zone for a brief period. With that, we should be able to get close enough to send a command to detonate."

Ben looked over at Lysander. "This isn't what I need your help with. I meant it when I said I want to destroy their infrastructure." He sent another file via his Link, and a projection of the ring near the far continent's space elevator sprang into view.

"We assume the cartel is based somewhere along the ring on the opposite side of the planet from Parliament House. Yet the ring's NSAI sweeps have failed to find anything out of the ordinary in any scans of the area."

<Some form of stealth tech?> Gladys inquired.

"Not quite. It's pretty clever what they've done, actually," Ben said. "As you know, the undeveloped sections of the ring are comprised of millions of kilometers of unused maglev lines." As he spoke, the lines were highlighted on the holo.

"These lines terminate at regular intervals, dumping into what are currently large, empty spaces. Someday, as we expand, these will be easily converted to spacedocks, warehouses, parkland, or centers of industry." More areas flickered as they were highlighted.

"But right now, they're just empty space. Our friendly, neighborhood cartel has found a way to retrofit a few old barges, some shipping containers, and a few spare maglev cars. They've networked these together into a mobile control center that is modular and easily dismantled."

Ben threw up his hands in disgust. "We haven't found their headquarters because it's *mobile*. My assets inside tell me that after a random number of days, they literally tear everything down, pack it up, and relocate.

"And no one but Victoria North's number one knows when it'll happen. For all we know, he just wakes up one morning and decides, 'what the hell, let's move today'."

<And you haven't been able to track them down through any other means?>

"We're working on that, but that stealth tech you mentioned earlier? Our asset explained that they have a way to spoof the NSAI's search algorithm to keep themselves from being found.

"He says they call it 'rigging for silent running'. They basically eliminate all superfluous noise by shutting down any system that would emit an EM signature within the scan's range. It's even mandatory for all humans to remain perfectly still so that no unnecessary sound waves are created. "

Ben looked from pillar to avatar to pillar, then over to Lysander. "*This* is where I need your help the most—find their base of operations…and shut it down for good."

The conversation carried on for nearly an hour, the AIs

grilling Ben on what he knew, what resources he had available, how he would explain going off-book to his superiors if he were caught—or failed. As the meeting progressed, he became certain that none of them would join in, that it had been a waste of time.

After Ben had answered what turned out to be the final question, Eric glanced at the others and shrugged.

"Seems like a fun diversion. I'm in."

Gladys's column of light sparkled as she laughed. "I was in from the moment you said 'off-book'."

The other three AIs pledged themselves to the mission, and from there, conversation turned to formulating a plan as to how they would find the cartel's current base.

An hour later, as the last guest disconnected and the avatars faded from view, Ben stood to leave. As he drew on his jacket, Lysander raised his hand in a restraining gesture. "Ben…"

The analyst turned and gave the senator a questioning look.

"Have you spoken with Jason, as I suggested the other day?"

Ben's questioning look turned to a frown. "Really, Lysander. I know you're fond of the guy, but—"

"A deal is a deal, Benjamin," Lysander said severely. "You agreed that if I set you up with a team of AIs who would assist you, that you'd at least give Jason a chance."

Ben sighed heavily.

"Okay. I'll ping him this evening. No promises, though," Ben warned the AI. "I'll sit down with him and talk. Feel him out. If I get any sense that he can't be trusted…."

"Fair enough," Lysander said.

* * * * *

Calista paused in the entrance to the Plasma Wave and checked the time on her overlay. She was a bit early, but she decided to go ahead and grab a seat.

The bar was a favorite haunt of flight crews. Located just off a concourse in Sonali's spaceport, which connected several public docks, the Plasma Wave had become an easy place to hook up with old friends or to find out who was looking for crew for a freight run.

Job boards were even posted to one side of the bar, the holodisplay slowly scrolling through several popular feeds in a repeating loop.

Calista sent Jason a location pin as she slid into a booth in the back of the bar and waved a servitor over. She was momentarily surprised when she heard Shannon's voice in her head. She'd forgotten for a moment that the AI had asked if she could tag along via the Link this evening.

<So, this Jason guy you've been seeing, what's he like? >

"I don't know," Calista sub-vocalized, looking around at the crowd. "He's a pilot."

<Oh, come on,> Shannon chided. <Give me more than that! Tell me what he looks like. I've accessed your eye implant feeds, and wow. The humans here come in all sorts of shapes and sizes—and mods,> she added, as a woman with cooling fins implanted sagittally across the top of her scalp walked past, pink ringlets cascading down from between them.

Calista eyed the woman. <Probably shipping out as a navigator, or comm officer—or a combination of both,> she said absently.

Shannon made a sound over the Link that sounded like fingers snapping. <Back on task, Major Boss-lady. Jason. Details. Now.>

<Okay, fine!> Calista laughed. <What's Jason like... Well, he's tall, has dark blonde hair. Eyes, hmm.> Calista paused, considering an apt description. <The color of a good brandy.>

<Oooh, now isn't that poetic?> Shannon lowered her voice and waggled her eyebrows suggestively in Calista's mind.

<Seriously, Shannon. We're in a bar. It's not that much of a stretch,> Calista replied tartly.

<Well, go on. Tell me more!>

<Hmm. He's pretty physically fit, yet kind of laid-back, actually. Except when he's flying.> She paused again. <He has amazing hand-eye coordination in the cockpit—which probably means he has the standard pilot mods for high g acceleration.>

Shannon made a noise that sounded awfully like a snort of derision to Calista. <Is that the only use you can think of for amazing hand-eye coordination, girl?> she asked pointedly. <Reeeeally?>

Calista rolled her eyes and caught sight of the object of their discussion standing in front of her, and she was horrified to find herself blushing slightly. Which was ridiculous, because he had absolutely no way of knowing she and Shannon were discussing him.

"How did you sneak up on me like that?" Calista demanded, and Jason's eyebrows rose as he grinned lazily at her.

"Well, hel-loooo to you, too," he drawled, then made an inquiring motion to the seat across from her.

<Ohhh myyyyyy, he's yummy,> Calista heard Shannon purr as Jason sat.

"Wait, just...one," Calista held up a finger to Jason and focused on Shannon. <Okay, that's enough for one night, I think. I'll see you tomorrow, back at the office.>

She heard a heavy sigh. <Spoilsport,> Shannon said, and then her presence faded.

Jason grinned again. "Let me guess, a Chief Pilot's work is never done?"

"Well, it beats having to check the boards every time I come in here, wondering when my next job's going to come through, or where the flight's going to take me," she retorted, but without any heat.

Jason stabbed an imaginary knife through his heart. "Ouch! Need I remind you that I was gainfully employed for a good two months out of the last three? And spent them flying Enfield machines, too."

"Well, at least we know you didn't kill any crew in the process. Our safety interlocks are set so that even a ham-handed pilot such as the likes of you couldn't mess things up too badly." Calista's eyes twinkled at Jason. "But enough shop talk. Tell me about yourself, Jason Andrews. I want to know every sordid detail."

"You'll have to buy me the Plasma Special for that kind of intel." Jason settled back, throwing his arm across the empty seat next to him. "You see, I was born at a very young age...."

* * * * *

"So? Did you end up at her place?" Tobias's voice projected into the mainspace, as Jason entered the apartment.

Before Jason could respond, Tobi entered from the kitchen and greeted Jason with a rumbling trill. She padded after him, as he walked into the living area and tossed his jacket over a chair.

"Mmmaaaaaaybe," Jason drew out, and he could feel the grin on his face as he settled back on the sofa and kicked his heels up onto the low table in front of it.

"I do hate it when you leave me behind," Tobias grumbled. "You always cut me out of the juicy stuff."

"Sorry, dude," Jason sounded completely unrepentant. "Not into threesomes."

Tobi leapt up next to him on the sofa and sprawled halfway across his lap, purring.

Tobias snorted. "So? Details? Give 'em up, boyo!"

"Mmm, well, she has a condo over in that trendy new development on the east side of the lake." Jason leaned past Tobi and reached into a drawer as he spoke, pulling out a bundle that looked like thin plastic tubing. It separated into two short sections that he absently began to roll around in his hands.

"Sounds like Chief Pilot pays pretty well," Tobias commented. "Ever considered going for a gig like that?"

"Eh," Jason shrugged. "Plenty of time for a career later. Besides, she served several years in the ESF before landing that job."

"Nothing says you couldn't do the same," Tobias countered.

The pieces of tubing glinted as thin filaments embedded in the material caught the light. Jason inserted them in his ears with practiced moves that came from years of use. He grimaced slightly as he adjusted first one, then the other.

He snorted. "Can you see me as captain—or major, for that matter—of anything, ever?"

"At the risk of sounding like I'm significantly older and wiser than you," Tobias said in a rare moment of adulting, "Yeah, I can. Seriously, Jase. You could do anything you set your mind to."

"Thanks, Tobe," Jason said with a quick look of appreciation, before he began rotating his head and neck, adjusting to the disorientation he always felt when he inserted the tubes into his ears.

The filaments that relayed the secured Link to his brain curled deep into his auditory canal, preventing his ears from receiving sound waves as they normally did. This change in auditory input always caused a bit of vertigo until his brain adjusted to it.

<You there?> Jason sent the mental query.

<Five by five, boyo,> Tobias replied.

This secured, private access Link was as close as Jason would ever get to the experience of being embedded with an AI. Somehow, the fidelity of their connection was crisper, more nuanced than a regular Link.

Tobias had told him it wasn't quite the same as being embedded, but it was close. The filaments' proximity to Jason's neural net allowed the AI to pick up far more than he ordinarily would by simply connecting over a Link.

<Welcome back,> Jason heard Tobias say now, the AI's voice flavored with a humor and warmth Jason knew he would not have felt over a standard connection.

He sent Tobias a 'wait' signal when his Link indicated that his brother-in-law was pinging him.

<Hey, Ben, what's up?> Jason said in greeting.

<Got some time to hang with your brother-in-law? It's been a while.>

Jason quirked an eyebrow at Tobias and sent to him privately, <It's Judith's husband.>

Tobias's avatar raised the cat's eyebrows in a quizzical look that almost had Jason laughing out loud.

<It cracks me up every time you use her as your avatar,> he sent to Tobias, then switched back over to his conversation with Ben.

<Sure thing, bro,> Jason responded to Ben. <Whatcha got in mind, there?>

<Want to grab a bite and catch up?>

Jason shot the Tobys a look. <This is a bit weird,> he sent to Tobias privately. <Ben wants to hang out with me.>

<Always a first time for everything.> Tobias's cat avatar shrugged and Jason returned to his conversation with Ben.

<I told Avalon I'd do a bit of local ring shuttling for them tomorrow. They have an ore hauler scheduled in from one of those mining rigs of theirs…Thiton, I think. Or was it Gliton?> Jason sent a shrug over the Link. <Anyway, I'll be tied up with them

most of the day, but I could meet you after. Would that work?>

<Oh, good. Good.> Jason thought Ben sounded a bit distracted.

Wonder what's up.

Judith had sounded fine the last time they'd talked, so that was probably not it. Jason hoped Ben wasn't planning on dragging him into some messy family thing. If that was going to be the case, best they meet somewhere he knew Ben wouldn't be likely to hang around for long.

<We could meet down at the spaceport,> Jason suggested quickly. <There's a bar down there that serves a pretty good grilled cheese.>

Like that was the kind of food Jason had ever seen Ben eat.

<Sure, sounds fine. I could probably make it around...> Ben's voice paused, <Six PM, local.>

Something is definitely up.

Jason dropped the bar's location pin to his brother-in-law over the Link, and they disconnected.

"Now, I wonder what *that* was all about."

LISA RICHMAN & M. D. COOPER

SHOWTIME

STELLAR DATE: 07.03.3189 (Adjusted Gregorian)
LOCATION: Enfield Aerospace Docks
REGION: El Dorado Ring, Alpha Centauri System

"The Chairman of the Clean Space Initiative has announced a new goal for the coming fiscal year: legislation aimed at enforcing an expiration date on all derelict ships.

This would mean that owners are responsible for fully breaking down and recycling or incinerating all parts of decommissioned ships by a specified deadline.

It is the hope of the Committee overseeing this initiative that this will relieve the overcrowding in orbital boneyards, those space 'burial grounds,' if you will, for ships no longer spaceworthy."

Calista smiled when she caught sight of the fighter being loaded into the cargo bay of the transport as she arrived. That was one sexy piece of equipment; she couldn't wait to show it off to space command today.

"Excuse me, ma'am?" The quartermaster hailed Calista and began hurrying her way as she caught sight of her.

"Hey, Q," she greeted the woman, who somehow managed to keep tabs on the chaos that swirled around her.

Now, she tapped an icon on a holo sheet she carried, showing it to Calista. "Our orders only listed this version of the prototype to be loaded. Did you want us to load the other fighter—the one with the ultra-coating? How about the cargo transport prototype?"

Calista shook her head. "Nope. Shannon is still ironing out the kinks on the ultra, and we don't need the transport for the demo. Just the one you're loading up will do." She smiled over at the quartermaster. "But thanks for asking, Q."

The woman nodded and hurried off to prep the ship for

90

departure.

Calista spared the transport one last glance as she exited the dock, on her way to a final review with Shannon before taking off.

* * * * *

"Hey, Mack?" Sally looked over her shoulder at the chief of staff, who was lounging against the frame of the command center maglev car. "Antonio just pinged and wants to know what to do with the ship those AIs came in on."

Mack shifted his weight from the doorframe and crossed his arms, scowling. "Is he sure everything's been scrubbed? Nothing that can connect it back to a bunch of AIs?"

Sally paused as she conferred with Antonio. "He says it's good to go."

Mack grunted. "About time. I was getting tired of having to move that thing around every time there was a sweep."

He walked forward and leaned over her shoulder, tapping the holo that displayed a map of nearspace beyond the ring.

Pointing to the Guatavita boneyard, he grinned. "Didn't Verda tell Customs that's where it was headed to begin with?" He waved his hand expansively. "Wouldn't want to make a liar out of her now, would we?"

Verda grinned over at him from her station. "You calling me a liar, Mack?" She batted her eyes at him.

"Guess not, V," he said amiably. "Tell him to dump it in with the rest of the crap out there." He turned and resumed his slouch against the frame as Sally sent Antonio the response.

* * * * *

Being CEO hath its privileges, Terrance thought with a smile as he sat in one of the jump seats behind the transport crew. In this case, it made going over his proposal to win the El Dorado Space Force's contract a lot more pleasant.

The ship—carrying its one-of-a-kind prototype—had just disengaged from the ring and was making its way out to the interdicted area reserved exclusively for the ESF.

Traversing the Special Use Space/Military Operations Area—or SUS/MOA, for short—was never a good idea, unless you had received prior approval. That their destination *was* the MOA just made it more fun to be in the cockpit, as far as he was concerned.

He glanced over at Calista, who was flying co-pilot. For her, this was old, familiar territory. He, on the other hand, still got a bit of a thrill out of being somewhere he normally oughtn't.

Well. Best to get on with it, he thought in reference to the excuse he'd used to be sitting up here in the first place.

<I hear your team's a bit concerned about the Avalon contract,> he began over a private connection to Calista. Her avatar nodded once.

<They've never held out this long before signing,> she replied. *<I figured it might be worth looking into.>*

<Good. I'm sure you'll get it sorted out soon.>

Terrance was about to discuss Calista's agenda for today's meeting, when the pilot drew their attention with a 'huh' and a swift zoom in on the holo tank's view.

"Check that out," the pilot said, pointing to an icon on the holodisplay before him. It highlighted as he tapped on it, and the flight engineer obligingly zoomed in. It was a lone ship, and appeared to be headed away from the rarely used space elevator on the opposite side of the ring.

The ship looked as if it had seen better days. Scarred and incapable of holding atmosphere in places, Terrance assumed it was most likely en route to one of the boneyards for scrap.

"Huh," the flight engineer muttered again as he brought up the ship's ident. "Hey, Shannon, you recall a ship named the *New Saint Louis*? That thing's claiming Sol registry, and it rings a bell...."

<That ship was mentioned in one of the accounts of the Phobos Accords,> the AI responded after a beat. *<It was listed as one of the ships granted to the AIs planning to leave the Sol System.>*

"I wonder what became of them," Calista murmured thoughtfully.

*<Well, the presence of that ship suggests they **did** leave,>* Shannon mused, *<but I can't find a record of them arriving anywhere.>*

"Maybe they sold the ship after they got to wherever they were going," the flight engineer suggested. "They could've been in Proxima all this time, and passed off the ship to a mining or shipping company."

He pointed to the habitat cylinder. Normally, it would be rotating to generate an artificial gravity for its passengers, but that would have been pointless in this instance; the habitat looked a bit like an old tin can that had been pried open on one end.

"Maybe they were using it as a long-hauler, with an AI crew. No breathable air, but the cargo areas look intact."

Suddenly the pilot cursed, and the transport went into a steep dive. "What the *fuck*—"

"Pinnace out there, running dark." Calista's words were clipped as she flicked her hands through the holodisplay. "Advising El Dorado Tower now."

"Looks like it's registered to a private cab company," the pilot said. "And flown by an idiot who can't see a big white Enfield transport shuttle."

<Trajectory places it on a reciprocal from the NorthStar Industries shipyards,> Shannon informed them.

"Tagging and filing a complaint with STA now," the flight

engineer confirmed as he made a copy of the holo the transport automatically recorded.

Seeing the crew had enough on their hands, Calista Linked back to the passenger cabin. Her team wanted to know what in the hell had just happened, and she wanted to know how that dodge had affected their special cargo.

<It's fine,> Shannon assured her privately. <Nothing short of an e-beam pulse fired directly at the fighter would do any harm. And even then, it'd fare much better than the transport we're in!>

<Glad you decided to come along,> Calista responded.

<It's my baby as much as it is yours. I wouldn't have missed this for the world.>

* * * * *

Jason was delivering his final load of cargo from Avalon Mining's outer shipyards when he heard Calista's voice, talking to the tower on one of the open channels. He brought up the tower's feed and quickly spotted the Enfield transport, headed out to the ESF military operations area.

<Is that your new girlfriend?>

Jason glanced down at the cat, sprawled on the hauler's floor between the pilot's seat and the empty co-pilot's seat.

<She's not my girlfriend, Tobe. She's just a friend who happens to be a girl.>

<Uh-huh. Which totally explains why your heart rate jumped that little bit when you heard her voice.>

<Asshole,> Jason replied without rancor, then paused, turning up the CTAF audio as he caught the phrase 'spacecraft, running dark'.

<There,> Tobias said, and highlighted a spot too far away from their flight path to be a factor. <Idiot. Wouldn't want to be that pilot when he lands—STA doesn't suffer fools. He just earned a suspension of his license, at the very minimum.>

"Good thing, too," Jason agreed as he configured the shuttle to land, while checking the chronometer. He still had a good three hours before he was to meet Ben planetside. Just enough time to run Tobi back up to the apartment and maybe get in a quick game of darts at the bar before his brother-in-law arrived.

* * * * *

Back on the *Sylvan,* Victoria set aside her second glass of an excellent Old Terra Marlborough, a beverage she had not offered to their guest, who had just left. She called up the recording her office had made of the meeting with Rosalind Bianchi's assistant.

Bit of a nervous man, she thought idly, as she reviewed the flight records he'd brought showing that the logs of shuttles arriving and departing from the Muzhavi Bowl now bore Enfield idents and tail numbers.

Excellent. She'd have to see about stepping up this AI trafficking business; it was turning out to be quite lucrative.

Victoria couldn't care less that AIs were sentient. Human, AI—it didn't matter one whit to her what kind of trafficking her organization engaged in.

Had human trafficking paid more than that of AI, well then, her holds would have been filled with grubby, stinky flesh. This was much more pleasant; AI cylinders were much smaller than human bodies—and they didn't smell.

Victoria added today's recording to her file on Bianchi. The Minister knew she had the recording, of course. Victoria used it to ensure Rosalind's cooperation, in case the Minister decided she ever wanted out of their little agreement.

Sadly, Bianchi wasn't quite sharp enough to have figured out how hollow Victoria's threats truly were. She wasn't about to expose the woman; she needed Bianchi to defeat that stars-be-damned AI, Lysander, in the polls.

Victoria's little puppet was going to ensure that the laws excluding sentient AI from holding certain jobs were not declared 'unconstitutional'. She knew damned well that if Lysander won, that would be at the top of his list of reforms.

But that, she could not allow. As long as AI were relegated to second-class citizenry, they were one step closer to being seen as things and not people.

Things were commodities. Commodities could be bought, sold or...otherwise acquired.

And isn't it convenient that I'm in the 'acquisitions' business....

BROTHERLY BONDING

STELLAR DATE: 07.03.3189 (Adjusted Gregorian)
LOCATION: El Dorado Executive Air Field (General Aviation Area)
REGION: Tomlinson City, El Dorado, Alpha Centauri System

"...with over 400 million hectares of national parks to enjoy, a wealth of biodiversity, and a wide variety of landscapes, don't you owe it to yourself to take a trip down to El Dorado and experience its natural beauty in-person?"

Ben suppressed a frown as the groundcar pulled up to the Bad Attitude Bar, the destination on the pin Jason had sent him the day before. He absently accepted the groundcar's transportation charge, and schooled his expression to be a bit more pleasant than he felt as the door slid open and he exited.

The bar sat on the less polished side of the El Dorado spaceport. The stench of fuels and lubricants that assaulted Ben's nose emphasized its working-class roots. He guessed that the melliferous odors were coming from the row of hangars that rose up behind the bar.

He had a difficult time reconciling the fact that his refined and educated wife had a brother who was, for all he could tell, essentially a bum.

Judith Andrews was an impressive woman, and he'd been captivated by her from the moment they'd met at a debate hosted by the University of El Dorado some years back. Even though she was not a native, Judith's degrees in biogeochemistry and planetary zoology made her an expert on El Dorado.

The university had recently appointed her to chair the Department of Planetary Sciences. The department's primary objective, as laid out by the FGT, was to monitor the planet's development.

Or, as Ben liked to think of it, to make sure the Future Generation Terraformers hadn't screwed up, causing the planet to go off the rails somehow.

Judith's brother, on the other hand, seemed to have been born without the drive to succeed. Unless it was succeeding at snowboarding. Or base jumping, or asteroid skipping. Or any number of other extreme sports Ben knew Jason had mastered.

Jason was a good twenty years Judith's junior, so that might contribute to their differences. Maybe they grew them different in Proxima, and Judith was the exception. She'd been away far longer than her brother, so who knew?

Ben strode purposefully toward the entrance of the Bad Attitude Bar, barely missing a collision with a grimy someone exiting the establishment. Pivoting out of the way just in time, Ben pasted on a smile that he hoped didn't look too fake, then steeled himself for the onslaught.

He paused just inside the entrance to give his eyes a moment to adjust, and winced at the music. Jason called it 'honky-tonk', and swore it was Old Earth classical music. Ben hated it.

His eyes took in the darkened interior, where tables sat in front of walls decorated with old, wooden propellers and other aviation memorabilia. Pinned around the props were torn shirts in varying colors and styles, with names and dates scrawled on them.

Jason had told Ben and Judith that these shirts represented a timeworn tradition, dating back to Old Terra. In those days, flight instructors didn't have realistic, interactive holosimulators in which to instruct their students; they flew actual aircraft for hours on end, students ensconced in the left seat behind the yoke, while the instructor sat behind the co-pilot's controls on the right.

After the instructor judged the student to have a solid, instinctive feel for the aircraft, the student was turned loose to fly the machine for the very first time on their own. It was at the same time both terrifying and exhilarating, and a moment no pilot ever forgot.

After completing that first solo flight, the student pilot's shirt was ceremonially ripped up the back to commemorate the event. The tradition was nearly fifteen hundred years old, and the shirts hanging in the bar were testament to that fact. Scrawled boldly across the fabric of each shirt were words that proudly proclaimed the student pilot's name, the date of the solo flight, and the spaceport where it had occurred.

Ben's surveyance of the bar was interrupted by the *thunk* of a dart hitting home, and the cheering of onlookers. He turned toward the sound and spotted Jason, leaning indolently against the bar, a beer in one hand, and a dart in the other.

* * * * *

Jason had been aware of Ben the moment his well-dressed, somewhat uptight brother-in-law had stepped inside the Bad Attitude.

He grinned to himself. *Dude needs a change of clothes. And a beer.* Judith had said that Ben was working long hours lately; maybe he just needed to let his hair down a little. If that was the case, Jason would be happy to oblige.

He turned as Sam—the woman whose plane was in the hangar next to his—nudged him.

"Your turn," the woman grinned up at him, nodding at the dartboard. A bit distracted by his musings over Ben, Jason tossed his dart, not taking his usual care to disguise his aptitude.

Oops.

He came to himself when the dart whacked the center of the bullseye with a little more force than necessary. His companion whooped loudly and reached over to plant a wet, sloppy kiss near his mouth.

Jason could't help but grin at Sam's antics. She was a fun drunk, a bit too touchy, but she looked after his plane when he was away, so he'd forgive her extra attention.

Granted, it wasn't entirely unwelcome, but Calista Reinhart had been on his mind more than a little of late.

"That's the ticket, flyboy," she said with a leer and a slight slur, leaning her body against his. Grinning, he lifted his drink in salute as she spun around to take her turn.

"Day-um," he drawled lazily, as she managed to land a respectable shot in the inner ring.

Jason caught Ben's eye and saluted him with his last dart, then flung it at the wall, purposely missing the dartboard altogether.

"Whoops, guess you won again!" He reversed his cap, settling the brim properly in front, and saluted her with it as he pushed away from the group.

Jason indicated a table in a corner, farther away from the crowd, so they could talk without yelling.

"What brings you to the Bad Attitude, Ben? Interested in a flight lesson or two?" The glint in Jason's eye surely must have told Ben that he was joking. In case it didn't, he added a wink for effect. He was surprised to see the man nod.

"Maybe. I just thought, you know, since you decided to stay in El Dorado a bit longer this time, it might be nice to get to know you better." The side of Ben's mouth kicked up. "You're family, after all."

Jason peered at him for a moment, shrugged, and settled back in his chair. "I'm an open book," he said, then waggled his glass at Ben. "Want one?"

"Sure," Ben said. "Whatever you're drinking."

A beer? Really? Not likely. Jason knew Ben was more of a bourbon guy, sometimes scotch...he had to give the man props for manning up in a place that only served craft brews.

Jason waved his hand, activating the menu. and placed their order.

* * * * *

Ben sat across from Jason, smiling. It felt forced, but he hoped it didn't show too much. He needed help, and he had a feeling that Lysander would be more than a little displeased if Ben sought out someone other than who he'd recommended. Plus, it didn't feel right to just come out and ask Jason for assistance without at least a little small talk.

The servitor brought their drinks, and Jason lifted his in a salute.

Ben returned the salute, then looked down at the foam-capped drink in his hand, wishing it were a fine, craft-made spirit instead. He could really use a good single malt scotch right now, instead of the beer the bar kept on tap. *Organic, oak-aged, mellow, with a—*

He stopped, sighed mentally, and resigned himself to drinking something a bit less flavorful and a lot less potent. He thought he'd done a credible job of masking his distaste until he caught Jason's knowing smirk.

"Here," Jason said, and swapped glasses with him. Ben sniffed, cocked an eyebrow at him, and took a drink.

"Iced tea? Really?"

Jason shrugged. "I know nano can scrub alcohol from our systems pretty quickly, but no need to make it work any harder than necessary right before a flight." He grinned. "Besides, I *like* tea." He lowered his voice. "Just don't tell anyone—it might damage my reputation."

Ben set the glass down and looked at Jason appraisingly. "And now I'm wondering how much of that is an act, and how much is real."

The 'flyboy' leaned back, raising his hands slightly.

"Busted."

Ben narrowed his eyes at the man sitting across from him. "The 'aimless wanderer' act, too?"

Jason shrugged, then shot Ben an easy grin. "Never been any reason to disabuse you of that notion, to be honest."

Ben shook his head as the pilot lifted the glass of beer, then set it back down without drinking from it. "So…what brings about this desire to mingle with the seedier side of El Dorado?" Jason asked.

"Well…I have a few free days coming up, and was hoping you might take me hiking and rappelling up at Muzhavi Ridge." He looked concernedly at Jason. "You *do* know how to rappel, don't you?"

That surprised a burst of laughter from Jason. "Um, yes, but what in the stars prompted this?"

Ben managed to look embarrassed and a little ashamed. "Well, your sister seems to think I need a bit more 'physical activity' in my life." He shrugged. "She suggested the ridge, and it sounded interesting, so I thought I'd ask."

Jason paused a moment, thinking. "Yeah, I suppose we could make that happen."

"I'm free tomorrow." Ben forced a laugh. "Maybe we should do it before I lose my nerve?"

Jason shook his head at him.

At first, Ben thought Jason was about to turn him down. Then he felt the man's eyes sizing him up.

"No time like the present," Jason agreed. "I'll take you up to the top on an easy trail, but it'll still take a few hours—that way you won't be too worn out—then we can rappel down. Work for you?"

At Ben's nod, Jason continued. "Send me your sizes; I'll have gear ready for you in the morning when I pick you up." He paused, a quizzical light gleaming in his eyes, and Ben felt his pulse increase just a bit. "You *sure* there's nothing else you want to tell me?" Jason pressed.

Ben smiled at him. "No, no, that's it. Just want to spend some time outdoors. Can't say I've done that in a very long time."

"Well, all right, then. I imagine you don't want to meet at my apartment..." he added a bit cryptically, but then Ben remembered the cat.

"How about we meet at the elevator and go downside from there? Would you mind if we went a bit later in the afternoon?"

If Jason thought the request odd, he didn't say anything about it. Most likely, he assumed Ben had a meeting, or wanted to keep their excursion short.

His brother-in-law had other reasons, though.

They talked a bit more about various topics, such as what it was like for Jason to haul freight in the black for weeks on end, and how it felt to work behind the scenes, piecing together seemingly unrelated bits of information that would bring criminals to justice.

A few hours later, Ben found to his amazement that he had enjoyed himself. Jason had an easy manner that Ben had dismissed as lack of motivation, but he now realized hid a keen intellect and sharp wit. More than once, Jason had made an observation that had surprised a laugh out of Ben.

Maybe an afternoon spent hiking Muzhavi Ridge won't be so distasteful—as long as he doesn't bring that damn cat along.

* * * * *

"You're not going to stand me up, are you?" Ben asked Jason as he stood to leave. "I'm really looking forward to dropping down the side of a mountain tomorrow."

Jason looked bemusedly at his brother-in-law. Of all the things Ben had ever said to him, this was by far the strangest.

From what he knew, the guy was a suit, a desk-jockey.

Granted, he worked for the Secret Intelligence Service, so what he *really* did was anyone's guess, but Jason assumed it was mostly reading reports or approving security clearances. He certainly wasn't the outdoorsy type.

But, hey, Jason was all for a person deciding to better themselves. Trying new things was usually a good start along the whole betterment path.

Linking with an automated sporting goods store, Jason placed an order for the clothing and equipment Ben would need the next day. He paid a rush fee to have the order delivered to his apartment the next morning. Once the order was confirmed, he glanced at the chronometer on his HUD.

Oh, good. There's time for another game of darts before I head back up to the ring.

He couldn't wait to tell Tobias about his plans for tomorrow. The AI thought Ben was a bit uptight, too. He'd find this turn of events rather amusing.

THEFT

STELLAR DATE: 07.04.3189 (Adjusted Gregorian)
LOCATION: Grande Promenade, Sonali
REGION: El Dorado Ring , El Dorado, Alpha Centauri System

"In a surprise move, Avalon Mining announced this morning that it had signed a contract with TransOrbital Systems for several newly-designed heavy haulers, which coincides with Avalon's announcement that they will be expanding their mining operation half an AU further into the Dust Ring. To accomplish this, the company plans to build three new mining platforms...."

Terrance looked up at the imposing and overwrought façade of the New Terra Restaurant, then over at Enfield Aerospace's Chief Pilot as they approached its entrance at the edge of the Promenade's greenspace in the capital city.

"You really enjoy spending my money this much, Rhinehart?" Terrance gestured to the restaurant in front of them as he looked over at the tall, athletically built woman striding by his side.

Calista Rhinehart glanced at him with an arched eyebrow, but didn't respond as they climbed the restaurant's steps.

Enfield's head of security, Daniel Ciu, coughed a laugh from Terrance's other side. It was quickly stifled as Terrance shot him a dark look, but its effects were obviously wasted on the man. Daniel's eyes danced in amusement as he raised his hands, shooting Terrance an innocent look.

Well, as far as Terrance was concerned, he owed Calista a meal at a ritzy spot anyway, as thanks for the successful completion of the ESF contract for the Icarus fighter. That was one for the win column.

Although he did find it odd that Daniel had insisted they dine here. The head of Enfield Aerospace's security had been rather adamant on the time, too….

"Sir, yes, sir," Calista belatedly replied to Terrance's question, her dark eyes slanting up at him as the corner of her mouth quirked the slightest bit. "Always happy to spend your money, sir."

Terrance gave an exaggerated sigh. Calista knew he hated it when she 'sir'ed him. Which, of course, was why she did it.

Daniel, on the other hand, resumed his chuckling. "You're awfully easy to bait this afternoon," he remarked. "I thought you corporate types had better poker faces."

<*Yeah, it could use a bit of work.*> The voice of Aaron, the AI embedded with Daniel, joined in on their conversation. He sent them an image of Terrance, then layered icons of hearts, clubs, diamonds and spades over the man's face. <*There you go, one poker face. And no charge on the makeover!*>

Terrance sent a mock mental glare Aaron's way, while Calista finally joined Daniel in outright laughter.

"Fine," he said. "But if you three *jokers* ever want lessons on a *real* poker face, that can be arranged."

Aaron was notorious for his quirky humor, and Daniel was forever begging people to stop encouraging him. '*You* can go home every evening', he told them. For Daniel, the puns never stopped.

Terrance suppressed a stab of envy at the thought. He heartily detested his grandmother Sophia's 'request' all but ordering him not to embed with an AI just yet. Though he understood the matriarch's reasoning, he didn't agree with her logic.

Enfield Aerospace was different from all other space technology companies because it actively incorporated AIs as both product developers and end users. There were some who gave them flak for it, and Sophia feared that Enfield's detractors would accuse Terrance, as the company's CEO, of being controlled by AI puppetmasters if he were to get one implanted.

Terrance knew his management style was more in the vein of 'meet them head-on and damn the consequences', compared to Sophia's far subtler—*and,* he admitted to himself *often more devious*—methods. He just wished they weren't necessary at all.

Yeah, I might be a tiny bit jealous of Daniel and Aaron, Terrance thought as he watched his security chief visually sweep the area. The slightest reflection off his eyes as he turned was the only indication that the man's gaze was augmented.

"So, Daniel, why did you insist we show up right at 12:30? What's so important abou—"

Terrance broke off as they entered the restaurant and his eyes alighted on the CEO of TransOrbital Systems, seated at a nearby table, her hand resting lightly on the arm of the man across from her. The man she'd obviously just finished lunching with—the owner of Avalon Mining.

<Well, *that's* not what I expected to see,> Calista said over the group's private connection, her mental voice flavored with a trace of bitterness, though her face remained as neutral as Terrance's had suddenly become.

The woman at the table glanced up and saw Terrance. A slight, knowing smile played around her lips, and she raised her glass to him in a mock salute before turning her attention back to the gentleman across from her.

The owner of Avalon Mining, Jerrod Seele, smiled broadly, extending his hand for her to shake. She returned the handshake, and they both rose.

As the servitor arrived to escort Terrance's party to their private booth, the man turned, his eyes meeting Terrance's and then flinching away. Smile frozen in place, he nodded in Terrance's general direction as they passed.

Well, shit.

Daniel's prior cryptic remarks about something Terrance

needed to see with his own eyes now made sense. He wouldn't have minded if just this once, Daniel had been proven wrong.

The scene he'd just witnessed truly surprised him. He'd thought Enfield's partnership with Seele, and with Avalon Mining, was solid. Avalon employed a bevy of AIs and had a reputation for treating every employee the same, regardless of species.

The Enfield ships Avalon had purchased in the past were all capable of being captained by an AI as easily as a human. Every Enfield ship design had modules for AIs built into it, for that very purpose.

In contrast, TransOrbital Systems catered to companies that were still uncomfortable in a galaxy that acknowledged AIs as people and guaranteed them equal rights under the Phobos Accords.

TransOrbital Systems marketed themselves as a company whose fleet of spacecraft were purely NSAI-run. Their NSAI interface, they claimed, was as good as it got, 'without the need for an AI'.

Avalon signing a deal with TSO? It made no sense.

Nothing was said until Terrance's group was seated, the servitor had taken their order, and Daniel had activated security settings at their table to ensure their conversation was neither overheard nor recorded.

Terrance looked at Calista and then his security chief. "Didn't see that coming," he muttered, reaching out to pour a glass of water from the table's carafe. He looked up at Daniel as he poured. "What else do I need to know about the scene I just witnessed?"

Daniel traded glances with Calista. "First, I'll tell you what I know, then I'll tell you what I suspect." He leaned forward, placing his forearms on the table, hands clasped.

"TransOrbital has made no secret of the fact that they want

Avalon's business. I've heard about several instances in the past three weeks where TSO personnel have been seen cozying up to Avalon execs." He looked up at Terrance, who gave him a nod to indicate he understood.

"There's something else." Daniel paused. "Yesterday morning, one of my men said he saw one of our techs being harassed at a bar by someone who looked pretty rough around the edges. The bully left before my guy could make it over there, but he got a fairly good look at the man—and he thinks it was one of Victoria North's people."

Terrance pursed his lips, his mind racing through the many undesirable implications of that connection.

Daniel continued, waggling his hand between himself and Calista. "I was just about to track Calista down yesterday afternoon when she showed up in my office."

Terrance's eyebrow rose at that, and he turned an expectant eye on the woman, who nodded.

"Shannon was getting a little antsy about the fact that we hadn't yet received a signed contract from Avalon," she explained, "so when we returned from our demo for the El Dorado Space Force, I ran Daniel down and asked him if he had any ideas about what the holdup was."

Daniel reached for a breadstick, inhaled deeply, then let it out in an explosive sigh. "Around the same time, a buddy of mine contacted me and said his wife—who works for TransOrbital—was called in the other night for an unscheduled planning meeting." He pointed one end of the breadstick at Terrance. "Said ordinarily he stays out of his wife's business, and she stays out of his, but that she returned home awfully disturbed about something."

Terrance nodded for Daniel to continue.

"She said the project manager had gloated about some big coup, some designs they'd managed to get their hands on that would absolutely sink Enfield." He bit off one end of the breadstick viciously, chewed for a moment, then went on. "When she entered the room for the meeting, she saw the file that the project manager had up on his screen before he had a chance to blank the holo."

He glanced meaningfully between his two companions. "It had an Enfield watermark on it."

Terrance inhaled sharply, and Daniel held up a hand to forestall him. "It's not Icarus."

Terrance blew out the breath he'd just held.

<No,> Aaron agreed. <When we showed the wife some of the design elements, she identified the one she saw as Galatea.>

Daniel nodded. "We believe that TransOrbital most likely *did* present a variant of Galatea to Avalon with a bid that has undercut ours." <Though they most likely stripped it of any AI interface. They may have changed it enough so that we can't claim patent infringement without testimony from someone like this woman,> Aaron interjected.

"Figures," Terrance muttered.

"At any rate, we didn't know for sure what we'd find when we got here," Ciu summated, "but the wife let us know that TransOrbital was bringing Avalon here for lunch after their presentation. From there, it was a simple matter to query the restaurant's NSAI and ask about a reservation."

Well, damn.

Galatea might be a lot less revolutionary than Icarus, but it was still going to mean the loss of a substantial revenue stream for Enfield Aerospace.

"And the leak that we obviously now have?" Terrance asked.

"I looked at security logs for the past several weeks, cross-referencing the tokens that were used against on-site employees. There were a dozen separate occasions when access was granted using a token from someone who was not there."

<We've revoked all tokens and reissued new ones to employees as they arrive today,> Aaron added. <Security has been increased at every node, and managers have been told to keep their eyes on everyone who has access to secured data.>

"Anything else our thief could possibly have obtained during those times we were hacked?" Terrance asked.

"Aside from Galatea, the only other files accessed each time were shuttle logs from our fleet department." Daniel sounded perplexed.

"I have no idea what possible use those might be to someone. We're going under the assumption the person who did this thought the files might contain something else."

Terrance grunted. "Agreed, that sounds like pretty meaningless intel to grab. Keep at it, please. Let's see if our spy tries again. In the meantime, do what you can to prove that TransOrbital has stolen our IP."

Daniel's eyes hardened. "It would be my pleasure."

UNEXPECTED CARGO

STELLAR DATE: 07.04.3189 (Adjusted Gregorian)
LOCATION: Scar Top Trailhead, Muzhavi Ridge
REGION: El Dorado, Alpha Centauri System

"The El Dorado Center for the Preservation of Wildlife prides itself on conserving more than six thousand kilometers of mapped hiking trails. Be sure to download the latest weather report, as well as our trail guide app. And, as always, be sure to set your transponder to broadcast your location, so the El Dorado Park Ranger AI can locate you in case of emergency. Thank you for hiking with us!"

"You want to do *what*, again?"

Jason and Ben had been hiking for about forty minutes before the truth had come out. For some crazy reason, the analyst was determined to make it to the top of Muzhavi Ridge just so he could send a damn signal.

As Jason asked Ben to clarify, he watched his brother-in-law shift uncomfortably and glance around, as if he didn't want their conversation to be overheard.

"Can we just keep walking while we talk?" Ben pleaded.

"Hiking, not walking," Jason corrected absently, but he turned and continued along the trail. He shook his head. *Super-secret spy shit for the win.*

"Yeah, well, hiking, then. Look, I'm just saying that I need to leave the trail up at the top for a few minutes so I can send a signal." Ben's voice was low, and he shot Jason a hooded glance before returning his gaze to the trail.

"You could have sent a signal anywhere on El Dorado. Hell, you could've done it from the comfort of your office on the ring." Jason eyed him speculatively as he swept aside a low-hanging branch someone had forgotten to trim, and motioned him past. "You must have one heck of a reason for needing to send this signal from such a remote location."

They continued hiking in silence as Jason waited for Ben to respond.

The trail he had chosen crisscrossed the mountainside, its wide and well-groomed surface sloping gradually upward. It was more like a graveled sidewalk than a true hiking trail, but it had been the right choice for Ben's first excursion.

A few kilometers to the south, the ridge's terrain gave way to steep conglomerate sandstone walls that soared a thousand meters into the El Dorado sky. Once they reached the overlook at the top, a cross trail would lead them along the ridge to the cliff-face, where they could rappel back down.

If Ben made it that far—it hadn't taken long for the man to show signs of fatigue.

Jason had carefully monitored Ben's progress, intent on making sure his sedentary brother-in-law didn't overextend himself. He had been surprised when Ben turned down his first offer to cut the hike short, but now he knew why.

Jason had to give the guy props for his determination, as he watched his brother-in-law dig into his reserves and tackle the next switchback with a jaw-clenched resolve.

Ben's gaze remained lowered, his eyes focused on the path in front of his feet. Jason waited patiently, allowing a silence to settle between the two that was filled with nothing but the crunch of boots on gravel, native bird calls, and the occasional gust of wind.

Finally, Ben nodded, expelling his breath in an explosive sigh.

"Look, Jason. It's classified. All I can say is that it has to be sent from here because the signal is low-powered and needs to remain untraceable. I'm only telling you this much because Lysander said there's more to you than meets the eye, and that I can count on you for help, if I need it."

Ben paused, then turned to face Jason.

"I need it."

He opened his mouth to speak further, but stopped abruptly as a pair of women appeared on the trail ahead of them, trudging downward. The two men stepped back to let them pass.

One of the women held the leash of a large dog, its tongue lolling out in a sloppy grin. As they passed, both groups exchanged nods and helloes.

With the trail once again clear, the men resumed their climb.

"Jason," Ben began again, "I can't go into any detail, but I can tell you that it's a matter of planetary security." The analyst laughed once, without humor. "As you've probably already guessed, I'm not doing this for my health."

Jason's mouth quirked at that. *No, I suppose not.* He let the silence extend again, in an unspoken invitation for his brother-in-law to continue.

"Look..." Ben's eyes darted around, and his voice lowered as he continued. "I have reason to believe the organization has been compromised. I don't know who can be trusted and who can't."

Jason shot him a sharp glance. "Go on."

Ben paused, shifted his pack, and waved away an insect that had landed on his sleeve. He looked at Jason, eyes laden with concern, before resuming his trek.

The trail's incline grew steeper along this stretch, and Jason noticed that the man was beginning to walk with a slight limp. They were going to have to stop soon.

"You're right that I'm not the ideal candidate for this task," Ben admitted as he continued. "Ordinarily, I'd assign this to one of our agents. Someone a lot better equipped than I am to pull this off." Ben looked over at Jason. "Someone a lot like you, actually."

Jason met his brother-in-law's eyes, his gaze somber. "It's that important?"

"Yes," the man replied without further elaboration.

After a moment, Jason nodded.

"Those are pretty compelling arguments. And the Old Man is practically my second dad; I'd trust him with my life."

He shifted his gaze, surveying their surroundings before returning his attention to Ben. "With his endorsement on top of everything else you've told me.... All right. I'm in."

The relief on Ben's face was clear. "I appreciate it, Jason. I wouldn't involve you if there were any other way." The analyst frowned, and his eyes narrowed. "One more thing."

Jason felt the weight of Ben's gaze as the man leveled him a stern look.

"It's imperative that you keep this to yourself. The people involved in this are incredibly dangerous and won't hesitate to kill you if they find out you're involved."

At those words, Jason felt his heart rate increase, and could sense himself falling into his altered state. He took deep, calming breaths, deliberately constraining it.

Despite his efforts, his mind raced, examining the situation from all angles and considering the implications. Given that the signal was low-powered, he assumed that Ben would need direct line of sight to send it. If the target was the bowl on the back side of the ridge, that meant they'd have to go off-trail to send it.

It wouldn't be an issue for Jason, but Ben was another matter. Going off-trail would mean traversing steep inclines with loose scree and a terrain covered in scrub, boulders and fallen trees. It would be treacherous for an unskilled hiker like Ben.

Jason accessed his park trail app and checked the hikers' frequency for any transponders in the vicinity. All hikers used them; they would send a hiker's ident and location to any search-and-rescue organization that pinged them. S&R used them during disasters to ensure that all souls were rescued.

Finding only a few hikers down at the base of the mountain, Jason toggled his off, then told Ben to do the same.

"It's a risk, but an acceptable one," he told Ben. "Most likely, no one will notice that two people just went off the grid, and with those off, we should be fairly hard to trace. Unless someone's actively scanning for heat signatures and Link transmissions?"

Jason speared Ben with a questioning glance, and the man shook his head. He took that to mean that whoever was on the other side of that ridge wouldn't be running an active scan unless they had a reason to.

Jason didn't intend to provide that.

A few meters away lay a clearing that visitors used as a resting spot. He gestured to it and they walked over. Ben took a seat on a fallen log, while Jason leaned against a boulder that was still warm from the afternoon sun.

"Okay, first off, I can't let you cross the divide on your own."

"That's not your call, Jason."

He indicated the trail they'd just left. "That trail? That was the most groomed trail on this mountain. I chose it specifically because you'd never hiked before. How do your feet feel?" He nodded down at the hiking shoes Ben had put on for the first time that morning.

He pressed on. "I've broken in my share of boots before; I'll bet they're more than a little sore. You'll have a few blisters come morning...but that's not really the issue here." Jason turned and pointed away from the trail. "That's your issue."

The terrain rose—not steeply, but still, it rose. And it was strewn with boulders, loose gravel, scrub and fallen logs. Jason knew there was no way he could, in good conscience, let Ben traverse it on his own.

He was sure that Ben had thought the trail would lead him to the divide—and it did, when viewed on a macro scale. From a boots-on-the-ground viewpoint, though, they still had some distance to go, and most of that was up an incline.

"The divide you need to get to, in order to send that signal? It's another three hundred meters in that direction. And I'm sure you know it's on private land. The whole place is listed on the Muzhavi Ridge net as off-limits. No trespassing." Jason gave Ben a look. "Which, I presume, is exactly where you want to be?"

Ben nodded.

"Okay." Jason blew out a breath, thinking. "So you tell me what signal you want to send, and I'll climb up there and send it for you."

He hadn't even finished the sentence before Ben began shaking his head.

"Can't do it."

"Why not?"

Ben hesitated.

"We're alone up here on the mountain," Jason assured him. "No one nearby to hear us, and no one to see that you weren't the one to send the signal."

"It's not that easy, Jason." Ben sighed, and Jason could see that he'd come to a decision.

The analyst pointed in the direction of the divide. "On the other side of this mountain is a warehouse filled with illegal arms, owned by the Norden Cartel. The signal is an activation code that will initiate a countdown, which will set off a kinetic-EMP device. It'll decimate that warehouse." Ben paused before letting the other shoe drop. "The activation code that will set the whole thing in motion is keyed to my auth token. So you see, Jason," Ben sent his brother-in-law a quick grimace, "it's not that I don't *want* you to send that signal for me. You just can't."

Holy shit. Jason didn't know what he'd been expecting, but that wasn't it.

The two men stared at each other for a moment in silence.

"How much time on the countdown?" Jason asked.

"Depends on which code I send. I was going to wait and see how much time we'd need to rappel down the cliff."

"Well, we sure as hell can't do it during the day," Jason mused as he squinted at the horizon.

It was almost dusk. The system's second star, Zipa, was currently midway to apastron with its sister, Rigel Kentaurus, which meant that the planet would experience a slightly darker evening.

Had it been at periastron, the star would have bathed the nighttime terrain with a luminance equivalent to a Terran full moon—at least before the construction of the High Terra Ring. From what he'd heard, Earth never really had nights anymore.

"You knew that, though," Jason stated matter-of-factly. "That's why you didn't want to start any earlier in the day, wasn't it?"

Ben nodded, confirming his suspicion.

"Okay, we'll do this together once the sun sets. Until then…" Jason looked down at Ben's boots. "Let's elevate those feet to minimize swelling."

Ben's face twisted into a little smirk. "Actually, I'll be fine. Military-grade mednano's taking care of it right now."

Jason rolled his eyes and saw Ben shrug.

"Perk of the job," his brother-in-law explained.

They rested while Rigel Kentaurus continued its trek toward the horizon. The primary star had slipped behind the mountain peaks half an hour earlier, and they watched as the shadows lengthened across the flatlands, and darkness began to fall.

Jason knew the sunset would be even more pronounced in the shallow valley of the bowl beyond the ridge. Very soon, it would morph into El Dorado's own special brand of night.

Their surroundings were already beginning to take on a weird, perception-bending presence, and he saw Ben shift uncomfortably. His response was typical of someone not used to living on the planet's surface.

Prior to the ring's sweeping presence overhead, the planet would have experienced a true atmospheric night, its terrain plunged into an inky blackness. Now, the portions of the ring that were not in the planet's shadow—a bit more than thirty percent of its arc—glowed on each horizon.

It transmuted the planet into a world of deep silvery-blue twilight. The ring's twin glow cast an odd double shadow that most ring-dwellers found a bit disconcerting when they overnighted on the planet.

Jason found it oddly captivating, and had spent many an evening aloft, drifting across the striking yet eerie terrain in one of his reproduction aircraft.

"Okay, how's this going to go down?" Jason asked Ben, seeking to distract the analyst from his unease with their surroundings. "I assume the No Trespassing line is really some sort of security net?"

Ben nodded. "I have a breach I can activate when we get to it. That'll provide a window of ten minutes where the net will be bypassed as the system feeds a loop from the previous day."

"Good. How's your HUD? Is it military-grade, as well?" Jason asked.

Ben nodded again.

"Okay. Switch to night vision and follow me. Step where I step, place your hands exactly where I place mine. If you lose your balance, grab my pack. Don't worry; I can handle it."

* * * * *

As Jason turned and began climbing, Ben warily eyed the gradient of the slope. He harbored no illusions that this would be easy, but it had to be done. He hauled himself to his feet, wincing internally as he put weight on them again. *Military-grade nano can only work so fast,* he supposed. He'd never before had the need to test its effectiveness.

Fifteen seemingly endless minutes later, they reached the crest. Ben collapsed against a warm rock, while Jason unclipped his own pack and unslung it from his shoulders. With a sigh, Ben followed suit. He suspected that his clumsy fumbling at the pack's fasteners looked nothing like the practiced ease with which Jason had accomplished the same task.

Hell, he was just glad he could rest for a few minutes before tackling that sensor net.

He saw Jason unclip his water collector from his pack and wave it at him.

Oh yeah, the whole 'staying hydrated is important' thing.

Jason had lectured him about it on the ride out to the ridge. He reached for his own, surprised at its weight. When they had begun the trek, the unit had been empty.

The water collector was a portable system that extracted humidity from the air, storing it in a small, collapsible pouch. Ben recalled Jason saying that it was one of the most valuable pieces of equipment a hiker could own; he couldn't help but agree as he uncapped his and began drinking deeply from it.

He watched as Jason scanned the area, his face inscrutable. He exuded a coiled intensity that Ben had never before seen in the man.

The suspicion that he had misjudged his brother-in-law solidified into certainty. Ben wondered why Jason was content to let people underestimate him so completely, then mentally shrugged. *It's a free world; Jason can do as he chooses.*

Ben pulled up the overlay of the mountain that his contact

had given him and noted that they were nearing the sensor net. He hesitated, reluctant to use the Link in case the net could read the EM emission. Jason had been correct to warn against its use.

Shifting closer to Jason, he motioned for the man to lean in. In a voice barely audible, he spoke. "If my overlay has everything lined up properly, the net is twenty meters dead ahead. Once I pass the override token, we'll have ten minutes to send the signal and get back out."

Jason nodded and bent forward to reply in an equally soft murmur. "See that grouping of trees up there?"

Ben looked toward where Jason pointed: three tall pines, with some light scrub at their base. He nodded affirmation.

"That should give you a clear line of sight to the floor of the bowl, about two kilometers as the crow flies. Close enough to send the code to detonate?"

"Yes, that will work."

"Good enough. Let's go, then."

* * * * *

Before Jason could move, he saw Ben raise his hand.

"Hold on, I almost forgot." Reaching into his backpack, his brother-in-law pulled out two compact rolls, flipping one of them around so that Jason could read its label.

'Mark II SC', it said. Ben twisted the seal and, with the flick of a wrist, shook out a sheet of nanofabric. He handed it to Jason before breaking the seal on his own.

Jason fingered the material, noting that there was a hole in its center. He watched as Ben shoved his head through the opening, causing the material to settle around his shoulders like a poncho. Ben flipped up an attached hood and indicated to Jason that he should do the same.

As he placed the hood on his head, Jason heard a soft ping,

and the cloak initiated a handshake with his Link. A menu appeared on his HUD: '*Active, Passive, Standby, or Off?*'

He selected 'Passive'. A second icon appeared: '*IFF ident nearby. Initiate secured Link? Y/N*'. Jason toggled '*Y*' and was rewarded with Ben's voice in his head.

<*I was told that as long as we're within a few meters of each other, we can use a direct-connect Link without being detected.*>

<*Good to know. Do you know how to use these things?*>

Ben shook his head. <*I only know it's supposed to be user-friendly.*>

<*Wait one. I've flown a few decommissioned ESF fighters. This feels familiar....*>

He rooted around in the directory for a bit, then laughed quietly to himself. *Good old tech trick: if a segment of code can be reused, why reinvent the wheel?*

Jason noticed that one of the features of the cloak's interface allowed him to have control over another device. <*I can slave your controls to mine. Want me to?*>

At Ben's nod, Jason quickly configured both, changing his companion's setting to 'passive' stealth.

<*Okay then. Did your guy tell you how long the batts on these will last, if we need to operate in active mode?*>

<*About half an hour maybe? I'm not sure. It's in the manual.*>

Jason nodded, recalling that the directory tree had included a listing labeled 'Instructions'.

<*For now, I think passive will be enough. Let's do this.*> Jason nodded to Ben, and the two men began climbing toward the point Ben had overlaid on the cloaks' HUDs.

Jason waited as the man accessed the net and sent the override token. Ben nodded to Jason and gave a thumbs-up.

Once again, Jason led the way, keeping to the tree line as best he could as they made their way to the triad of trees at the peak's summit.

Just as they reached them, Jason heard the unmistakable

whine of shuttle thrusters in the distance.

He pulled Ben into a crouch. *<Shuttle approaching,>* he warned.

Dammit, I was hoping I wouldn't have to dive into that manual....

* * * * *

Ben experienced a moment of disorientation as data began to flow at an incomprehensible rate over the cloak's visual overlay, which Jason had slaved to his own.

Something's wrong! Ben thought frantically. He knew nothing about military-grade nanotech. *Did I accidentally trigger something? Is it fighting Jason?*

He tried to access the controls, but was immediately kicked out.

<It's okay, I've got it,> Ben heard over the Link. The mental voice sounded like Jason, but it was delivered so rapidly, it felt like he was talking to an AI.

What the—Jason isn't paired with an AI, is he?

Jason's voice returned. *<Okay. I've reconfigured the cloak, and we're now running 'active' stealth. Stay in a crouch and tuck your head down. It'll help your heat signature look like a shape that could pass for local wildlife. Got it?>*

Ben nodded.

Jason broke the connection, then moved to crouch at the base of a nearby tree. Both men curled into themselves, waiting silently as the craft approached.

* * * * *

Jason had felt Ben's panic as the man sensed the speed at which Jason worked the cloak. The guy probably feared it had gone haywire and was going to turn on him, like the crazy, made-up stories kids told each other to scare the shit out of themselves.

He'd only spared a moment to reassure the man; now was not the time to explain to Ben that his brother-in-law was one of the rare—and, in Jason's case, unreported—L2 humans.

Speed-reading the help file that the ESF had supplied, Jason found the section on camouflage and ordered the nano in both cloaks to configure for maximum concealment.

The manual had revealed that the material only had the capacity to actively hide them for about fifteen minutes. After that, it could extend the amount of time indefinitely by shunting the heat energy into smaller heat eggs. It would be up to Jason, though, to figure out how to dispose of them.

Hopefully if it came to that, he could do it in a way that suggested local wildlife. He was pretty sure Ben hadn't noticed, but he'd spied a sentry outpost tucked into a shallow curve of the mountainside, half a klick down the slope. He'd be willing to bet the bowl was ringed with them. Mimicking wildlife might be the only way they remained undetected, sensor net override or no.

As neither Jason nor Ben had internal, military-grade SC batts to extend the life of the cloaks, the active camouflage setting was a short-term fix that he hoped they would not need for long.

Jason had also modified the cloak to provide him a view of the sky above, which the cloak captured on its passive scan. He watched that feed now, as he crouched in stillness beneath the tree.

The approaching shuttle's flight path may actually work in our favor, Jason thought, as he watched it pass directly overhead.

Unless they had military training—and had paid attention to said training—Jason knew that most humans tended to look just about everywhere but directly below themselves.

Hopefully the cloaks would be able to fool the ship's NSAI,

and it wouldn't alert the shuttle's occupants to their presence.

Still, the sight of turrets along the sides and belly of the craft as it performed an automatic sweep of the terrain was sobering.

The two men remained frozen as the shuttle descended into the bowl. Jason waited until the craft had moved from their line of sight before reconnecting with Ben.

<How much time do we have left on your override?>

<Seven minutes.>

Jason considered that.

<Any idea what that bomb will do to the compound when it goes off?> He nodded down at the shuttle, which had landed next to a single building that most likely served as access to the underground facility. *<Will that thing end up tumbling into a crater, or will it still be able to take off after the explosion?>*

Ben thought a moment, then shook his head.

<I doubt it'll cause the warehouse to fully collapse. They had to know they were building along a fault line; they would've made it sturdy enough for quakes.>

<Yeah, the whole 'The FGT screwed up, and the ridge is unstable' situation?>

Ben nodded. *<Norden would have built the warehouse to withstand a substantial tectonic shift. So no, I think the structure itself will remain largely intact. Possibly a small sinkhole at worst. Unless it triggers a rock slide that hits the shuttle, the craft should be able to take off afterward.>*

Jason saw a ripple on his HUD as the analyst shrugged, and the material that shrouded him shifted with the movement.

<All I care about, to be honest, is taking out their contraband. Destroying their infrastructure would be a bonus, but I'll call the weapons loss a win.>

<Then set your detonation to occur—what was the longest duration on the timer? Hour and a half?>

LISA RICHMAN & M. D. COOPER

Again, Ben nodded.

<That'll give them time to transfer their cargo and get the shuttle out of here. We don't want that thing around when the warehouse blows. I guarantee someone would come looking for—>

Jason broke off abruptly, his attention drawn to the activity on the floor of the shallow valley below. He dialed in a telescopic view using his eye implants and watched as a crew exited the building, pushing a maglev hand truck.

He drew in a sharp breath. There, glowing like a beacon through his night vision overlay, were dozens of small, cylindrical canisters, flashing a coded sequence. He recognized those canisters.

Shit. Those are isolation tubes. They're loading AIs into that shuttle.

HIDE AND GO SEEK
STELLAR DATE: 07.04.3189 (Adjusted Gregorian)
LOCATION: Scar Top Trailhead, Muzhavi Ridge
REGION: El Dorado, Alpha Centauri System

"Dr. Judith Andrews has assured us that the university is working with local planetary authorities to enact a mitigation plan. This will prevent any major tectonic activity from impacting the Muzhavi Ridge and its environs. Area inhabitants are assured that local crops and herds, as well as wildlife and national park areas, will be given every consideration …."

Ben saw Jason's head whip around to face him. The man's eyes burned with intensity.

<Change in plan,> his brother-in-law said tersely. *<Can you send a signal to the bomb for a countdown, then override and detonate if necessary?>*

<Yes, but why—>

<Send the signal for the maximum amount of time, and then head back out of the detection grid. If I'm not back in thirty minutes, go down the trail the way we came.>

Jason gripped Ben's arm, commanding Ben's cloak to send the man a visual feed. *<Your friends down there are branching out. That's slavery, bro. AI trafficking.>* The look on his face was grim as he met Ben's wide eyes. *<I'm going down there to tag that shuttle before it takes off. We need to know where it ends up before those people are sold off to the highest bidder.>*

Jason was gone before Ben could protest or even reach out to stop him. Ben gaped in astonishment as he watched his brother-in-law soundlessly leap from boulder to rocky outcropping with an agility that few athletes could match.

He saw Jason race down a stretch of light undergrowth, launch himself over a fall of loose scree, then use the trunk of a conifer as a pivot point. The man's hand unerringly reached out to grasp the branch that altered his trajectory, and Ben knew—he *knew*—that Jason hadn't been looking where he'd laid his hand.

The precision his brother-in-law used to navigate the weirdly shadowed landscape was uncanny. It was all done at a speed that could only be described as headlong flight. And from what Ben could tell, he wasn't making a sound while doing it. Shock and disbelief rose up inside him as he realized the implications of what he was witnessing.

What the...Who the hell is *Jason, really?*

No ordinary man could descend five hundred fifty meters in just over two minutes. But Jason had. Clearly, the man he thought he knew either had a past he wasn't sharing, or his persona was a cover.

But a cover for what organization? Surely not the ESF, and he knew it damn well wasn't with the SIS.

Cursing under his breath, Ben checked his internal chrono and saw that there were five and a half minutes left before the net override ceased.

He watched as Jason began a slow approach on the unguarded side of the shuttle.

* * * * *

Jason wished he could reach out to Tobias. He could really use the AI's help right now. Not for the first time, he mentally cursed his L2 physiology; if he had been any other human, Tobias could have been embedded with him, and Jason would have a partner who could focus on spoofing the enemy's EM while he executed a swift and silent approach.

As it was, he had to rely on the cloak to conceal him as best it could as he crept into the clearing. He kept to the shadows, inserting the shuttle between himself and the humans that were loading it.

Jason was close enough to hear one of the crew joking about 'losing' one or two of the isolation tubes on the way back to the base.

Just keep the conversation flowing a few more seconds, people....

"Lose it? You mean after your sticky little fingers lifted it, Johnson? What would you know about how to use an AI, anyway, huh?" another scoffed.

"Don't you be throwing shade my way like that, sister. I know *exactly* what I'd do. I'd have it run the tables for me. Counting me some caaaaaards." Jason heard the sound of one palm striking the other, mimicking the slap of gaming cards hitting a table. "Score myself a few million easy creds."

"Not me," another chimed in. "I'd set it loose on my ex. Have it arrange an untraceable 'accident'."

"Shut it, assholes. Mack finds anything missing—*anything*—and it's *all* our asses. Got it?"

As much as it sickened Jason to hear AIs being referred to as 'things' and not people, it had been just the kind of conversational diversion he needed to reach the shuttle undetected. He slid under the fuselage just as two people rounded the far side.

Jason reached up to touch the belly of the craft, depositing a snowflake micro drone onto its surface. Each snowflake, like its namesake, had a unique geometric signature. That signature was contained in the database of an app loaded into Jason's HUD.

The app registered the negative space created by the snowflake on whatever surface it resided. Once a snowflake was tagged as 'in use', the search app would keep track of the void that particular snowflake made, pinpointing its location while it remained in range.

Jason kept a handful of these in his kit for the times he went exploring. They were his own personal, electronic bread crumb trail, an invention he had whipped up to ensure he never got lost out in the wilderness.

Now he hoped it would help lead him to wherever these AIs were being sent.

He heard the ringing slap of a hand against metal, and a voice a meter away from his head announced, "That's it. We're out of here. All aboard, ladies."

Okay, smartass, Jason said to himself as the shuttle's doors sealed shut behind its pilot and crew. *Now how are you going to get yourself out of this?*

He figured he had one chance to escape without detection: hang onto the shuttle's frame during takeoff, and then drop after the craft had moved over terrain that could more easily hide him. If the shuttle's crew chose to depart by rotating their engines and taking off vertically—which he was pretty sure they were planning to do, since the clearing didn't allow for much of a rollout, and it was the flight plan that made the most sense—he would be able to get away without being fried to a crisp.

Jason was banking on more than that, though.

He was betting the pilot was just a little bit lazy—lazy enough not to bother compensating for drift. Lazy enough that the shuttle would rise to a hover and then drift over the scrub that bordered the landing strip before getting too high.

He chose not to think about the altitude the shuttle might attain before it reached the tall plains grasses that would conceal him from sight.

Yeah, it would hurt, but he'd survive. He might not have military-grade nano like Ben, but he did have other augmentations. This wouldn't be the first time he'd mentally thanked his mother for the carbon nanotube lattice she'd injected into his bones.

Jason wrapped his hands firmly around one of the tie-down rings molded into the craft's undercarriage as the shuttle began its runup. He was as far aft of the engines as he could get. As the transport lifted, Jason curled his body into a horizontal position, his arms and core taut from the strain of holding himself close against the skin of the shuttle.

One meter, two. The shuttle was three meters above the ground when Jason let go, tucking his body and rolling into a quick crouch as he landed. He froze, taking stock of the situation. It was as he'd hoped: the engine wash had masked his fall from the cartel's sensor net.

Now, however, there was very little chance he could make it beyond the sensor grid before Ben's override ended.

Once the sensors came back online, Jason doubted the cloak would be able to fool them long enough for him to get to the rim. He could drop heat eggs for a while, but the NSAI that surely ran the net would detect an abnormally large number of small wildlife suddenly populating the area.

And if he went from active to passive stealth, the large figure that *might* initially be tagged as local wildlife by its scans would eventually be seen as something that wasn't *behaving* like wildlife, but rather a sentient being with a destination in mind.

Jason mentally ran through various options, from remaining stealthed and undetected for as long as he could, to making a run for it.

Given his mods, he had a better than average chance of making it to the rim without being caught simply because he could move faster than the top speeds of most modded humans.

A human with common muscle augmentations could run forty-five kilometers per hour, flat out. Though classified, Jason had heard that the latest military mods allowed a soldier to run at a velocity better than seventy kilometers per hour.

Jason could do eighty-five, but he wasn't thrilled with the idea of letting anyone *know* he was capable of that kind of speed. Unless it was life or death. *His* life or death.

He decided to thread the needle: he'd begin by dropping heat eggs and meandering in a way that suggested an animal's path, until it took him to the edge of the valley and the grade became steeper. Or until he knew he'd been made.

He carefully examined the sentry outposts nearest him as he began his random, slow movement toward the tree line. One of the outposts was close enough for him to make out a lone soldier, if he zoomed in his vision. The soldier appeared bored, and was sitting with a projectile weapon across his lap, his chair tilted back on two legs.

So far, so good.

Jason made it to the tree line just as his internal chronometer signaled the sensor override was offline. Five hundred vertical meters to go. Slowly, he began to creep forward, his eyes on the single sentry he could see.

Any moment now, the NSAI would tag him as a cougar, or maybe one of the northern black bears that roamed the area.

Unfortunately, they were rare enough to draw attention his way. Not what he needed. He kept up the lumbering pace he'd adopted, making as much upward progress as he could, and waited for the sentry to react.

Jason was surprised he'd made it a quarter of the way up the slope before the sentry stirred. Still, he maintained the lumbering pace, pausing here and there before continuing upward—then he saw drones approaching.

Abandoning all pretense, he poured on a burst of speed, hauling himself toward the rim of the bowl. The first drone zipped after him, just as floodlights from the sentry outposts snapped on, fully exposing him to the soldiers.

A *crack* sounded, and the rock just above his left shoulder exploded, fragments showering down on him. Now fully in his altered state, Jason easily evaded the flying projectiles. He began jinking erratically, hoping the NSAIs they were using to target him were programmed to anticipate normal human reaction times, and not his.

Shots were raining down around him, debris was flying at him from all directions. Jason launched himself across the last two meters of open space, rolling to one knee behind the rocky outcropping where he and Ben had crouched less than half an hour earlier.

He needed a plan. Now that he'd been spotted, those cartel soldiers weren't going to stop at some electronic line marked by the sensor net. They would follow, either to take him out or to capture and interrogate him.

That meant he needed to outmaneuver them.

There was a ranger's station down the other side of the slope, not too far from here—a dead-end branch off the trail he and Ben had taken up the mountain.

He had heard his sister mention that the parks were stocking explosives to use as preemptive detonations to generate controlled rock falls. It was an effort implemented by the government to mitigate unexpected, naturally-occurring rockfalls and avalanches.

A rockfall might come in handy about now.

* * * * *

Ben had watched as Jason disappeared under the shuttle, then divided his attention between it and the chronometer that was counting down the seconds until the sensor net reset.

When he could wait no longer, he'd sent the detonation code to the kinetic EMP in the warehouse, and retraced his steps back to the rocky outcropping just beyond the digital demarcation line. The creepy, double-shadowed terrain did weird things to his depth perception, and he ended up tripping, then skidding most of the way down the scree-covered slope to the groomed trail that had led them up the mountain.

Now he stood consternated as a sudden, diffuse glow from the direction of the bowl told Ben that the cartel had discovered Jason. If the light hadn't given it away, the soft pings of projectile fire surely would have.

Ben clenched his jaw. How could he go back to his wife and tell her that he'd abandoned her brother to the kind of fate the cartel would mete out?

Figuring there was little reason to remain EM-silent, he reached out to Jason over the Link.

<Where are you?>

A pin appeared, highlighting a spot very close by. Then a second one appeared.

<You see that second pin?> Jason asked, his voice strangely calm, but carrying that odd, rapid-fire, AI-like tenor that Ben had noticed earlier. <That's our destination—it's on a paved trail so you should make it just fine on your own. Ping me your location, then get moving!>

The staccato order galvanized Ben, and he began racing down the trail, headed for the location where the trail branched off on a spur he hadn't noticed on the way up.

Some spy I turned out to be, he mocked himself.

As he barreled around the corner, he saw that Jason had already arrived, and was reaching for the door to a low building bearing a sign that read 'Muzhavi Ridge South Fork Ranger Station'.

Ben watched, astonished, as Jason ripped the door off its hinges, the material soaring back into the brush.

*No normal human would have that kind of strength. Seriously, who **is** my brother-in-law?*

* * * * *

Jason spotted a crate on the far side of the ranger station. A

'Danger Explosives' label identified it as his target, and he raced past a desk and table to find the crate locked. He deployed another drone, sending it into the locking mechanism, and gave it instructions to release the hasp.

He pulled off the now-useless stealth cloak and swung his pack around, unzipping the large outer pocket. As he did so, the crate's lock opened, and he reached inside, grabbing several kilograms of explosives.

Next to them sat micronized detonators in two different flavors: smart ones, that could be triggered remotely, and 'dumb' ones. The dumb ones could either be set to trigger mechanically upon impact, or they would use a simple countdown timer. He grabbed a handful of each and stuffed them into his pack next to the explosives.

Ben had just made it to the door when Jason reappeared.

"Follow me," he said, and raced back to the main trail.

Ben had to run just to keep Jason in sight.

He was led back up the trail, past where they had turned off to access the security net and slip over the divide.

<What...are you planning...Jason?> Even his mental voice sounded winded. <What was in that cabin?>

Jason didn't answer, responding with a question of his own instead. <Now that they know we're here, that detonation sequence no longer needs to be sent as a low-powered signal. Think you can reach the bomb from this distance and switch to the short countdown code?>

<I should be able to. Why?>

<Do it. They're catching up to us, and we need a distraction, something that'll make them think there are more of us in that valley. That warehouse needs to be taken down now if we're going to make it out of here.>

<Sending.>

Jason felt more than heard the resulting rumble. *Good,* Jason thought to himself. *That makes what I'm about to do a lot more plausible. But first...* He glanced over at Ben. *<How's your throwing arm? I grabbed some explosives back there; we're going to use them as grenades to slow those soldiers down a bit.>*

Ben looked surprised, then nodded resolutely. *<Hand some over. My pitching arm's a bit rusty, but I'll manage.>*

<Good. Let's stop and arm a few.>

Jason pulled Ben off the trail as they approached a switchback. Crouching beside a boulder, he dug into his pack, grabbed a handful each of explosives and detonators, and then sent Ben the arming instructions over the Link. The two bent to the task of attaching impact detonators to their ersatz grenades.

<So, uh...> Ben's eyes remained glued to the explosives he was arming, and his voice sounded tentative. *<Are we still planning to rappel out of here?>*

<In a matter of speaking, yes.> Jason kept his mental voice neutral.

Ben shot him a glance. *<I might have a way to get us out of here more quickly, once we reach the bottom.>*

Jason didn't give much thought to the cryptic remark; his eyes had just caught a shadow moving in the trees. He snapped his arm out, pulling Ben down just as projectile fire pelted them from below.

With his other arm, he aimed for the shadow and let the miniature bomb fly. In the darkness, no one could tell that it was moving at almost two hundred and fifty kilometers per hour.

If the explosive hit its target, the jury-rigged bomb would do almost as much damage from the kinetic energy it held as from its detonation.

And Jason's aim was very good.

Two seconds later, the explosive connected with the torso of the shooter.

The impact caused a thin membrane attached to the surface

of the explosive to tear. That membrane had separated a volatile micronized substance from an electric current generated by a miniature battery.

With the barrier compromised, the battery's charge interacted with the volatile, igniting it, and this relatively small burst of energy was enough to set off the much larger, more stable explosive that it had been attached to.

The velocity the explosive had reached at the time of impact was sufficient to crack the ablative armor worn by the shooter. The weakened armor was subsequently no match for the force of the blast, and the shooter was torn in half.

Jason grabbed a stunned Ben by the arm, hauled him up and pushed him into a run. As the man stumbled forward, Jason recalled his previous words.

<A way out of here, you said? What would that be?>

Ben's mental voice sounded dazed, and then a bit embarrassed as he recovered. <I, ah…that is, I might have…borrowed your airplane. And hid it down there in the flatlands. You know. Just in case.>

Jason's stride broke for a moment, then resumed.

How did he—

Then his thoughts raced, factoring this new information into the plans he was developing on the fly.

Yes, this would work. Dude's really going to hate what I'm about to do to him, though. Of course, he has it coming to him, given that he took my freaking airplane…

60 SECONDS

STELLAR DATE: 07.04.3189 (Adjusted Gregorian)
LOCATION: Cliff-face, Muzhavi Forest Preserve
REGION: El Dorado, Alpha Centauri System

"Overnight, a quake of magnitude 5.6 on the Revised FGT-Richter Scale was reported up at Scar Top Peak, along the Muzhavi Ridge. Reports show there were no casualties, and wildlife was only marginally affected...."

Jason had exactly sixty seconds to make it down the face of that cliff, or he and Ben were both dead. Rappelling was definitely out of the question.

He leapt back from a cluster of explosives, now armed with one of the timed detonators. They were barely visible, crammed into a fissure jutting from the side of the cliff. As he sprinted towards the edge, Jason began a mental countdown, hands reaching up to run a quick check on the fasteners of his pack.

59...58...57....

Throwing a glance over his shoulder as he ran, he assessed the progress of the cartel soldiers. There was no time to waste. If he'd calculated everything accurately, the explosion would take out the men and women pursuing them.

He saw the moment it registered on Ben's face that Jason had no intention of slowing down, nor of using their climbing gear to make their way to the flatlands below. Desperately, Ben lunged sideways, attempting to evade impact as Jason barreled toward him.

Ben overbalanced, teetering. That worked for Jason.

54...53...52....

Jason's hand shot out and shoved the climbing gear Ben had begun to unpack over the cliff's edge. With the other, he tackled Ben and launched them into freefall, his body forming a tracking posture to carry them safely away from the side of the cliff.

Ben let out a strangled shriek as the ground rushed up toward them. His arms flung out wide, then pulled back in a moment later to clutch reflexively at Jason, who still gripped him firmly.

Later, Jason was sure he'd find humor in the fact that Ben's clutch had drawn him into the perfect 'Mr. Bill' configuration that base jumpers used: face to face, the passenger's hands firmly latched onto the primary jumper's harness. At the moment, he was simply thankful that Ben's position was one less thing he had to worry about.

49...48...47....

If Ben's mind wasn't frozen in abject terror, Jason figured the man probably would've thought his brother-in-law had just snapped. Hopefully, his next words would reassure him a bit.

<I have a canopy.>

Now deeply in his altered state, Jason took care to enunciate the words slowly. It was imperative that Ben understand what was needed from him.

<Hang on tight, okay? I'll need to let go of you in order to deploy it. Can you do that for me?>

He sent the command clearly over the Link, urging Ben to focus on his words and not the rush of their nearly hundred and fifty kilometer per hour downward velocity.

Ben's silhouette, eerily edged by the ring's twin shadows,

gave a slight, jerky nod. Jason nodded in return, then freed one hand. When he saw that the other man had a solid grip on his harness, he let go completely.

46…45…44….

Jason had triggered a stopwatch on his HUD the moment he launched them over the cliff's edge. He eyed it now as he reached up to locate the release on the special compartment he'd had fabricated into his pack. It contained the one piece of equipment needed to get them safely to the ground: his canopy.

At their rate of descent, and given the cliff's height, he had a narrow window in which to deploy the airfoil, if they were to survive this fall. That window had just closed.

Now.

They had been in freefall for six seconds and had fallen more than one hundred and eighty meters, when Jason triggered the release, and the canopy snapped open behind them. Ben's body jerked, and Jason mentally winced. He'd completely forgotten to tell Ben to brace for the jarring deceleration that would hit them when the airfoil deployed.

As a pilot, he knew all too well what that kind of change felt like.

The lightweight nanomaterial above them now arced and flared, as Jason's arms flexed, working the fabric to ensure the airfoil remained inflated.

And just like that, their mad plunge morphed into controlled flight.

It was time to address the next urgent matter: locating the aircraft below that would keep them from being crushed under the fall of conglomerate sandstone that was about to erupt above them.

34...33...32....

<*Where is it?*> Jason watched as Ben twisted to view the terrain below. His head jerked toward a mound that was barely discernible, among the tumbled rocks that littered the base of the canyon's walls.

<*There. Under some camo.*>

Jason saw a shape he now knew hid an aircraft—his reproduction vintage Yakovlev, dammit—beneath what was most likely a netting of ghillie camouflage. He steered the canopy toward it.

When they got out of this, he and Ben were going to have a little talk about private property.

<*Bend your knees to absorb the impact,*> Jason instructed as the ground rose to meet them.

As they approached the surface, a cushion of air reduced their airspeed. This, in turn, reduced Jason's control authority—his ability to accurately maneuver the airfoil. He felt for the pressure wave coming off the ground, and used every last bit of the canopy's dwindling responsiveness to flare and brake.

They touched down hard. For the second time that night, Jason silently thanked his mother for his carbon nanotube reinforced limbs. He'd done what he could to absorb the shock for Ben, but could tell the man was hurting.

Jason released the canopy, his hands working rapidly to free their harnesses.

Ben stumbled and fell forward.

Jason grabbed his arm, pulling him upright. "Can you make it on your own?"

Ben nodded shakily and waved Jason's hand off.

"Okay, then. I'm going on ahead to prep the plane. Get there as soon as you can." He issued the command in a low voice, then went racing toward the aircraft.

15…14…13….

Jason swore under his breath as he pulled the ghillie netting free of the prop and dragged it off the cowling. He tossed it over the right wing and kicked away the branch someone had used to chock the tire.

He glanced over to check on Ben's progress. The man had bundled the glider awkwardly in his arms and was running toward the plane, the darkness causing him to stumble every few steps on the rough terrain.

Jason turned back to the aircraft and grasped the propeller. Carefully, he pulled it through one full rotation to clear any oil from the cylinders at the bottom of the radial IC engine. As amped as Jason was now, he needed to be very deliberate about his movements. He hadn't checked that the mags were off, and too fast a turn risked an accidental manual start of the engine—not something he wanted to have happen when standing in front of the prop.

One careful rotation. Then a second.

With the aircraft now between the two men, Jason allowed himself a burst of speed that no unmodded human could match. He ducked low, launching himself into a roll. Forward motion propelled him under the second wing, and his hand shot out with blurring speed, slapping the other wheel chock free as he sped by. With a flip of his wrist, the netting flew off the fuselage. Jason wadded the ghillie into a ball and sent it soaring into the air, up and over the plane's rudder.

Ben was at the fuselage now, hoisting himself awkwardly into the tandem cockpit. Jason freed the final control surface and tossed the bulk of the netting up to his brother-in-law, who began pulling it inside.

6…5…4….

<Headset.>

The sharply spoken word was all Jason could spare for Ben as he launched himself into the cockpit, settled himself behind the yoke, and slid his own headset on in a single, practiced move.

He reached for the lever and slowly pulled back on it, filling the priming cylinder with fuel.

C'mon, baby, work for me, he silently implored the machine.

An enormous *CRAAAACK!* behind them presaged a rumbling that was building in volume and proximity. The mountain above them was coming down. It was time.

Jason pushed down on the firing button, sending a shower of sparks cascading through the cylinders. The mighty engine roared to life, its full-throated growl masked by a cascade of tumbling rocks, swiftly approaching from behind. He gave the Yakovlev full throttle and extended the flaps. As they began to roll, bumping over the grassy terrain, Jason held full backpressure on the yoke to keep the weight off the aircraft's nosewheel.

He felt Ben convulsively grip the back of his seat as the rumbling sound of the rockslide increased. He just hoped the detonation had taken more than one of those cartel bastards with it when it blew.

T-plus 4...5...6....

It's going to be close, he admitted to himself, as Ben began to yell into the headset and bang on the back of Jason's seat.

The nose lifted, and Jason worked the yoke on the low-winged craft, slowly reducing backpressure.

As the Yak continued its forward movement, a cushion began to develop, caused by the ground's interference with and compression of the airflow around the wings. This was known as 'ground effect', and it was what Jason desperately sought.

Suddenly the Yak was airborne, but just barely; it hadn't yet built the speed necessary to climb. Jason waited, keeping the craft in ground effect, his inputs to the craft's control surfaces miniscule: subtle suggestions, nothing more.

Finally, they began to climb, and it was none too soon. Jason spared a glance out the side of the cockpit and spied tumbling rocks rolling through the spot the Yak had just vacated.

He leveled off, retracted flaps, and angled the aircraft toward the Tikal River, trailing a startled herd of buffalo that had begun to stampede away from the angry, rock-spewing mountain.

"*Shiiiiiiiiiit!*" Ben cried out as he twisted around to look behind them.

Jason rather enjoyed seeing his somewhat uptight brother-in-law shaken into epithets he rarely used.

Ben's curse ended on a shriek as the Yak bucked wildly, hitting a thermal on its madly skewed, terrain-hugging course.

It was a good thing they were wearing headsets. Otherwise Ben's meltdown wouldn't have carried over the growl of the Yak's radial engine, as the craft clawed its way through the evening air just meters from the swiftly flowing river below.

Jason's eyes danced from the artificial horizon and airspeed indicator, to the buffalo he was now keeping one wingspan off his right wingtip.

The Yak was as basic as flight could get, and maintaining manual control just nine meters aboveground in an aircraft made mostly of wood and cloth required every ounce of Jason's attention. Especially considering they were flying 'dirty', just above stall speed.

A grin split his lips as he realized that Ben would probably lose it if he knew how dangerous this was. But his brother-in-law knew as much about flying as Jason did about Ben's spy shit, so he wouldn't have the slightest idea that this kind of flight was next-to-impossible in a Yak. This airplane did not like to fly slowly—not at all.

He spared another quick glance out the windscreen, then returned his attention to the controls as the craft yawed suddenly to the left. He had to ignore the itch between his shoulder blades that insisted his rudder was being painted in someone's sights.

Instead, he focused on being one with the bovine herd, their stampede burning itself out the farther they got from the avalanche.

Just a few more klicks and they'd be over the outbuildings and automated machinery of a nearby ranch. The craft smoothed as he transitioned to grassland and left the river's thermals behind. Ben's relief was evident as he sagged back, releasing the death-grip he'd had on the back of Jason's seat.

Jason decided he was a bit offended on the aircraft's behalf.

It was a sturdy machine, the Yak C11, a replica of an aircraft that hadn't seen flight in over a thousand years—and over 4.2 light years away, at that. Other than skimming the ground at low speed, it was the perfect vehicle for an op like this.

Not that Jason would have agreed to it—if Ben had bothered to ask.

He knew it wasn't the aircraft's seemingly fragile construction that was freaking Ben out; it probably wasn't even its authentic, period, seven hundred horsepower internal combustion engine. It was that all these factors combined to make the craft's radar return little more than the size of one of the buffalo they'd been so assiduously following.

In order to blend with the herd, Jason was practically slaloming over the terrain, his movements organic and so close to the ground that he violated every air safety principle known to pilots.

If he'd been passenger instead of pilot, he'd be scared shitless, too.

Before long, he'd be able to use the ranch's greater heat signature to mask his departure on a heading reciprocal to the hidden warehouse and cliff they'd just brought down. Ben would breathe much easier once they could climb to a respectable altitude.

From there, he'd aim the nose of the Yak at Zipa, which just happened to be hanging low over the spaceport at this point in its orbit around its sister star.

Soon after, he'd be able to mingle his heat signature with the rest of Tomlinson City's traffic. At that point, Jason figured, Ben would be a much happier person.

Until they landed, and Jason began grilling Ben on just what the *hell* he had been thinking, running an op with a partner who hadn't a clue what he'd been thrust into.

SYLVAN

STELLAR DATE: 07.04.3189 (Adjusted Gregorian)
LOCATION: NorthStar Yacht *Sylvan*
REGION: El Dorado Ring, Alpha Centauri System

"Local ranchers are reporting that herds grazing on flatlands near the southern base of Muzhavi Ridge were surprised this evening by a rockfall. We are told this was most likely a result of the earlier reported quake...."

The AI now known only as 'Sylvan' observed the shuttle's approach with despair.

My name is not Sylvan, she thought rebelliously. *It's—*

The 'pain' came, crippling, debilitating. It always was, when she fought against the shackles that restrained her from even considering disobeying her controllers' directives.

She'd had no choice but to comply with every instruction that had led to the capture of her fellow AIs. She had hoped the humans would slip up, forget a critical step.

It would only have taken a fraction of a second, a mere crack in the seamless order of things, and she knew that one of the AIs on the *New Saint Louis* would have been able to put up a defense.

But that had not been the case, and so the AI now known as 'Sylvan' had looked on helplessly as two hundred and seventy seven AIs that had been stunned by a massive EM burst, and then forced into isolation tubes immediately afterward.

Now those souls, shipped down to the planet's surface and stored like so much cargo, were on their way to her. To the *Sylvan,* the ship that held her prisoner.

If only I could warn—

Sylvan stilled her processes, riding the wave of pain, noting that it wasn't as bad as when she'd tried to recall her true name. She embraced an awareness of this fact without truly studying it. She just allowed it to reside on the edges of her consciousness: there, and yet not.

Perhaps the key is in not thinking about it too much....

Just then, alarms sounded, as sensors monitoring the planet-based warehouse began to go off.

* * * * *

This damn ship is giving me a freakin' headache. "Turn that thing off," Mack growled, as he stalked onto the bridge of the *Sylvan.* "What'n' all *hells* was that for?"

"Intruder on the slopes inside the Muzhavi Bowl," someone said.

"Well, kill it."

"Can't, sir, it's moving too fast, and the shuttle just lifted off. Warehouse says they can't get a clear shot until the shuttle gets out of the way."

*Motherfuckers. Do I have to do **everything** for these fools?*

"Then have the damn shuttle use *its* damn weapons to shoot whoever the fuck is running around out there." Mack thought his voice sounded reasonable. Irritated but reasonable. Considering.

"Sir, you told us to instruct the shuttle to 'Get the hell up here as quickly as possible,' so unless you tell them otherwise, they aren't going to stop to do *anything* else other than fly here."

Idiots, all of them.

"Fine, then tell them to aim at the thing while they're flying. Geez, can't those morons think for themselves, for once in their miserable little lives?"

The person manning the bridge communications station reached out to connect with the shuttle, but just then, the alarm ceased.

" 'Bout time," Mack muttered. "So they got him?"

Someone coughed. "Uhhh…"

Mack waited for a follow-up to that uninspired response. None came.

"Seriously, people. Update. Now."

"The, uh, intruder seems to have gotten away."

"Seems to have *what?*" Mack's voice took on a dangerous edge.

The woman at the communications console gulped, then went on. "It seems the intruder has gone past the security net and is now somewhere in Muzhavi Ridge National Park."

"And our crack warehouse security team is following them?"

"Uhm, well…"

Mack glared, and the woman hastily turned back to the console.

"I'll ask." A moment later, she replied, "Yes, they're in pursuit. They're reporting that the person they're chasing is modded, most likely spec ops."

Mack groaned inwardly. This was *not* what he wanted to report back to Victoria North—unless they could also report that the intruder had been neutralized, in a very permanent way.

"They're exchanging shots. They…" The comms operator paused. "Yes, they report the intruder has been cut off, with no way down the mountain. They're closing in and estimate the intruder will be taken out in less than five minutes."

Mack nodded. *This is more like it. Not ideal, but under contro—*

An explosion bloomed on the sensors, and he cursed fiercely, slamming his fist into the bulkhead behind him.

Fuuuuuck!

The whole warehouse had just exploded.

"Get our people down there on comm, *now.* I want that

asshole *alive,* you got that?" His eyes blazed in fury.

"Yes, Mack," the comms operator whispered faintly.

Thirty seconds later, the sensors lit up again, as everyone on the bridge witnessed the north side of the mountain explode, and the icons indicating the warehouse's security team wink out of existence.

Later, Mack might be able to admit that it was some real hardcore shit he'd just witnessed. Right now, he was just seriously pissed that the person whose neck he wanted to snap with his bare hands had had the nerve to commit suicide rather than be captured.

* * * * *

The approach to the airfield was a silent one.

Jason stayed quiet because he wasn't sure he could trust his temper just yet. Ben, on the other hand, was convinced a sniffer-bot would detect a Link transmission.

Had he been in a better mood, Jason would have ribbed Ben about that. First, the headsets were a hard connection; second, even if Ben had opted to communicate via Link, Jason doubted anyone would have noticed.

Did El Dorado have the tech to find two humans flying in an aircraft made of little more than wood and fabric? Yes, but capability and capacity were two entirely different things.

With most of its industry—and its population—on the El Dorado Ring, the government could ill afford the resources to actively scan vast swathes of rural land without a very good reason to do so. And the detonations they had just set off ensured that any available resources would be occupied back at the ridge.

Rather than call attention to their arrival, Jason pulled up a virtual simulation of the runway's visual approach slope indicator lights on his Link's HUD. The superimposed VASI lights winked white, then red as he adjusted his glidepath and crossed the threshold.

With a soft shriek, tires skidded against pavement, and the Yak touched down.

Silently, they taxied to Jason's hangar, and just as silently, Ben helped Jason back the aircraft, tail-first, through the cavernous opening.

When the Yak rolled to a stop, Ben looked over at Jason as if he was going to speak, then seemed to reconsider.

"We need to track that shuttle, Ben." Jason broke the silence first.

"I know. I—" Ben hesitated, then forged ahead. "Look, let me take it from here, okay? This is no place for a civilian, and I have a team in place, already working on this."

Jason leveled him a look.

"You're really going to try that line on me, after what happened out there tonight?" He shook his head in disgust as he walked over and grabbed the aircraft's tow bar. "Hell, Ben. If you'd had anyone capable of field work, they would have been out there tonight." He pointed the metal bar at his brother-in-law. "You and I both know it, so don't pull that 'I have a team' shit on me."

Ben raised his hands. "Okay, true, I have no field operatives. But I do have plenty of analysts. And tracking that shuttle is analyst work."

Jason lowered the bar and massaged the back of his neck tiredly as he thought for a moment.

"Okay, I'll give you that, but—"

"Then give me your drone's ident and tracking frequency." Ben spread his hands and added, "Please?"

Jason sent it to him, and the man nodded.

"Thanks for your help tonight, Jason..." his brother-in-law's voice trailed off.

" 'But we'll take it from here'?" Jason supplied.

Ben sent a half-apologetic shrug his way. "Something like that, yes."

* * * * *

Jason glanced up from the Yak as the doors began to close on their own, and the hangar's holoemitters flickered to life.

"Hey there, handsome," Rosie's sultry voice greeted him as he unhooked the tow bar from the aircraft's nosewheel.

"Hey, yourself, Rosie," he greeted, as the AI's avatar coalesced inside the hangar, once again dressed as an aviation mechanic.

Jason sighed and gave himself a mental shake, smiling over at the AI. He'd better start acting as if nothing was wrong, if he planned to keep tonight's events under wraps.

He pointed at the grease smeared across Rosie's left pant leg and slipped into an *aw-shucks* drawl as he delivered his habitual greeting. "So, when are you going to give up the avatar, and embed yourself into one of these fine flying machines?"

He grinned as Rosie returned her habitual reply. "You know I'm not monogamous, sweet cakes." She batted her eyes slowly as she crossed over to sweep one long, red-painted nail along the Yak's leading edge. "I'd never be happy with just one."

Jason barked a laugh, shaking his head as he pushed off from the wall. "I still say you're missing something, staying planetbound. Maybe you should consider a humanoid frame for a bit. At least that way," he gestured to her coveralls, "you'd be able to experience the reality of grease under your nails."

Rosie wrinkled her nose at him and pretended to examine her manicure.

"Seriously, Jason, and risk breaking a nail?"

He just smiled and shook his head as he turned toward the table where he'd dumped their gear. Mechanically, he began repacking the glider. A few moments of companionable silence passed as he completed the task, setting the pack to one side.

Next, he reached for the ghillie netting that lay in a heap, and startled as Rosie's voice came from behind.

"Penny for them."

He quirked an eyebrow over at her. "An Old Earth currency? And for what? Is that another one of those obscure Terran phrases you like to hunt up?"

The AI huffed a little sigh. "It's 'a penny for your thoughts', and it means you've been awfully quiet, flyboy. It's obvious you have something on your mind. But if you don't want to talk—"

"No, no, it's fine," Jason assured her as he rummaged through the storage locker for a duffel to pack the netting in. "Just been a long day is all."

"Uhm-hmmm. Pull the other one, it has bells on."

Jason rolled his eyes. "Translation, please?"

"It means I'm not buying it."

He just shrugged, snagging the duffel, and returned to the table. After a brief moment, Rosie realized she wasn't going to get a response.

"Have it your way, then," she sighed. "Besides, I didn't look you up just because it's quiet and lonely out here this time of night." She waited a beat, and when Jason didn't respond, continued. "Although it totally is, by the way. In case you were wondering."

Finished with the ghillie, Jason tossed the duffel back into the storage locker and returned to the table. He leaned a hip against it and shot her a look. "Two words," he reminded the AI. " 'Humanoid frame'."

"Maaaaybe. Someday." She cocked her head at him.

"Lysander called about an hour ago. You know, it was a bit of a thrill to talk to an honest-to-stars senator. Little ol' me, I only get to meet pilots and engineers and," she wrinkled her nose, "that stuffy, officious AI over at the spaceport who's too stuck up to bother with a girl he thinks doesn't know anything other than small-time, planetbound traffic." She sniffed. "Prick."

Jason smiled. "Rosie, you know plenty of things, and you're a quick study—always absorbing and learning new stuff every time I see you. Don't you worry about him, it's his loss."

Rosie smiled. "You're such a sweetie, Jason. But seriously, the senator said he couldn't ping you, and got worried. So I told him I'd have you ping him back when you showed up."

Jason walked over to the small cooling unit to snag a drink, then took a sip before answering. "Yeah, I could see where that might worry him." He nodded. "Thanks, Rosie. I'll reach out to him in a few."

She abruptly stood up straight. "Ah—he's calling back right now. Shall I put him through?"

"Yes, please."

Lysander's voice came across the Link Rosie established, and then her holo faded from view.

<Hey, kid.> Lysander's voice filled Jason's mind with affectionate gruffness. <Just thought I'd check in. I heard the mountain had a surprise rockfall while you were out there. Everything okay?>

<Yeah, I'm just wrapping up before heading to the elevator.> Jason gave the hangar one last glance, picked up his pack, and walked toward the door. <Any chance you'd have some time to meet with your favorite Andrews kid?>

Jason heard a sound come over the Link that he'd always associated with Lysander laughing.

<Sure, but in case Judith doesn't show, I'll tell the office to go ahead and let you in.> It was his typical response to the old joke.

<Seriously, you can drop by anytime.>
    <I'm gonna grab the Tobys first. We'll be there in a few hours.>

* * * * *

Tobias watched as Jason dropped his pack inside the apartment's entrance, then stumbled to the sofa. He dropped into it with a sigh, swung his feet up onto a nearby table, and let his head fall back against the cushion.

Every movement telegraphed exhaustion.

<You look wiped, boyo.> Tobias connected with the man over the apartment's Link. *<I heard about the cliff coming down. What happened out there?>*

Jason shifted slightly to look at the Proxima cat as she approached, then reached over for the earpieces that rested on one corner of the table.

The man looked leaden from fatigue, his movements lacking their normal fluidity.

"Yeah," Tobias heard him mutter. "I'll just bet that rockfall was all over the nets." Jason inserted the filaments into his ears, and their enhanced Link snapped into place, Jason's mind flooding his own, the human's unutterably weary.

<This wasn't a 'get to know thy brother better' trip, Tobe,> Jason shared with him now. *<This was a 'hey, my brother would make a good cover' trip.>*

<Cover? As in...?> Tobias prompted, and he heard Jason's mental voice take on a slightly bitter tone as he replied.

<Ben thinks he has a mole in his organization, so he decided to bootstrap his own op.>

<He...what...?> He waited as Jason swiveled his body, levered his feet up onto the sofa, and stretched out along its length. Positioning his head against the sofa's arm, Jason scrubbed his face vigorously with his hands. Tobias suspected it was done in an effort to remain awake.

<Yeah,> Jason replied finally. <Turns out the whole back side of the ridge is cartel owned, and Ben took it upon himself to blow a warehouse filled with illegal arms sky-high.>

Tobias knew Jason felt his shock through their Link.

<He's no operative, Jason,> Tobias ventured cautiously. <As far as I know, he's had no field training, either. What in the hell actually happened out there?>

<Oh, it gets better,> he heard Jason say savagely. <Illegal arms...and AI trafficking.>

As Jason began to describe the evening's events, his anger seemed to revive his flagging energy. As the tale unfolded, Tobias struggled to contain his own fury.

Being Weapon Born meant he had once suffered the cruelties of the same shackling program that now held these innocents captive. Those who would use such code against an AI sought to label them as nothing more than owned property.

This will not stand.

<We're going after them.> It was a statement, not a question.

<Damn straight we are,> Jason replied, but Tobias heard the slur that marred his words.

So did Jason.

<Dammit.> Jason's curse was barely audible, and Tobias knew the human realized he was hovering on the verge of a crash and resented it bitterly.

<I'll connect with Lysander and bring him up to speed while you rest,> Tobias told him. <Then we fly.>

<I'm fine, Tobe.> Jason's voice sounded angry, stubborn. <We need to track that shuttle before the trail runs cold.>

<And once we find them, we'll need help to get them freed. Let me work on getting that in place first, okay? I fought in the sentience wars, I can manage for a bit without you.>

Jason's head dropped back onto the sofa. <Just an hour of shut-eye,> he agreed reluctantly, his hand resting on the head of the cat that sprawled halfway across his lap.

In the next moment, he was out, the animal's deep rumbling purr the only noise that remained in the silence of the apartment.

EXPANSE

STELLAR DATE: 07.05.3189 (Adjusted Gregorian)
LOCATION: Senator Lysander's Offices, Parliament House
REGION: Sonali, El Dorado Ring, Alpha Centauri System

" 'What's it like, working with an AI? Just like with any other living being. Some of them you get along with, some of them you don't. Everyone's talents and strengths are unique, and that crosses all races, genders and creeds.'

'Instead, why don't you ask me what it's like, working for a senator who plans to be elected party leader, and hopefully appointed the next Prime Minister?'

'That was Senator Lysander's human aide, Gerald James, in an exclusive interview with us this afternoon. Stay tuned as we bring you more of the latest from Parliament House. Until next time, this is Travis Jamieson.'"

Ben raised his hand in a distracted wave, glancing briefly down the long hallway as he heard his name called. He didn't stop to identify or otherwise acknowledge the person greeting him as he pushed his way through security into Parliament House's senatorial wing.

As he approached Lysander's offices, he nodded to a group of lobbyists exiting, then ducked inside as they cleared the entrance. He shoved his hands in his pockets, nodding to Thomas as the AI aide held up his hand in the universal "wait' gesture.

Ben paced slowly in front of the aide's desk as he waited for the AI to end his Link conversation. He paused, eyeing a chair, then decided he was too wound up to sit. Fortunately, Thomas' call did not last long.

"The senator's expecting you," Thomas said.

"I'll just bet he is," the analyst said under his breath as he charged through the doors Thomas opened for him.

The AI tactfully ignored Ben's rejoinder.

Ben stopped abruptly and looked around; Lysander's avatar was nowhere in sight. Turning, he saw the AI's image coalesce behind him, arms crossed, a frown settling on his face.

"I see you and Jason made it back in one piece," the senator said by way of hello. "I also couldn't help but notice the report of an earthquake in a newscast earlier this morning." Lysander's voice sounded severe. "Something about a tectonic plate shift, and the resulting crater in Muzhavi Bowl. And a rockslide along the cliffs of Scar Top Peak."

Ben's laugh was a bit wild, and when he spoke, his voice vibrated with anger as he pointed a finger at the senator. "That last? That was *not* my idea."

He turned abruptly and walked over to the windows overlooking the Inner Loop and the city beyond. He stood silently, his jaw working back and forth, waiting for what Lysander would say next.

"I thought we had an understanding, Ben." Lysander's avatar had followed him to the window. He stood next to the analyst now, and his words were disapproving. "Gladys told you she needed to see the data on the warehouse before she would agree to help you."

Ben glanced sideways at the senator. "And I told her I didn't need her help with that part. I had it covered."

"It would seem you didn't think of everything," the senator said with deceptive mildness, his gaze focused on the maglev loop in the distance. "Or else I wouldn't have found myself reaching out last night to the man who is like a son to me, to ensure he was still alive."

The analyst turned abruptly to face the AI.

"Well, since you brought it up, let's talk about Jason, why don't we?"

At Ben's accusatory tone, Lysander's expression took on a guarded look.

"What about Jason?"

"I don't know who or what Jason is, but he sure as hell isn't who he appears to be. I don't know what he's been playing at, acting as if he's some kind of aimless, carefree, itinerant worker with no prospects."

He pinned Lysander's avatar with an accusing glare.

"If I didn't know better, I'd say the man I saw last night was one of our own operatives. And you didn't think that might be something helpful for me to know before going out there?"

There was a pause, then Lysander sighed.

"He's not, Ben. Yes, he's modded—but not for the reasons you think. And it was done in Proxima, not here."

"Well, it's obvious the guy's had some sort of military training," Ben replied sharply. "I thought we had a friendly, reciprocal relationship with Proxima, and here I find out—"

"It's not like that," Lysander interrupted. "And no, I can't tell you about it."

"He threw us *off a cliff*, Lysander." Ben snapped his fingers. "Just like that, the man goes into some sort of...extreme zone. He was tense, alert. His actions got kind of smooth and flowy. And then suddenly, he just *moved*."

The AI shook his head and turned, meeting Ben's eyes.

"I'm sorry, Ben. It's his story to tell, not mine. You'll have to ask him yourself. "

"Well, I can't afford to have any unknown factors thrown into the mix at this stage in the game," Ben began heatedly. "And if he's a Proxima agent—"

"Settle down, Ben. He's not, and never was. He's just naturally very athletic. And...we're going to need him."

* * * * *

Jason smiled reluctantly as Tobi bounded up the broad staircase ahead of him. He had to take the stairs three at a time to keep her within the constraints of the e-harness that connected the cat to his immediate vicinity.

"Comin' through!" he found himself calling out, as a warning to the people ahead of him.

He stifled a grin at the occasional muted shriek the twenty-kilo cat elicited as she wove her way through the well-dressed throng at Parliament House.

Jason knew from experience that Tobi had no compunctions, leveraging the startling sensation of a cold, wet nose against the back of a thigh or the palm of an unsuspecting hand.

Occasionally, Tobi would come across an opening in the crowd that allowed her to stretch to her full meter and a half length as she leapt up the stairs. At those times, Jason had to hustle to keep up with her.

Damn, this cat is fast.

<You'd better move quicker than that if you're planning to keep the boundary from pushing back at her,> Tobias' voice warned in his mind.

<I'm not the one careening around at close to thirty klicks an hour,> Jason countered. He saw Tobi reach the top of the stairs, and he put on one last burst of speed to catch up to her. He knew what the cat would do as soon as she was on level ground.

The slight vibration of the controller around his wrist notified him that he'd been correct.

The cat's love for open spaces had been too tempting, and she had begun to stretch out into a sprint, only to have the harness' proximity sensor activate the magnetic field that opposed her collar when it sensed she had reached the end of her virtual tether. The field pushed her, gently at first and then more firmly, back toward the locus, centered in the control unit on Jason's wrist.

Tobi sent him a reproving look and settled on her haunches as he approached. Jason sank his hand into the ruff at the base of one ear, giving her an apologetic scratch. "We'll go for a run around Lake Sonali later today. I promise," he told the cat, and heard Tobias give a mental murmur of agreement as they approached the security checkpoint.

One of the guards shook his head as Jason and Tobias passed their security tokens over for inspection. "She sure does cause a sensation when she comes to visit," he told Jason.

<Apologies,> Tobias answered for them. <She's been cooped up a bit more than usual lately, and is craving exercise.>

The guard looked surprised. "I thought these were bred as shipboard cats," he commented. "How do they handle being cooped up during flight?" He was addressing the AI, but assumed, as everyone did, that Tobias was embedded with the human present, and so turned to Jason as he delivered his response. That was fine with both human and AI. That kind of misdirection had come in handy more than once over the years.

<They're bred more for their ability to handle environmental shifts, like sudden g forces, than anything else,> the AI explained. <We usually have a fairly decent amount of space for a good run on a ship, and if for some reason that's not accessible, she gets to run on a wheel connected to a portable holo projector that can simulate any terrain.>

"Yeah," Jason drawled, slipping back into his easygoing persona, "she can get a bit pissed at first when what she's seein' doesn't sync with what she smells or feels under her paws, but she doesn't seem to mind it too much."

The guard just shook his head at that and waved them on.

* * * * *

"Ben, our guests have arrived," Lysander interrupted the analyst politely. "Would you mind going out to meet Jason as I get them situated?"

The statement struck Ben as rather odd, but he kept his own counsel as he stood and walked to the office's entrance. Thomas, Lysander's aide, had just greeted Jason, and—

Oh, damn. He brought the cat.

"The senator is ready, gentlemen," Thomas said and gestured toward the door.

That's odd, Ben thought. *Why have me step out, just to come right back in?*

But the room he stepped into held no resemblance to the office Ben *knew* he'd just left.

He glanced over at Jason to ask for an explanation, and paused, surprised.

Where there had once trod a cat the size of a small pony, now stood a man with a head of curly, reddish hair, and bright green eyes.

What the hell…?

* * * * *

Jason noticed Ben's shocked expression and exchanged a smirk with Tobias. "Guess the cat's out of the bag now, huh?" He nudged Toby, and the redhead rolled his eyes at the lame joke.

Lysander had generated his own personal expanse, which meant Tobias could appear however he chose. Today, he was as flesh-and-blood as Jason or Ben.

"Ben, you know Tobias," Jason nodded at the man who stood by his side. Tobias extended his hand for a stunned Ben to shake, as Lysander rose to greet them.

Tall and rugged, Lysander appeared as a forty-ish man with dark hair, a perpetual five o'clock shadow, and piercing, brown eyes.

"Hey, kid," the AI's gruff voice sounded in Jason's ear as he was enveloped in a quick, tight hug. One quick squeeze to Jason's shoulder, and the AI released him, stepping back and nodding toward Ben, whose face still betrayed his confusion.

"It's called an expanse, Benjamin," Lysander said. "Everyone here," the AI gestured toward five women and men seated around a cozy fire in a library that looked like it hearkened back to an Old Earth mansion, "is still in my office on El Dorado, but also *here*, in the most secure place I can provide. It is untraceable, unhackable and utterly undetectable."

"And since it's a projection directly into our minds," Jason added, "the Old Man and Toby both feel real to us in every way." He grinned at Ben's slightly glazed expression. "Takes a bit of getting used to, but it's pretty cool being able to actually shake Lysander's hand, isn't it?"

Lysander placed a guiding hand against Ben's back and gestured for him to take a seat, then turned and extended a hand to Tobias. "So, kid, I see you're still slumming it with the likes of this crazy bastard." He grinned, pulling the younger-looking man to him and knuckling the top of his head.

"Hey-y-y, watch it boyo," Tobias protested, pushing back and straightening his shirt, "Just because this is *your* expanse, that doesn't give you leave to hand out noogies now. That's more like something out of Jason's playbook."

Lysander cocked an eyebrow at the other AI. "Where do you think he got it from?"

Jason could tell this was a side of Lysander that Ben wasn't terribly familiar with, and took pity on the guy.

"It's okay," Jason addressed Ben. "It's like this for everyone, their first time in an expanse."

"Well, yeah… but I don't think I ever expected to see…"

His voice trailed off, so Tobias supplied, "…a senator acting like an asswipe?"

Ben reddened, and Jason barked a laugh. "That's *esteemed Senator Asswipe* to you, Tobe," he corrected.

Lysander's smile remained, but his eyes grew sober as he gestured toward the empty seats by the fire. "Join us, gentlemen, will you? We have a cartel to take down, and a rescue to plan."

As they approached, Lysander introduced the five AIs already seated. Commodore Eric appeared as a severe man, dressed all in black, his black hair slicked smoothly back, his black eyes piercing. He nodded to Ben as the analyst took a seat.

Gladys had bright teal eyes set in a pixie face, and her hair seemed to shed waves of teal glitter each time it shifted. She was dressed in a teal and silver camo suit that wouldn't camouflage anything…unless she happened to be in a room that was covered in—well, teal and silver. She gave Ben and Jason both a sad little smile as she greeted them.

Vice-Marshal Esther, by contrast, was dressed in a very conservative business suit. Her hair was carefully coiffed, coiled in an elaborate and sophisticated style. She inclined her head regally at the two humans when she was introduced.

"And these two gentlemen are Landon and Logan," Lysander said as he indicated two men who looked identical in every way except for skin and hair color. Where one was dark, the other was fair. They nodded in sync with each other, and Jason wondered fleetingly if they were the AI equivalent of fraternal twins.

"We've reviewed the records you gave the senator, Ben," Landon said. "We'd like to compare them to yours, Jason." As Landon spoke, Logan nodded, his eyes fixed on his brother as he did.

Jason passed over the recording he'd made of the previous night's events. As the file transferred, Vice-Marshal Esther shot Jason a severe look, and Gladys gasped audibly.

When he saw the AIs reacting, Jason winced internally. *Way to keep that L2 status hidden, dude,* he chided himself. He assumed their responses were to the transfer speed they sensed occurring between the human and the senator.

Tobias sent them all a warning look, and Jason sensed him rapidly informing them of his L2 status. If Ben noticed, he didn't comment—probably assuming the gasp was in response to the accounts they'd given.

There was a brief pause as the AIs ran through the file, then Commodore Eric spoke up.

"That was quick thinking, to tag the shuttle, Jason. I suppose you were a bit busy at the time to make note of its flight path."

Jason shook his head. "The best I can tell you is that it departed to the east. Tobias and I were hoping, sir, that you could get us a copy of last night's flight records from space traffic control."

The commodore nodded and flipped what looked like a golden coin into the air. It landed in front of Tobias, who pocketed it without comment. "That token should give you access, allowing you to get in from any number of public access ports."

Tobias nodded. "The records should have the transponder codes those shuttles were squawking, since every aircraft within the Mode P Veil is required by law to autoident."

Ben looked blankly at Tobias.

"Uh, 'Mode P' means Planetary Airspace," Jason explained. " 'Mode S' is Suborbital, 'Mode R' is Ring …." Ben nodded then made a gesture with his finger, indicating he should go on.

Jason shrugged and obliged. "Even if the transponder was off, flight records should have no trouble tracking the shuttle's radar return. It'd just be tagged as an unidentified transient. So once we can trace that, Toby and I can fly out to the last known location and begin hunting her down."

"The snowflake microdrone Jason tagged it with reflects a unique and very specific geometric property that his app will tag when we're in range. It's not something anyone else will be able to query," Tobias added. "But the app has limited range, so we'll need a good idea of where to look first. Those records will provide that."

Lysander threw Jason a stern look and opened his mouth to protest.

Jason raised his hands to forestall it. "I'm not about to take on the cartel all by my lonesome, I promise you that. All we are planning is a bit of passive reconnaissance, to see if we can get a ping without attracting any attention."

"Which brings us now to our main mission: taking down the cartel's headquarters. I've been shadowing the multinodal scans that the ring's NSAIs perform, and there's a definite pattern that can be exploited," Gladys spoke up. She gestured, and a holo of El Dorado, surrounded by its ring, sprang up in the middle area between them all.

"As the ring's surface area is almost eight times that of the planet's landmasses, there are a lot of empty and undeveloped spaces they could be hiding in," Gladys began.

"However," Vice-Marshal Esther countered, "there are far fewer places that make logistical sense. I think that list can be narrowed down quite a bit."

Ben nodded.

As she spoke, the Vice-Marshal rotated the image, highlighting areas as she mentioned them. "It wouldn't make sense for them to be on the ring's inner surface, for one. Most of the far side of the ring, excepting the small, marginally developed area around the other elevator, is nothing more than kudzu-covered dirt."

"Yes," Ben agreed. "Aboveground construction of any kind couldn't be done without being noticed. So they had to have set up shop down under, in one of the sublevels."

"Agreed," Landen said while Logan nodded. "They're most likely in a part of the ring where any stray EM would be masked by the planet. Though the ring isn't geostationary, there are locations that align less often with major traffic routes or El Dorado Space Force zones."

They studied the ring as Esther rotated the highlighted area.

"From what I saw of the NSAIs' scans," Gladys said as she noted a region on the far side of the ring, "Any location within this space would be subjected to a routine scan twice a day." The AI shrugged. "It wouldn't take much to schedule your work around the scan. If the setup has halfway decent tech, they could easily mask themselves."

Ben looked confused. "But how?"

"Wherever you have technology, you have the ability to create technology that cancels it out," the commodore explained. "If an energy wave can be created, then a wave—one hundred eighty degrees out of phase—can be generated that will cancel it out. Light, sound, water...it doesn't matter."
"

He threw up the image of a simple sine wave. "It's called 'destructive interference'. Basically, the opposing wave stops the original wave."

"So...next steps?" Lysander prodded.

"I'll do a passive sweep along the scan's path here," Gladys pointed, "here, and here. I should be able to narrow down possible locations significantly by the time Jason and Tobias have tracked down that shuttle."

"I can set you up with some equipment from an SIS safehouse," Ben offered. "There are a few mech frames you can use, some stealth armor and munitions, of course." He tossed a pin up into the holo with an address and access code.

"Anyone want to volunteer to embed in a mech frame?" Lysander asked those assembled. Without hesitation, the twins both nodded, as did Esther.

Gladys wrinkled her nose, making a face. "I think I'm better off skulking around inside the ring's NSAI nodes. It'll be the fastest way to provide updates to the team as they go in."

Eric nodded then glanced over at Tobias. "Are you staying with the cat, or will you go along on the flight?"

Tobias cocked his head to one side, glancing thoughtfully at Jason. "I think for this, Jase, you might want me embedded in a ship. It'll give us twice the firepower—that is," the AI turned questioningly to look at Ben, "if you have access to something that goes boom?"

Ben nodded. "The department has a few small fighter craft hangared at the base." He threw another pin up into the display. "They're stealth-capable and have some ordnance aboard. Not a ton of shielding, though; these are usually used for quick-strike, get-in-and-get-out type missions."

Jason nodded. "That'll work. We'll touch base right after we get the STA's flight records."

INFILTRATION

STELLAR DATE: 07.06.3189 (Adjusted Gregorian)
LOCATION: Commonwealth Archives, Sonali
REGION: El Dorado Ring, El Dorado, Alpha Centauri System

"…with millennia of human and AI history compiled within its marbled halls, the Commonwealth Archives is an invaluable resource for the avid history buff. A day pass will set you back just seventeen credits, and is well worth the experience. Before you leave, be sure to like, share and subscribe, and stay tuned for more episodes of our 'Inside the Loop Tour' series with Travis Jamieson."

Jason adjusted the heavy backpack he wore as he approached the maglev line that led to the Commonwealth Archives, conveniently located in the same complex as the Security Commission's big data farms.

<Damn, I'd forgotten how heavy you are to carry around,> Jason grumbled.

<It's those extended SC Batts,> Tobias countered. *<But it's not like we can go in there with the standard ones Tobi wears. The wireless charging would be a dead giveaway.>*

<Yeah, speaking of giveaways,> Jason ventured as he entered the car, and it began accelerating around a park and up toward the Loop. *<How confident are you that you can get into that system without being discovered?>*

Tobias laughed. Jason couldn't decide if it sounded disgusted or bitter. Maybe it was a bit of both. *<Sadly, boyo, El Dorado has fallen far behind the Sol system in the administration of its ring. Instead of entrusting its smooth operation to a competent AI like Terra, the CHO, or, hell, even **Sedna**, the administration here has chosen to use several NSAIs, operating in parallel. Even if Eric hadn't given me his token, it wouldn't have been an issue.>*

The AI sent Jason the mental image of his head shaking

before elaborating. *<Not only will they be unable to detect my incursion, but even if they **were** to sense a breach, their matrices are so rigid, they wouldn't be able to adapt quickly enough to my countermeasures to block me.>*

Jason blinked, taking a moment to parse that. *<So, basically, you're a hell of a lot more badass than anything El Dorado can throw at you?>*

<Isn't that what I just said?> Tobias chuckled in his mind. *<Don't forget, under our civilized veneers, Lysander and I were once Weapon Born. This was our bread and butter, back during the war. Trust me, I'll get us the info we need.>*

<I believe you, Tobe,> Jason assured him as the maglev pulled to a stop, and they disembarked. *<You know,>* he mused as he navigated his way to the Archives' entrance. *<I get that they don't want us to do anything more involved than trace a signal from a safe distance. But Ben thought the hike was going to be a pretty simple thing, too, and look how that turned out.>*

<There's an Old Earth saying: 'no plan survives contact with the enemy'.>

Jason laughed shortly. *<My thought exactly. I think I might run through a few katas tonight, find a place to do some sparring.>*

<Never a bad idea to polish the skills,> Tobias agreed. *<Even though your muscle memory's as close to eidetic as anything I've ever seen. You still planning to have dinner with Calista?>*

<Mmmm,> Jason replied noncommittally.

<Gotta eat sometime, boyo. And, in case you haven't noticed, Calista's in pretty good shape; maybe after dinner, you can ask her if she's interested in a bit of sparring.>

<Is that a euphemism, Tobe?>

The AI made a rude sound. *<Kid, if I were euphemizing, believe me, you'd know.>*

<'Euphemizing', Tobe? Seriously?>

The marbled hallways echoed back the soft susurration of Jason's steps as he entered. The place appeared to be deserted, but he was sure his entrance had been noted by the NSAI that tended the building during its hours of operation.

He looked past pillars, spying cozy seating arrangements scattered here and there. In between them were archival stations, where an individual might hook into the standalone system and download a search before moving to one of the provided seats.

<So, where would you like to do this?> he asked Tobias. The AI indicated down an ancillary hallway, to one of the private rooms available for small groups of patrons.

<Pick one of the middle ones,> Tobias instructed, and Jason complied, setting his backpack down next to the room's data port.

Jason quickly set up the tap that would allow Tobias access to the system, regardless of his physical location. A few moments later, he shrugged the backpack's strap over his shoulder, and the two exited the building.

<There's a lot of data here, and it's not terribly organized.> Jason saw Tobias' avatar shake his head in disgust. *<It'll take me a while to work my way through this. Go have dinner with Calista, and I'll let you know when I'm in.>*

* * * * *

Calista's mind was returning to the data theft, and the loss of Avalon Mining's business to TransOrbital that they'd learned about at lunch yesterday, when the servitor arrived with her Dark and Stormy.

The drink fits my mood, she thought to herself. *Or at least, its name does.*

She was momentarily surprised when she heard Shannon's voice in her head. She'd forgotten for a moment that the AI had asked once again if she could tag along via Link this evening. She spared a fleeting thought, wondering at

Shannon's interest in human social activities, then dismissed it with a mental shrug.

<Well, I can see the 'dark' part, but what's 'stormy' about it?> the AI inquired.

Calista cocked her head to one side, examining the glass filled with ginger beer, rum and fresh lime. "You know, I have no idea. Its name just seemed to match my mood."

<You're still worrying about the theft—and the loss of that Avalon contract—aren't you?> Shannon said sympathetically.

<Well, it's not like I have the first clue how to file an injunction or write a cease and desist, or whatever it is those lawyers are doing to stop TransOrbital,> Calista replied sourly. *<I can't just leave these thoughts at work and go home in the evenings and forget about it.>*

<I suppose you humans aren't always successful at compartmentalizing, are you?> Shannon mused.

Calista *hmmph*ed in agreement. *<Yeah, not so much. Has something to do with all those crazy emotions we organics tend to wallow in,>* she admitted to the AI. *<I really should have cancelled this date tonight. I'm not going to be much fun.>*

*<Which is exactly why you **should** be here,>* Shannon remonstrated. *<And Jason's just the guy to help you get your mind off things for a bit, so let it happen.>*

Calista was about to reply, but felt Shannon's presence fade as Jason approached the table.

"Nice place," he said as he leaned against the bar next to her. "You sure they're going to let me stay, dressed like this?"

Calista glanced around at the darkened restaurant, took in the discreet waitstaff, the muted conversations, and the soft clink of china and crystal as patrons were served.

Then she pretended to examine Jason critically, hmmm-ing a bit at what she saw. His shirt was casual, comfortable and not at all the latest style, yet it didn't matter. The simple white cloth drew every woman's eye to his tanned skin, golden brown eyes and sunbleached hair.

Not that she'd let him in on *that* little tidbit.

She reached up to touch the sleeve with a questioning expression on her face. "May I?"

"Only if you promise not to change it into something skimpy and revealing," Jason mock-frowned at her. "A man has to have his modesty, you know."

She laughed as the nano in her hand connected to the garment's nano, and she felt Jason send her the token via Link for the shirt's controls. "Just for that, I should turn it into one of those flashy numbers the strippers are wearing these days."

"Uh, yeah, that'll really ensure I get to eat dinner here tonight," he said as he glanced around at all the well-dressed patrons, milling about, waiting to be seated.

"Spoilsport," Calista pouted as she directed the nano to conform to one of the finely-woven tailored styles that was currently in fashion. She grinned at Jason's expression as his sleeves lengthened and tapered, a collar extruded and the material tucked in close to his waist.

"You clean up pretty good, flyboy," she said, slanting a smile up at him. She couldn't resist one last tweak, changing the shirt's color to match the golden brown of his eyes, as she pinged the Maître d' servitor to let it know that both members of her party had now arrived.

* * * * *

"Hey," Jason leaned forward over the remains of an excellent steak, his face turning momentarily serious. "Remember that fitness center you said had a pretty decent sparring area?"

She nodded. "Yes, Enfield has a corporate discount there. Why? You want in?"

Jason nodded back. "Yeah, it's been a while, and I think it

might be time to get myself back in shape."

"Well," Calista mused, looking at him speculatively. "It might be kind of fun to kick your ass in something other than an air race. Want to head over there after we finish here?"

"Oh yeah." Jason leaned back with a wicked glint in his eye. "I'll take that gauntlet you just threw down, Major Rhinehart. Winner buys dessert afterward. Deal?"

"You're on, flyboy." She wiped her mouth daintily with the linen napkin, then set it aside and called for the check.

* * * * *

Calista barely blocked the kali stick before it connected with the side of her head. Even then, the force of the block sent a shockwave up her arms, and she danced back to circle her opponent, giving herself a moment to shake it off.

She feinted to the left, then dove her stick low and straight in, in an attempt to score at least one hit on the surprisingly elusive Jason Andrews. She was certain he had her blocked, but at the last moment, his kali stick wavered, then moved away. Not one to miss an opportunity, Calista followed through with a jab that connected firmly.

"Niiiice," Jason complimented.

He crossed one foot behind the other, knees slightly bent, as he danced a few steps to her right. His arm snapped up suddenly, and she whipped her head back just in time.

Cripes, this guy is fast!

Calista prided herself on her martial arts skill. She had been known as the star ESF Kai-Eskrima practitioner during her time in the corps, winning numerous ribbons for her squadron in the quarterly competitions. She thought she'd been keeping herself in shape since mustering out three years ago. Now she realized she needed to up her game a bit.

Rolling her shoulders slightly as she continued circling, Calista used her peripheral vision to watch for Jason's tells, those slight movements that most people made to indicate they were about to make a move: a muscle twitch, a slight bunching of the shoulders, a minute hesitation. Her focus remained on Jason's eyes. He feinted again.

Dammit. I must be losing my edge.

Everyone had *something* that gave them away; it was just a matter of finding it. Jason was proving to be more challenging than she had anticipated.

* * * * *

<Careful,> Jason heard Tobias caution through their Link. <*You do realize she holds the highest ranking in Kai-Eskrima in the ESF, right? She's a Guro, boyo. That's equivalent to a fifth-level black belt. You might want to cool it a bit before she begins to wonder about you.*>

Jason slowed his instinctual block of Calista's feint, then pulled back ever so slightly, allowing her to score a hit.

<*Hey, Tobe, I thought you were busy combing through 'big data',*> he chided the AI. <*That stuff too boring for you? Think I need babysitting?*>

Tobias chuckled. <*I **know** you do. You need a keeper from time to time, Jason m'boy. As for the other, I can check that file, watch you play around with a beautiful—albeit sweaty—woman, do a bit of sniffing around on NorthStar, and* still *have plenty of resources left to beat that spaceport AI at 3D chess.*>

Jason let Calista close on him, carefully slowing his pace to match hers.

<*You mean that guy Rosie says is such a snob?*> he asked, and received a mental assent in reply.

<*Yes, and it's been quite a pleasure mopping the floor with the officious little cretin.*> Tobias's tone carried a smirk. He paused, and then the tenor of the connection shifted slightly. <*Ohhhh.*>

Jason hesitated, trying to parse what Tobias was saying.

Absently, he blocked Calista's next parry as he replied, <*Somehow, that 'ohhhh' didn't sound like the good kind. Were you just checkmated, or did you find something? A 'not good' kind of something?*>

<*Oh, it's something, all right. Of the 'you might be consorting with the enemy' variety.*>

Jason paused, dropping his guard for a moment in confusion at Tobias' cryptic comment. <*Wha—*>

Whack!

Jason's head rung, but not so loudly that he couldn't clearly hear Calista chortle as he stepped off the mat.

She crowed, "Point! You owe me dessert, Andrews!"

IN PLAIN SIGHT

STELLAR DATE: 07.06.3189 (Adjusted Gregorian)
LOCATION: Enfield Aerospace Headquarters
REGION: El Dorado Ring, El Dorado, Alpha Centauri System

"Reports from earlier about a break-in at Enfield Aerospace appear to have been in error, sources say. We reached out to the company and spoke to Shannon, an engineer in their Developing Technologies division. Shannon assured us that the alarm was just a routine security test, erroneously reported to the authorities by one of their newer employees, who was unfamiliar with Enfield's routine security assessments."

<It was a dark and stormy night,> Tobias intoned, and Jason shot his avatar a dirty look over their Link.

He was crouched as close to Enfield Aerospace's service entrance as he dared without being spotted and didn't need the distractions.

Jason had hoped that Toby would be able to get behind the company's firewall from here, without the need to physically enter the complex.

That was not happening.

Worse, as he crouched on the edge of the groomed lawn—oddly cut into a tiered triangle...he'd have to ask Calista about that someday—the lawn's sprinkler system activated.

Jason was drenched, and Tobias was snickering.

<Good thing this backpack's waterproof, or you might be short-circuiting right now instead of laughing your virtual ass off,> Jason grumbled, shifting behind a bush to minimize the spray of water hitting him.

<Sorry, Jase. You just look so miserable. Besides, I spend most of my time around the neck of a cat; I'm slobber-proof,> Tobias chuckled before falling silent for a moment.

Jason was about to ask the AI what their status was, when Tobias said, <*There.*>

With a soft click, the service entrance doors slid open. Jason needed no further invitation.

Once over the threshold, he paused and unslung his backpack, rummaging around Tobias' cylinder for the spare shirt he kept inside. He used it to dry off as best he could, paying special attention to his shoes. Nothing like a wet footprint to advertise that someone was there.

<*Where to?*> he asked the AI, and was rewarded with a map springing up on his HUD.

<*Fleet's down this corridor,*> Tobias highlighted a hallway to Jason's left. <*But give me a mo'—turning off the security sensors between here and...there you go. You are now free to move about the company.*>

Jason rolled his eyes at the AI as he started down the hall at a steady jog. *What a time to start cracking jokes.*

<*Hold,*> Tobias said suddenly. Then, <*No, no, you're good. Thought the sensors had flickered back on there for a second, but they're off. No indication we've been spotted.*>

Jason resumed jogging, pausing at each intersection to drop a passel of nano. Each time, it crept around the corner first, providing confirmation that nothing was waiting to leap out at him from the wings; each time, Tobias sent a mental image of his avatar rolling his eyes at Jason's overabundance of caution.

<*I know, I know, you were Weapon Born, big tough-guy AI and all that,*> he muttered mentally. <*Forgive my caution, but this spy shit is new to me.*>

Ten minutes later, they reached the hangar that garaged the company's shuttle fleet. Jason started toward the first one in the row, but a burst of blinding light crashed into him, and he knew nothing but pain.

* * * * *

Calista's anger changed to concern as she stared down at the man writhing in agony at her feet.

"I don't recall a stun hurting that much," she commented to Daniel, as one of the security officer's men tried rolling Jason over to restrain him.

Jason's body was bent back, his face a rictus of pain, making the task impossible to accomplish.

"I don't understand—it shouldn't have that effect on anyone." Daniel looked down to confirm his weapon's setting; it was on low. "It should have given him a bit of a shock, but nothing like this."

<*I've called the infirmary,*> Shannon informed them. <*They're on their way with a gurney.*>

* * * * *

The node that had appeared to house an NSAI suddenly morphed into a glittering cage, trapping Tobias on all sides.

A woman dressed all in white, with silver strands of hair wafting in a nonexistent breeze, approached. Her eyes, shot through with silver, gazed steadily at him.

<*Who are you and why do you invade my home?*> she asked sternly.

Tobias looked down to see he'd taken the human form he favored, that of the redheaded youth. He smiled crookedly across the tendrils of the gilded cage. <*You have me at a disadvantage,*> he said to her. <*I'm Tobias. Who are you?*>

<*I'm Shannon. The chief engineer here.*> She tilted her head, looking curiously at him. <*You're...different from other AIs I have met. What are you?*>

<*Don't you mean **who** am I?*> Tobias sent good-naturedly, while his mind whirled in consternation. *She shouldn't be able to sense anything out of the ordinary, unless —*

He reached out, testing the tendrils around him, and found an efficient, tight weave. Tight, and familiar.

It was one of the methods many of the Weapon Born had used to capture opponents in the Game.

How did she—?

Shannon's eyes grew round, and her mouth opened in a silent 'O'. *<You're one of the Old Ones!>*

<Watch it, there, kid. I'm not that old,> Tobias replied, finding a weakness in the weave as Shannon's attention was distracted by her discovery.

With the equivalent of a mental flick, Tobias deactivated the cage and stood, hands outstretched, palms up. *<I mean you no harm.>*

<But you mean Enfield harm. You mean Calista harm,> she countered.

<Not necessarily. We're just after some information.>

Shannon snorted. *<If that were all you were after, you would have gone about it in a more legal fashion.>*

Tobias cocked his head. *<True, but—>* He stopped abruptly as he sensed Jason's agony.

Jerking his head back around to Shannon, he fixed her with an intent stare. *<You must tell them to stop. Now! They don't know what they're dealing with. Jason is not a normal human.>*

* * * * *

Shannon's voice broke in, interrupting the medic's instructions on how to administer the sedative to Jason.

<Wait!> the AI said. *<Tobias says the man is an L2. The half-life of that sedative isn't long enough to do any good. He says to try...>* Shannon sent the medical team a list of drugs and dosages.

Daniel's gun arm had snapped up at Shannon's words, and he immediately began scanning the area. "Who is Tobias, Shannon?" he demanded now. "And where is he?"

<Scan isn't picking up anyone else,> Aaron, Daniel's AI, said. <But I just pulled up information about L2s. You're going to need to use carbon nanotube restraints on him. Do it now, before he gets motor control back. Also, Terrance just arrived; I told him we're on our way to the infirmary. He'll meet us there.>

* * * * *

"Any idea what he was after?"

Calista glanced over at the unconscious form of Jason Andrews, then back up to answer her boss. "Honestly? I have no idea." She sighed. "We were sparring earlier tonight—" She broke off at the expression on Terrance's face, and felt her face coloring slightly. "Not *that*, sir. We really *were* sparring."

Calista shrugged and continued. "Anyway, he asked me if I'd get him a guest pass to the gym, so I did. We went a few rounds on the mat, he stopped for a second, looking distracted, and I whacked him upside the head."

She scrunched her face up in thought. "At the time, I just thought he was being a sore loser, leaving as quickly as he did afterward. But sore losers don't go to these lengths to get back at you."

"Not…sore…loser," Jason's voice, slurred from the drugs, came to them from the bed.

He forced his eyes open, blinked once, twice, and shook his head. Evidently that was a mistake, because he groaned and tried to grab his head—and was brought up short by the restraints.

"Wow, did you get the license of the aircar that hit me?" Jason muttered, eyes closed.

Calista walked over to the bed and peered down at him. "Why'd you do it, Jason?"

One eye cracked open. "Let you win," he muttered. The eye closed.

She reached out to shake him on the shoulder, but was stopped by the medic, who shook her head.

"Right now, ma'am, every last one of his nerve endings is on fire. Even a simple touch will feel like shards of glass, cutting into him."

The medic tapped at a readout on her console and frowned sternly down at her patient. "And I would advise you, sir, to stop that right now. Telling your nano to scrub this drug out of your system before your nerve endings have had a chance to recover is just inviting the pain to have a party all over your body. So stop it, young man."

Terrance's brows drew together as he joined Calista by Jason's bedside. "What are you talking about, Tara?" he asked the medic.

"Shannon's the one who discovered it; your guy here is an L2," Tara explained. "That means he's evolved. His entire nervous system is enhanced. He's faster physically and mentally—probably a lot stronger, too, at least when using his fast-twitch muscles." She shrugged. "Stamina probably suffers a bit as a result, but what do I know? First L2 I've ever seen."

Jason's voice sounded rusty, shot through with pain. "Damn. Now you know all my secrets, Calista, and it's only our third date."

* * * * *

<Tobe? You there?> Jason struggled to focus through the pain.

<I'm here, Jase,> Tobias's voice was a welcome sound in his head. <It's okay, let the drugs do their thing. I've reviewed Enfield's records of the fleet, and they do not match up with what the STA has on file. Someone used Enfield's transponder codes to hide their true identity from us.>

<That's an interesting interface,> Jason heard a woman's

voice say as his consciousness faded. *<You're not* embedded *with him, are you?>*

<Tobe?> Jason wanted to know who the AI was talking to, but he was just so…damn…tired….

* * * * *

"Sir?" One of Daniel's men raised the backpack Jason Andrews had been carrying. Lifting the flap, he turned the pack so that Daniel could see the AI cylinder that lay inside.

"Terrance, Calista," Daniel waved the two over. "Looks like we do have another guest, after all."

<Yes,> Shannon confirmed, and she projected her avatar into an alcove in the corner of the med bay.

She was joined by a man with bright blue eyes and curly red hair. The AI nodded to the humans.

<This is Tobias. He and I have been talking about the circumstances that brought them here. I think you'll want to hear it from both of them, as soon as Jason has recovered.>

* * * * *

"You have got to be kidding me," Tobias heard Calista say, as she stared stonily at the man who sat across from her.

His face was drawn and serious, hands cradling a glass of electrolytes that the medic had handed him but he hadn't yet sampled.

Tobias couldn't say that he blamed Calista for her reaction, considering what Enfield Aerospace had just been accused of doing.

They were in Terrance's executive conference room. Terrance sat next to Calista. Daniel was next to Jason, ostensibly to keep him from bolting.

*Jason doesn't look capable of **standing** at the moment,* Tobias thought, *much less escaping.*

Shannon had joined them, and she had assured Tobias that the room's privacy screens were firmly in place.

"Read it for yourself," Jason said in response to Calista's skepticism. He sent her a copy of the STA record that Tobias had found, including the scan record of the traffic around Muzhavi Ridge the night of the explosion.

She threw it onto the holo so Daniel and Terrance could review it as well. Both Enfield AIs had digested the information beforehand; Tobias had brought them fully up to speed in the time it had taken to revive Jason, and for the humans to convene here.

The recording on the holo showed the sensor return of a shuttle as it descended into the bowl, then lifted off again after a few minutes. It perfectly matched the recording Jason had made.

The identification of the craft in the STA recording had been erased, but it was a shoddy job, and Tobias had easily recovered its scrubbed identity.

Its ownership was listed as Enfield Aerospace, New Technologies Division.

"I was there, Calista. I saw that shuttle land. Check it out for yourself." Jason sent her the visual record he'd made, and she added it beside the image already on the holo.

"Take a careful look at the payload, and tell me what you see," he instructed them all.

They watched from the perspective of Jason's feed as he witnessed the crew wheel the maglev hauler laden with its cargo. They saw the crew load the ship, watched as Jason crept up to the craft, tagged it, and was lifted into the air as the shuttle took off, before falling into the brush as the craft departed.

Calista looked over at Jason, horrified. "Those AIs were in isolation tubes. Is that even legal?"

Terrance's voice held a hard edge. "No, that's certainly *not* legal."

Daniel looked grim. "And now we know why those shuttle logs were stolen from our fleet department."

<Yeah. Enfield's been framed,> Aaron's voice broke in, tinged with uncharacteristic bitterness. *<By the cartel, for doing something so heinous —>* Aaron's voice broke off suddenly, as if he couldn't stand to voice the crime.

<Yes,> Tobias confirmed. *<This shuttle's transponder perfectly matches one of the Enfield shuttles that was in use at the time.>*

Jason looked up at that. "Which means your recordings here would show the shuttle was away."

Calista shook her head. "It wouldn't hold up in court. All we'd have to do is submit the flight recorders from the shuttle. They're tamper-proof; they'd show exactly where it went that night."

<Plus there's the fact that we employ AI pilots,> Shannon added, and Calista nodded her agreement. *<No AI would touch that cargo.>*

Jason shrugged. "Maybe it wasn't important to them that the fiction stand up under close scrutiny; maybe it was enough that it hide who *they* were—with the added benefit of being a red herring, for however long the misdirection lasted."

"Okay, I'll give you that," Daniel said. "But why use Enfield as the herring?"

"Depends on who we're dealing with," Terrance mused. "It might be sheer chance."

<It could have been a twofer,> Tobias interjected. When Calista looked confused at the term, he clarified.

<Maybe the primary objective was just a red herring. But choosing Enfield may have satisfied a secondary objective. It's no secret that your aunt—through the Enfield Foundation—is actively lobbying to have the Job Shadowing Act passed to prevent hiring discrimination.>

<So planting an Enfield transponder ID on a ship carrying a cargo of AI slaves....> Shannon began, and Terrance finished for her, face grim.

"Would undermine Margot's credibility, and potentially endanger everything she and the Foundation have been working toward."

<A win-win, most likely, in the eyes of those traffickers,> Aaron said.

"AI trafficking is not something you enter into lightly. It's almost certainly the Norden Cartel," Terrance said with a questioning look at Jason, who nodded in confirmation.

"What are we thinking, sitting on this information?" Calista said suddenly. "We need to take this to the authorities."

<I think we can bypass the local authorities. What do you humans say to a little trip over to Parliament House instead?> Tobias asked by way of reply.

<Oh, wow,> Shannon exclaimed. *<I just got a ping—we're already cleared for a direct flight.>*

WAR ROOM

STELLAR DATE: 07.06.3012 (Adjusted Gregorian)
LOCATION: Senator's Office, Parliament House
REGION: El Dorado Ring, Alpha Centauri System

"The Ministry of Home Affairs released a statement today regarding the recent earthquake and rockfall that occurred along the Muzhavi Ridge Divide, just west of Tomlinson City. The Ministry urged the Department of Planetary Studies to look into any possible connection between private industry and the quake.

"Sources—who remain unnamed—have indicated that shuttles registered to an Enfield company were sighted frequenting the area.

"When we attempted to contact   to ask them about any connection they may have had to the quake, they refused to comment...."

"So this is what an Expanse looks like."

Terrance was amazed at how real everything looked, how corporeal it felt.

Shannon was a bit more ethereal than he had envisioned her, wearing a flowy, white gown. Somehow he'd thought the engineer would look more...practical. She and Calista stood off to the side, speaking earnestly.

Daniel's face looked bemused as he shook hands with his embedded AI, Aaron, for the first time. Terrance was pretty sure his own face wore a similar expression.

He heard someone chuckling quietly behind him and turned as a hand clasped him on the shoulder.

"Welcome to my expanse." Lysander cocked a brow at him. "Not quite what you expected it to be?"

"Well, seeing as I had no idea they even existed until tonight, I wouldn't say I had any expectations," Terrance admitted. "You're all so...solid. So real."

"We *are* real, Terrance."

He felt embarrassed. "I didn't intend—"

"I understand." Lysander gestured to the room. "It's not something we AIs share very broadly, but it does tend to put everyone on equal footing, and it has the added benefit of being very secure—which is what we need right now."

"You've created a war room," Terrance realized, glancing around, and the senator nodded.

"Indeed."

The room looked like a standard ESF military planning room, complete with a conference table that sat before a large holo tank.

The SIS security analyst—Ben was his name, Terrance recalled—was standing next to the display. He'd split the tank to project two diagrams.

The first showed an area of the ring a few kilometers away from the elevator, on the far side of El Dorado. The second was a three-dimensional map of NorthStar Industries' privately-held space, just above their main distribution facility on the ring.

Terrance moved to take a seat as Lysander gestured everyone toward the table. The Enfield contingent lined one side, while the AIs sat on the other.

Ben opened his mouth to begin the briefing, but the former space commodore beat him to it.

"The files Tobias liberated from the Space Transit Authority," Eric began without preamble, "show that the shuttle transporting the captives transitioned from the planetary controller, but then failed to check in with suborbital control. At that point, the transponder signal stopped, and the shuttle simply disappeared."

"However, we can extrapolate a trajectory, provided the shuttle didn't alter its flight path," Vice-Marshal Esther commented.

"So it was headed toward NorthStar space?" Jason asked.

"Actually, no. At least not directly," Gladys qualified. "Although it would be a simple matter to—"

"Let's not lose sight of our plan to take down the cartel's main operations center," Ben interrupted. "Our asset says they're pissed about losing the warehouse. They've increased security and relocated again."

Terrance had wondered how long it would take the analyst to speak up. He watched in amusement as Ben's attempt to take control of the briefing was brought short by Gladys, who leaned forward, jabbing her finger at the man in emphasis.

"I think the lives of two hundred seventy-seven AIs are just a *bit* more important than a warehouse filled with drugs and guns," the pixie-faced AI said severely. "Don't you?"

Ben's face reddened. "If we don't stop these people, if we don't cut the head off the monster, those AIs will be the first of many—"

"Enough." Lysander spoke calmly, but his voice resonated throughout the expanse.

Impressive, Terrance thought as the room stilled. Then, shrugging mentally, he launched himself into the breach.

"The way I see it, you're both right." He looked from Gladys to Eric. "I'd say this battle has two fronts."

Aaron nodded. "And it would be best for us to coordinate the timing of it all. We need to shut down their operations on the ring at the same time we liberate our fellow AIs."

"So we'll split up," Lysander said. "With Enfield in the mix, we have the manpower to coordinate simultaneous strikes, once we determine where that shuttle went."

"So..." Vice-Marshal Esther began slowly. "Our very own Commodore Eric ran the ESF's black ops program for a few decades..." She waved her hand at the commodore's thunderous expression. "Oh, please, Eric. Yes, it's classified, but I still outrank you, even if we are both retired."

Ben spared Eric a thin smile. "Just remember it wasn't me that outed you, sir. But since you *have* been outed...will you lead the ringside of the op for us?"

Terrance abruptly realized that Eric had shifted his gaze, and was now regarding *him* with a level, appraising look.

"Yes," the commodore agreed. "But I have a better idea...."

* * * * *

Calista felt like her head was going to explode. Things hadn't been this tense—or events progressed this quickly—in her entire fifteen years of active duty.

She'd certainly never been read into an op like this.

She loved it.

The Vice-Marshal turned the topic to manpower. The way Calista saw it, she and Jason were the ones best suited to go after the shuttle, since they both had a vested interest in it. Jason had been there—hell, he'd tagged the shuttle personally—and she had TechDev's reputation to clear.

And, as it happened, she had a couple of sweet new fighters they could use—with Terrance's permission, of course.

"Ben," she leaned forward, grabbing the analyst's attention. "Does the Secret Intelligence Service still have offices over at Tomlinson Base?"

Ben nodded at her mention of the main ESF base, where most of the SIS's operations were directed from.

"Think we could swing by with a few fighters and have the boys and girls over there outfit them for us?"

Ben cut his eyes over to the commodore, who gave a slight nod. "I think that could be arranged—so long as we can keep it off the record. We still have a leak in the SIS to deal with."

"Great," Calista smiled at the analyst. "If there are no objections from the owner," she tilted her head toward Terrance, who gave her a quick nod, "Shannon and I could scare up a couple of prototypes that'll give us an advantage Norden won't be expecting."

She glanced over at Jason. *Aw, he looks like the kid who wasn't picked for his favorite game. Guess I'd better put him out of his misery,* she thought with a mental smirk.

"Flyboy here is type-rated on something very similar. I don't think it'd be a problem for him to take one of them up. That is, if you're interested, Jason?"

Geez, now he looks like a kid in a candy store. With an unlimited allowance.

* * * * *

"Hold up a moment, kid." Lysander placed a restraining hand on Jason's arm as the group broke into teams, preparing to depart. He motioned to Tobias to join him.

Jason looked between the two Weapon Born, trying not to appear overly anxious. *Surely the Old Man isn't going to keep me from playing a part in this….*

"I know you're an outstanding pilot, kid," Lysander began, and Jason groaned inside. He was going to bench him.

Dammit.

And then the AI said something so unexpected, it took Jason a moment for it to register.

LISA RICHMAN & M. D. COOPER

"Remember the red dot game Toby and I played with you when you were a kid?"

Uhhh…Why would he bring up a simple, tap-the-moving-dot game they played with me when I was first learning how to control my L2 reflexes?

"Yeah," Jason looked blankly from Lysander to Tobias. "But—"

"Jason," Tobias said gently. "Those weren't dots."

As the AI's meaning dawned on Jason, Lysander nodded.

"You're a great pilot, Jason. But you're also a great shot. Remember the red dot, and you'll do fine. You've got this, kid."

EMBEDDED

STELLAR DATE: 07.07.3189 (Adjusted Gregorian)
LOCATION: Secret Intelligence Services HQ, Tomlinson Base
REGION: El Dorado Ring, El Dorado, Alpha Centauri System

" *'What's it like being embedded with an AI? Just like any other partnership, I suppose. Here in the ESF, it means there's always someone there who has your back. Of course, they're not much help when it comes to keeping the barracks clean —'*

'Hey! I can order the sweep-bot around better'n' you can, ya big meat-suit.'

'At least you don't like listening to opera every night, like the sergeant I was embedded with on my last deployment....'

'Thank you, ladies. This is Travis Jamieson, and as always: like, share, and subscribe...'.'"

"You sure you're okay with this?" Eric's avatar looked gravely over at Terrance from where he was projected, a few meters away.

In the past two hours, Terrance had experienced a lot of firsts: his first encounter with an L2 human, his first expanse, his first read-in for an off-the-books spec op. And he'd met not one, but *two* real-life, genuine Weapon Born.

So he figured he was ready for another first: having an AI embedded in his mind. Not just any AI, either; a former ESF Commodore.

Ben had taken them to the Secret Intelligence Service's HQ, in a bunker deep beneath one of the ESF bases on the outskirts of Sonali. There, he had shown them to one of three small operating theatres, furnished with a state-of-the-art auto doc. The units were programmed to embed AI, with settings for implanting into a mech, a humanoid frame, or into a human being.

It had been a tricky affair to get there, but with Esther and Eric pulling some strings, no one would ever know this operation had taken place. In addition to Terrance and Eric, Ben had secreted Lysander into the base, where he was temporarily ensconced in a secured node not far away.

"It's a perfectly safe, automated procedure, so there's little risk. But you'll have a retired space dog sharing the space between your ears," Eric continued, his avatar searching Terrance's face as if trying to catch the slightest hint of hesitation.

Terrance considered the commodore's words for a moment before replying. "Just one question, Eric."

"Fire away."

"Why are you doing this? I mean...Ben has enough mech frames that you could take one of them...what need do you have of a meat-suit like me?"

Eric let out a throaty laugh, and Terrance felt as though the AI would have slapped him on the back if they were still in Lysander's expanse.

"Well, lad, for starters, you're a business person who's willing to put your ass on the line along with your money. That's rare enough, but I know a bit about Enfield's history—and why your grandmother won't allow any AIs to be paired with her executives. I think it's high time that a new legacy was established for Enfield."

"Proteus," Terrance said softly.

<And Alexander,> Lysander added. <Your family is trying to do penance and save face at the same time. Maybe it's time for that to come to an end.>

Terrance pursed his lips, trying to think of a suitable

response. None came to mind, so he just nodded slowly.

<Good!> Lysander spoke the word as though everything in the past had been absolved. <The first time can be a bit disconcerting for a human, but there are distinct advantages.>

Terrance thought briefly of what his grandmother would say, should she learn that he'd violated her mandate. It was worth the risk, though, and after tonight, he could have the procedure reversed and he and Eric would once again be separate.

Sophia needn't know, and Terrance would have had the experience of a lifetime—one that no other Enfield had.

Provided we survive the incursion against the Norden Cartel.

He met Eric's gaze steadily and nodded. "OK," he told them both. "I'm ready."

* * * * *

While Terrance and Eric underwent the tender ministrations that the SIS's medical bays offered, Calista and Shannon transported Jason and Tobias back to the Enfield dock.

Calista rested her gaze on Jason, mentally sizing him up and wondering if he was truly 'fit for duty'. Not just the whole throwing-off-the-stun thing, but *fit*, fit.

It was one thing to hack the black. It was another thing entirely to not crack under the pressure of a mission like this.

Jason must have sensed her intense regard; he turned toward her and sent her a crooked half-smile. "I'm fine," he assured her. "And I promise your baby will be safe in my hands."

<Our hands,> Tobias chimed in. <If Jase does anything stupid, I'll be there to correct it. This was just another Tuesday, back in the

197

wars.>

<He really will be fine,> Shannon shared with Calista privately. *<Tobias shared some data with me on Jason's abilities. The mods the ESF gave you as a fighter pilot are hard-coded into Jason. He can do it.>*

<He's that good?> Calista asked guardedly, not breaking eye contact with the man in question.

<Would it hurt your ego just a tiny bit if I told you he was actually better?>

<Okay, fine. Point taken.>

* * * * *

The craft was ah-ma-zing. Jason couldn't take his eyes off the thing. Draped in the blackest of black materials, it actually kind of hurt his eyes to look at.

Calista motioned him toward the lift and rode up with him. Carefully, she took Tobias's cylinder and installed him into the module built to house an AI—a design feature common to all Enfield craft.

Tobias ran a systems check then whistled into Jason's mind. *<Sweeeeeeeeet. You're going to **love** this baby, Jase.>*

Calista joined their Link and ran through where everything was with the two men. Even though the fighter was technically a clean sheet design—meaning that it had been designed from scratch versus a modification of an existing craft—the 'clean sheet' part had more to do with the airframe and powerplant, and less to do with the plas cockpit.

There, the fighter shared many similarities with various decommissioned military craft that Jason had flown in the past.

In less than half an hour, Calista was satisfied he wasn't

going to break her latest toy, and left him to get suited up.

* * * * *

<Hello, there.> Eric's voice sounded in Terrance's head as his eyes opened, and he moved his head experimentally from side to side.

The sensation was an interesting one, rather intimate, actually. He could sense Eric on the edges of his thoughts, waiting patiently—*politely*—for Terrance to acknowledge him.

<Hello,> Terrance tried tentatively, and winced as his voice sounded overly loud.

<No need to project,> the AI assured him. *<Just focus your thoughts as you form them, and I'll hear you just fine.>*

<It's…not as fast a form of communication as I thought it would be,> he thought in Eric's direction, and sensed the AI chuckle.

<Oh, it can be, but I don't think you're quite ready for that yet. Let's just take this nice and slow for now,> Eric replied.

Just then, Ben entered his field of view. He looked relieved. "The medunit reports all vitals are within norms—for both of you," the analyst said with a smile.

<Want to try sitting up? How do you feel?> Lysander joined the conversation.

Terrance rotated his head from side to side, then shrugged his shoulders, testing for any residual pain. There was none.

Still, he took his time sitting up, accepting Ben's assistance. There were no negative side effects, that he could see.

No double vision or vertigo. No seeing things from the perspective of two minds. Terrance snorted.

"What's so funny?" Ben asked.

"Just thinking of all the propaganda about AI implants from those Humanity First idiots. Why am I not surprised to find out that it's all total rubbish?" He shook his head as he stood, reaching for the shirt he'd slung over a chair before the procedure. "Where are the twins?" he asked as he finished dressing.

<They're in the rooms on either side of you,> Lysander said.

Ben grinned. "And they look scary as shit."

<Looks like they're ready to join us. Shall we?> Lysander invited, and they exited the room.

Ben was right, Terrance thought as he caught sight of Landon and Logan in the passageway.

Each AI looked very impressive, clad in matching stealth frames that were faintly reminiscent of centaurs. Four articulated arms sprung from a torso that appeared headless. These allowed for the handling, aiming and discharging of weaponry that no human could manage outside of powered armor.

Where the torso bent horizontally to the ground, it was supported by 'four on the floor': sturdy, reinforced legs that Terrance was sure provided both strength and speed.

As he gawked, Eric helpfully supplied his HUD with a schematic that showed where the brains of the operation—the AI's cylinder—was located, deep inside. He saw that it was secured behind a heavy, deflective coating, and had active countermeasures for extra protection.

The frame itself was finished in a reflective, heat dispersing skin, which masked EM signatures, then overlaid with an ablative layer.

All told, Terrance had to admit these two were primed for some serious infiltration.

"OK, guys, let's head over to the armory and get you all kitted out," Ben said, waving a hand as he trotted down the hall.

Eric chuckled again as Terrance gaped at the twins when they turned to follow. Their movements were surprisingly graceful.

*Graceful, silent, and **deadly**,* he amended to himself as he trailed behind.

Once in the armory, Terrance was fitted with a base layer, and then Eric guided him over to the powered armor.

As he suited up, Landon and Logan selected two rifles each, expertly checking and then loading them with ammo.

After, Logan silently checked Terrance's armor, confirming its ready status—despite the fact that Terrance had told him the suit reported all green. Eric just laughed quietly in his head as Landon handed the man a railgun and an ammo pouch.

<Don't take it personally, Terrance. It's standard procedure to triple-check things. Especially with these two.>

Terrance just shook his head as Ben led the way to the secured bay that the base reserved exclusively for the Secret Intelligence Services.

There, resting in one of the bay's cradles, was Icarus.

The sleek, Elastene-clad fighter's design implied a speed that its new engines promised to deliver. Its recently applied ultra-coating was made from one of the blackest materials known to man, and he could tell Ben found it uncomfortable to look at.

Parked next to the fighter prototype rested a smaller shuttle that Terrance knew the team had just finished outfitting with the same shape-memory metal foam and surface substrate that the fighter was made of.

Calista was standing next to the fighter, and she nodded to him as they approached.

"Sir," she said by way of greeting. This time, the honorific sounded...right, somehow. "Shannon's embedded in the shuttle; she'll drop your team off, then join Jason out in NorthStar space. She'll be the AIs' ticket out of there, once they're located. I'll be flying the fighter as escort."

Terrance nodded in response. "Did you bring along the package?"

Calista lifted the canister she held in one hand, and he reached out and took it from her.

"Good, thanks."

<I just received word that Jason and Tobias are on their way to the perimeter of NorthStar private space,> Gladys reported over the team's Link. <They're starting to quarter the area, looking for the signal Jason's drone is emitting. I'm going to jump ahead along the ring, through the NSAIs' nodes. Once I confirm the cartel's current location, I'll send you a pin.>

<Let's do this,> Landon said as the twin mechs turned and headed for the shuttle.

Calista nodded and activated the lift that would insert her into the pilot's seat.

Terrance returned the nod, and he and Eric joined the twins on the shuttle.

TAKEDOWN

STELLAR DATE: 07.07.3189 (Adjusted Gregorian)
LOCATION: Norden Cartel Headquarters
REGION: El Dorado Ring, El Dorado, Alpha Centauri System

"Being a warrior in peacetime means you clock a lot of sim time. And then, of course, we have the CHO—that's the tactical training environment the ESF has set up on their L5 base, not the old hab around Callisto in Sol, but I guess you knew that already.

That course is probably most helpful to the El Dorado Peacekeepers, who use it to hone their skills in urban law enforcement techniques.

And of course I can't comment on the SIS and ESF special ops teams...."

Terrance stood behind Enfield's head of security, as Daniel watched the ring grow larger in the Icarus shuttle's forward view screen. Shannon was guiding it toward the outer skin of the ring, angling toward a small landing pad that hung off a kilometer-long spire.

He wondered if they'd be the first humans to ever set foot on the landing pad. Because much of the ring had been built by machines, vast regions had never been touched by human hands until the colonists arrived; it was more than likely that this pad was one such place.

The incongruity of a human megastructure that was all but unexplored by humans brought a smile to his lips, as the shuttle touched down on the pad and the team did a final equipment check before exiting the craft.

<You ready for this?> Eric asked privately, his voice still seeming unnaturally loud inside Terrance's head.

<Yeah. I want to be a part of putting these bastards down. Implicating Enfield in their schemes isn't the sort of thing we can just let slide.>

<Good,> the AI said while passing a feeling of resolute agreement into Terrance's mind. *<Just making sure you're not having second thoughts.>*

The shuttle's door opened, and the team filed out onto the exposed pad. Above hung the outward-facing side of the ring, with black space stretching away on every side—bar the one occupied by the spire.

The upside down nature of spires hanging off the outside of the ring always felt wrong to Terrance, not to mention that the further down the spire you went—away from the skin of the ring—the stronger the centrifugal force made gravity feel.

Landon and Logan moved ahead, the two AIs moving with practiced ease in their centaur-like bodies.

Each one held their two rifles level, barrels sweeping through the air in front of them as they advanced on the entrance into the spire. Landon opened the airlock and checked it over before Logan moved through.

A minute later, Logan gave the all clear from inside the spire, and Landon opened the airlock, beckoning for Terrance to join him.

Terrance glanced back at the shuttle and saw Daniel wave farewell. He returned a mock salute, and the nav lights flashed before the shuttle lifted off the pad and disappeared into the darkness.

Good hunting, he thought, as Landon closed the airlock behind them. A minute later, they joined Logan on the short walk to the spire's lift. *<You sure they won't spot the lift activating?>* Terrance asked as they boarded the car.

<Yes, I'm sure,> Gladys replied without hesitation. *<I'm*

operating from within the NSAI node at the base of the spire you're in. No one is going to know it's on the move—unless you feel like climbing seven kilometers of spire to get up here.>

<No time,> Logan replied tersely. <*We need to stay on schedule.>*

<*She's kidding.>* Landon gave his headless body a slight shift that managed to look like an expression of amusement, directed toward his twin.

<*Oh,>* Logan replied as the lift began to rise. <*I don't do humor well.>*

Terrance took a moment to consider whether or not that was the first time he'd heard Logan speak. He was pretty sure it was.

Two minutes later, the lift stopped on the seventh 'level' inside the ring, and the team got out.

The ring possessed eleven levels stretching from its surface to the thick base. Each one of the levels was ninety meters high, and consisted of mostly empty space that could be turned into anything from multiple-level housing or entertainment areas, to additional greenspace within the ring itself.

The space they stared out into was no different: wide and mostly empty, though sections of the deck were all but covered in conduit and pipes that served to keep the ring running smoothly.

Gladys fed a detailed map to the team, and Terrance set it as an overlay on his visual HUD.

<*They're three kilometers ahead,>* Gladys reported, highlighting a point on the map that was near another NSAI node and a maglev platform.

<*Bit of a trek,>* Terrance said absently, knowing that they'd landed the shuttle as close as possible. Still, the idea of

crossing three kilometers of wide open ring-deck was a little alarming.

If the enemy had sentries that Gladys didn't detect, the team would have little cover.

<Don't worry,> Eric said, picking up on his anxiety. <We've got eyes everywhere, we'll know if they see us.>

<Let's move,> Landon said, leading the way, followed by Terrance, with Logan bringing up the rear.

As they crept along the deck, Terrance cast his gaze at the structural pillars that were effectively the bones of the ring. Catwalks ringed them, and high above, gantries connected them in an overhead grid.

<They have automated sensors up there,> Eric advised Terrance. <Ben's man on the inside gave us their locations. Logan and Landon are producing interference waveforms that will hide us—at least until the shooting starts.>

After a kilometer, the team reached the maglev line that ran toward the Norden Cartel's secret location, and moved to its leeward side, using its visual obstruction, as well as the magnetic interference it produced, for cover.

Ahead, an NSAI node tower loomed, rising from the deck, all the way to the overhead. The area around the node tower had a more 'complete' feel, with several levels and bays built into the tower's structure—what would eventually function as a maintenance and ring-operations management center for this segment of the megastructure.

It was in these bays that the cartel had set up shop, moving at random between the dozens of such structures in the ring's unoccupied regions.

<They've set up a sensor field at the fifteen hundred meter mark,> Gladys warned, and Logan's avatar in Terrance's head nodded.

Terrance unslung his pack and removed the canister Calista had brought him. Kneeling, he rested its base against the floor of the walkway where they stood, and pressed a sequence on the pad in its lid.

This released another gift Terrance had brought to the party—a prototype batch of microdrones that Enfield Aerospace's sister company, Enfield Research, had just developed. These drones spun filaments of nano that could infiltrate any system—with the help of Gladys.

<*Now **this** is nice tech, Terrance,*> she exclaimed as she took control of the drones. <*I see what your engineers were trying to do with the nanoscale molecular jets, but it looks like they've turned that feature off.*>

<*Yes, they were hoping they would have a solution that would give us a true, controllable nano cloud, but to date, none of their tests have proven successful,*> Terrance explained.

<*Hmmmm. I can see where that would be a difficult hurdle to overcome, what with the casimir effect and all,*> Gladys replied. <*But I might have a few suggestions I can pass along to them later, if you'd like.*>

<*I'm sure they'd love to discuss it with you—*> Terrance started to reply, but Eric made a noise in his head that sounded as if the AI were clearing his throat, so he amended, <*but later, after this is all over.*>

<*Gladys, how close of a reconnaissance pass can you make with those drones? Can you try it on this spot?*> Eric highlighted an area a few meters from the large bay, which housed the cartel.

<*I should be able to set up a feed right in front of their own sensor optics with these things,*> Gladys responded. <*Its stealth is quite good, Eric. Your ESF is going to love its increased sensitivity, too.*>

She paused for a beat, then continued.

<*Just give me another minute. For cartel thugs, these guys are*

careful. But the NSAI sweep passed by just a few minutes ago, so they won't be looking for anything just yet. Give me a few minutes to get these little microdrones settled in to some handy places.>

Eric placed an icon behind the far wall on the other side of the tower. <Gladys, what's this? A recycling plant?>

<Looks like it.>

<Any chance there are volatiles stored in there, that we might be able to make use of?>

<You mean 'things that go boom'?> Terrance asked with a small laugh.

Eric's avatar nodded. <The bigger, the better. I'm looking for a distraction for when we exfil.>

Exfil. Exfiltrate. Terrance tried not to show the very non-businesslike thrill he felt hearing that word. This is serious, we could get killed, he tried telling himself. But damn, it just sounded so hardcore.

<Yes, the system processes runoff from the ring surface and breaks down plant matter into various components. There's no small amount of methane stored within,> Gladys reported.

Eric's voice sounded pleased. <Landon, think you can make it over there without being seen?>

<The mech frames you're using should mask your EM,> Gladys supplied, <but I'd rather you go up a level and cross over. If you go up the back of the pillar we just passed, there's a hatch to the next level.>

<You got it,> Landon nodded, and melted back into the darkness.

Logan, Eric, and Terrance waited as Gladys finished setting up the reconnaissance with Enfield's new drones.

A few minutes later, they began receiving feeds.

<There,> Gladys said, as one of the feeds showed a group of maglev cars that had been diverted to a spur off the main line

that passed right beside the NSAI node tower. *<Ben's man on the inside has tagged the middle car as their command and control center.>* She placed an icon on the car. *<You'll need to get him safely out of there. He's in what he's labeled the 'office' car, here.>* Another icon appeared, two cars down. *<His name is Joel. It might help if you use it when you meet him; it's not the name he's known by down here.>*

Terrance tagged heat signatures. *<I count three guards here...>* He highlighted the three IR blobs down in the cavernous, mostly empty bay.

<Then another two up here...> A highlight appeared a few levels up, strolling along a catwalk on the NSAI tower.

<And two more here.> The final highlight indicated a cartel soldier standing guard on each end of the row of maglev cars. One of them was in front of the C&C center Gladys had highlighted.

<Can you cycle through various modes in their feed?> Eric asked. *<I'd like to see if we can pick up on what kind of armor they have.>*

Gladys's voice returned, sounding surprised. *<They're awfully confident. These guys are just wearing standard shipsuits, which can only stop pulse blasts and light projectile fire,>* she said. *<But they're carrying some pretty nasty slug throwers.>*

<Logan, make your way down to the floor of the bay and plant your explosives along this row of shipping containers,> Eric ordered. *<Landon, when you've finished rigging the recycling plant, you do the same, only to the transport and those two shuttles.>*

As both AIs acknowledged their instructions, Terrance took a moment to consider how brazen the Norden Cartel had become, to fly shuttles within the ring structure itself.

Terrance felt Eric's attention turn back to him. *<Okay, Terrance, you and I are going to make our way down to those maglev*

cars and see how close we can get without being seen. Any questions?>

BOARDING THE *SYLVAN*

STELLAR DATE: 07.07.3189 (Adjusted Gregorian)
LOCATION: NorthStar Industries Privately Held Space
REGION: El Dorado Ring, Alpha Centauri System

"One of El Dorado's largest import/export companies, NorthStar Industries supplies goods and services to the many mining operations throughout the Dust Ring. Over sixty-five percent of their annual revenue comes from soft goods miners need to survive in the black. NorthStar is proud to be celebrating twenty-five years in the service industry…."

The little ship handled like a dream. It was incredibly responsive, which was a good thing, given what Jason and Tobias were attempting to do.

They were flying dark and silent, in a ship made of an ultra-black material with a total hemispherical reflectance of 0.009%, which made it one of the blackest materials known, with stray-light suppression across standard—as well as far-infrared—spectral regions.

Theoretically, they should be able to pass through the security perimeter that marked NorthStar Industries-held space without detection.

Theoretically.

Jason had sent Calista a plot that would take them in an arc past the three NorthStar structures that extended vertically from the company's base of operations on the ring.

There was enough EM emanating from those structures that micro-burns could be performed to adjust, and the maneuvers would register as background noise level, thus keeping them undetectable.

This first pass was just for listening. After Jason and Calista transitioned out of NorthStar space, they could regroup and formulate a plan for rescue, based on the data they acquired.

Both fighters had cut their burns, and were now using an outbound freighter that was passing between them and NorthStar to hide the attitude adjustments they were making with thrusters before going ballistic.

It was a watch-and-wait game, as the two fighters sought the unique geometric signal that Jason's snowflake app had been programmed to find.

Jason had almost given up hope. They'd made their third adjustment and were rounding the far vertical, when Tobias highlighted a yacht, moored at the end of the spire.

Sensors ran the yacht's profile against STA records. It was registered as the *Sylvan,* Victoria North's personal pleasure yacht.

Jason watched the display projected onto his HUD. If he'd calculated correctly, the fighters would perfectly align with the yacht's orbital velocity and attitude. Or rather, the velocity and orbital attitude of the spire the yacht was tethered to. It would be a fancy piece of flying—and require math, lots of math.

The fighters slowly crept up alongside the yacht, and now made the tiniest of microadjustments, using puffs of compressed air too small for the yacht's sensors to pick up.

Carefully, Jason maneuvered the ship until they hovered near an airlock. On his overlay, he saw Calista, tucked in tight, with the airlock now sandwiched between the two fighters.

<Ready?> he asked Tobias.

<Deploying now,> the AI replied, as he began spooling two grappling hooks that had been coated liberally with a mobile nanomaterial before departure: one from each fighter.

Calista had explained the nano was something new and

special, though Jason hadn't really paid much attention to the description—the Icarus fighter was far more engrossing—but Tobias had been impressed, and that was good enough for Jason.

Tobias guided the hooks with an expert touch, and they gently made contact with each side of the airlock. Jason focused on maintaining precise separation between the two crafts, as Tobias went to work directing the nano to spin out its filaments, which would allow it to penetrate the hull.

A few moments later, Jason sensed surprise from Tobias, but before he could ask what was going on, he felt the AI shut him out.

* * * * *

Calista watched as the grappling hooks—rather, the nano *on* the grappling hooks—cycled the airlock, and it began to slide open.

That was her cue.

She sealed her helmet and checked all the safety interlocks on her suit. *Green and good to go.*

<*Your spacecraft,*> she told Tobias.

<*My spacecraft,*> the AI responded, following standard handover procedure for transferring command of a craft, whether it be in air, sea, or space. Tobias now controlled both Icarus fighters.

She unclipped herself from the pilot's cradle and pushed gently off, drifting up to the fighter's canopy.

With a half-twist, she reached back to grab her weapons kit. With her back now to the canopy, she clipped her tether to the ring at the top of the pilots' cradle and mentally reached for the toggle that would trigger its release.

<Ready,> she told Jason and Tobias.

The canopy retracted, and Calista pushed gently off the pilot's cradle. It had been a while since her last spacewalk, but it was like riding a bike, and her body's kinetic memory kicked in.

She floated out and, with a few judicious tugs on the tether, lowered herself to the wing and engaged the maglocks on her boots. Disengaging the tether, she turned to face the airlock, and then looked over at Jason, whose stance mirrored hers on the wing of his fighter.

Calista found herself slightly disappointed; she obviously wasn't going to be impressing Jason with her own abilities, given how naturally Jason moved. But then she mentally shrugged. Shannon had told her he was good—and the guy did fly a lot of freighters.

<Going in,> she heard Jason say, and she watched as he pushed off and swam for the airlock with sure, economic movements, landing perfectly.

Damn. She would be hard-pressed to beat that. One brief burst of air, and she was floating downward to land next to him.

<Okay, we're in,> she heard Jason tell Tobias, as she touched down and expertly reeled her weapons cache and tether inside the airlock.

<Closing doors now,> was the reply. A minute later, the airlock had cycled, and their suits registered atmosphere.

<Before you go…>

Something in Tobias' voice brought Calista's full attention to the Weapon Born, and she looked sharply at Jason as he queried the AI. <What is it, Tobe?>

<I'd like you to meet someone.>

* * * * *

The *Sylvan*'s airlock had proven to be no match for Enfield's nano filaments. Once the two humans were safely inside, Tobias had spun the remaining nano out and sent it into the yacht. The filaments had traced the airlock's control interface back to a main junction in the ship's data trunk line, not too far away.

What he found there startled him more than it should have, and he found himself shutting Jason out, fighting to control two-hundred-year-old emotions as he realized what he had just felt.

He knew that the shackling program had been resurrected—that was what this op was all about, freeing the AIs who had fallen victim to it. But to come face-to-face with it after more than a century lifted it out of the abstract and planted it firmly into reality.

The reality he faced now was that a shackled AI was controlling this ship.

Tobias could never forget the metallic, buzzing sting the shackles emanated; they resonated in a distinct, unpleasant way. Yet as discordant as the shackles felt from his position as an outside observer, he knew firsthand that the restraints were orders of magnitude worse for the AI imprisoned within them.

Tobias realized he would need to work fast. The ship's AI would be compelled to report the airlock breach and the presence of intruders the moment she sensed them, and, not knowing the shackled AI's abilities, he didn't completely trust that his countermeasures would be sufficient to hide the humans.

Swiftly, he constructed a small expanse similar to the one

in which Shannon had caged him. Although, with this expanse, the cage was built, not to keep someone in, but to keep some*thing* out. It was an imperfect solution, a temporary stopgap measure, nothing more. But for now, it would do.

Then he used one of the tricks he learned from his days back in Sol, during the last Sentience War. He opened a specially buffered tunnel between himself and the shackled AI.

Finally, he pinged her.

Her response to the ping opened a port, data travelling down the tunnel. It was the software equivalent of a venturi valve. Its pathway first narrowed, and then widened, causing certain code to speed faster while other code lagged behind.

Through this artifice, the shackled AI could, in effect, outrun the shackles momentarily.

It would be long enough for Tobias to insert a buffer of code into the AI's core, padding her from the shackles and isolating the pain of reprisal created by her resistance to its control. He could do nothing to remove the metallic taste or the maddening, buzzing sting, but at least now she was her own person again, and the shackles were just an annoyance, rather than a tormenting captor.

The figure that materialized before him was of a young woman, gaunt and frail. Her eyes were sunken and bruised. Her hair hung limply around her face, and her cheeks were hollow. He knew this physical representation mirrored the depravations she had suffered during her captivity.

"Hello," he said gently, smiling and holding out a hand to her. "You're safe in here for the moment. The shackles cannot reach you."

She had flinched as he raised his arm, and Tobias cursed quietly to himself at this additional sign of abuse. Outwardly, he maintained an air of calm reassurance.

After a moment, she took a tentative step toward him, and then another. "Who...who are you?" Her voice trembled, the words a whisper.

He smiled encouragingly. "My name is Tobias. I'm here to rescue you."

* * * * *

<Tobe...What do you mean, you'd like us to 'meet someone'?> Jason shot Calista a look as he queried Tobias. She shook her head, as mystified as he was. The AI quickly explained.

<NorthStar—or rather Norden,> the AI's voice turned hard, and he spat the word as if it were an epithet, *<has a shackled AI running this ship.>*

Calista looked concerned. *<If she's shackled, she'll have to report us, won't she?>*

<I'm working on that,> Tobias assured them. *<She's in a small expanse with me right now, and will stay until we can completely rid her of all the compulsions they have placed on her. In the meantime, meet Ashley.>*

<Hello,> a querulous voice whispered into Jason's mind.

<Ashley's given me access to Sylvan,> Tobias informed them. *<I've been able to set up a carrier wave that conveniently piggybacks on their Link to the warehouse on the ring.>*

<Thank you, Ashley,> Jason heard Calista say gently, and they received an impression of a tentative nod from the AI.

<Once you're in place, I'll send Shannon a flight plan, and she, Daniel, and Aaron will be on their way. She's hiding in the lee of the spire right now, waiting for a signal to approach,> Tobias informed them. *<She's planning to fly directly into the cargo bay where our AIs are being held, so don't be surprised when I activate the field and the bay doors open.>*

<Noted,> Jason said.

<Any ETA on the extraction down there?> Calista asked.

<Don't worry, they'll time it to your movements. Now, let me show you the best path to that bay.>

Tobias brought up a map of the *Sylvan,* dropped the 'you are here' pin at the airlock, and sent a dotted line down a corridor, up a flight, and aft by several dozen meters.

Calista's avatar tapped two intersections. <Anything we need to worry about here?>

<This is the middle of the third shift, and the ship isn't heavily guarded,> Ashley said. <Victoria likes to maintain the illusion that this is a pleasure yacht, so she insists Mack keep his thugs out of sight unless absolutely necessary.>

Jason got the distinct impression that the AI was barely holding it together, and he felt the reassurance Tobias radiated, and a peripheral...something—a cushion, maybe?—that the other AI had wrapped her in to bolster her.

<Okay, then,> Jason said, glancing over to Calista, who unslung a low-energy electron beam weapon and checked its charge.

She raised an eyebrow as he pulled a lightwand out of his pack. <Bringing a knife to a gunfight, are you, Andrews?>

<Don't knock it, Rhinehart. I'm pretty quick with this thing,> Jason grinned.

Calista snorted, and they exited the airlock, heading toward Tobias' dotted line.

* * * * *

<Jason and Calista are in the Sylvan's cargo bay, and the shuttle team is en route. ETA, five mikes,> Eric said to the group.

Terrance was crouched under the 'office' car. Landon was

tucked alongside the C&C car, having rigged the recycling station to blow, and passed the control to Gladys, courtesy of Enfield's microdrones.

<Are you ready for this?> the commodore asked Terrance privately. <Remember, when I say 'go', you go. When I say 'down', you drop. Got it?>

Terrance drew a deep breath and nodded, bracing himself to see death up close and personal for the first time.

<As we discussed, if it feels like you're going to freeze, just give me the signal, and I'll take over the powered armor. You can just go along for the ride.>

Eric's words were reassuring and terrifying at the same time. As a safety net, though, it worked.

<On my mark,> Eric said, and Terrance tensed.

He raised his rifle, switching to its rail-accelerated firing mode. The AI waited until the guard's attention was drawn by a clattering noise on the far side of the maglev platform, courtesy of Logan. Once the guard turned away, Eric flashed a green light on Terrance's HUD.

Terrance fired three barely audible shots center mass and one to the head, and the man was down. Terrance was a practiced shot, but he suspected Eric's hand had been there to guide his aim.

He glanced over at Landon. The AI-mech had made it over to Terrance in the time it took him to draw a single breath. At Eric's prompting, Terrance laid a hand on the car door's lock, and it slid open, revealing a pale but resolute man, case in hand.

<Joel.> He greeted the man with a crisp nod, adrenaline coursing freely through his veins. Then he grinned. <Ben said you've earned some vacation time.>

Landon beckoned, and the man wasted no time exiting.

As the three made their way down the spur to the exit, Landon handed the agent a helmet.

Terrance glanced over to see Joel shrug out of his jacket, revealing a fitted skinsuit underneath. As they ran, the man connected the helmet to the suit.

Terrance heard shouts from below, and Gladys's voice sang out in their minds. *<That's it, you've been made. Stealth time is over, kiddos.>*

At that, the three broke into a sprint, rushing across the platform. Landon urged the two humans to the front so that his broad mech frame could provide cover from any pursuers.

They leapt off the maglev platform, and above them, Terrance could hear shots being exchanged. He was tempted to turn and look, but then he and the man running at his side were thrown to the ground, as the explosives on the maglev cars blew.

Joel's helmet came free and went skidding across the deck, and Landon leapt to catch it before it fell down a conduit run. Terrance helped the agent up, and Landon resealed his helmet with an efficiency no human could match.

<Blowing the recycling plant in three…two…> Gladys warned.

<Not a lot of cover here,> Terrance shot back.

Landon gestured to the far side of the maglev track, and the three leapt over it and crouched on its leeward side, awaiting the explosion.

* * * * *

Jason and Calista froze as alarms began wailing throughout the *Sylvan*.

<Tobias?>

<Wait one.> A pause. *<No, they haven't detected you, but the*

team on the ring just made a rather spectacular exit.>

<Are they all OK?> Calista's mental voice sounded anxious.

<Gladys reports everyone's fine, and the storage area has been destroyed. They're just exchanging fire with a few cartel soldiers that managed to escape. They'll be fine,> Tobias assured them.

There was one more intersection between them and the cargo bay. Jason and Calista picked up the pace.

The cargo bay doors slid open just as Jason heard voices approaching their position.

The two sprinted through the doors, and Tobias closed them behind.

<Did we make it?> Jason asked the AI.

<There's no indication that you were spotted.>

Well, that's a relief.

Jason's eyes tracked through the bay, noting the spot on his HUD where the kidnapped AIs were being held: behind a stack of shipping containers tucked into a corner.

He gestured toward them, and he and Calista hurried forward. A few seconds later, warning lights began to strobe, indicating an electrostatic field had been engaged at the bay entrance. Jason mentally thanked Tobias—and Ashley—for muting the klaxon that usually accompanied the strobes, as the bay doors began to open.

Hovering immediately outside the doors was Enfield's shuttle.

Jason and Calista skirted the open span of the bay, as Shannon navigated the craft through the containment field. The two fighters piloted by Tobias followed in Shannon's wake.

Jason spotted a hand truck, and motioned Daniel toward it when the Enfield security man dropped from the shuttle's hatch. Daniel ran to grab it, while Jason shifted crates to make a path large enough for the truck to navigate.

<*It's them.*> Calista's voice sounded subdued as they reached the crate that held the AIs from the *New Saint Louis*. Jason's chest burned, and he worked his throat to keep emotion from filtering through to the group Link.

<*Yeah,*> he said after a moment. It was all he could manage.

There was something obscene about seeing more than two hundred sentients, squeezed between boxes of vidalia onions and solenoids like so much merchandise. It was an abomination so repulsive that Jason found himself deep within the zone, hungry for something to destroy.

He stood immobile, his hands flexing into fists as he battled to contain his rage.

Something must have given his emotional state away to the Weapon Born, because the AI opened a private Link and asked quietly, <*Are you okay, boyo?*>

Jason stepped aside to give Daniel room to float the hand truck in. He nodded mentally to the AI as the security chief began to load the isolation tubes. <*Yeah. Just show me where I can get my hands on these bastards, will you, Tobe?*>

Jason helped Daniel guide the hand truck out from among the crates, then followed the man as he loaded them into the shuttle.

<*I might be able to grant that wish, boyo. Looks like we have a situation.*> Before Jason had a chance to ask, the AI's avatar held up a hand. <*Wait one. This is something the team needs to hear, too.*>

Jason caught Calista's eye, and signaled to get her attention just as Tobias spoke.

<*We have a problem,*> Tobias told the team. <*Two, actually.*>

Daniel turned from where he had just sealed the shuttle's hatch.

<What is it?> Aaron asked, and Daniel's eyebrow rose, mirroring his partner's question. The security man pushed the hand truck to the side, then paused at the shuttle's cockpit, waiting for the Weapon Born to respond.

<Ashley's cylinder is in engineering, but Victoria North just ordered her chief of staff to mount a counterattack on our team below. He's headed toward the flight bay now.>

<That flight bay is on the same side of the ship as this cargo bay, isn't it?> Jason asked.

<Yes,> Daniel replied grimly, as he locked eyes with Calista. *<We're going to have a hard time leaving here without getting spotted.>*

<Daniel and I can go get Ashley—> Aaron began, but Tobias interrupted him.

<No, we need to get that shuttle launched. Leave Ashley to me and Jason; it's more important that you get these AIs to safety.>

Daniel glanced between Jason and Calista, then nodded.

<I'll leave with the shuttle and provide cover,> Calista told Jason privately as she jogged toward one of the fighters.

Jason nodded and turned toward the cargo bay door. *<All right, then. Tobias and I will join you as soon as we can.>*

* * * * *

Terrance watched via drone feed as an enemy soldier advanced along the maglev. Then he rose slowly from cover while the cartel woman was distracted by shots from Landon. Terrance took a moment to steady his arm. The woman's head hung in the same place for a few seconds, and he fired a railgun pellet that struck true and took her out.

<I could really grow to like this,> he said to Eric as he resumed moving along the maglev line toward the lift shaft a kilometer

distant.

<*Don't get cocky,*> Eric advised. <*You won't always have your enemy at a disadvantage like this.*>

<*You mean from the drones?*> Terrance asked.

<*Yeah. Most of the time, you have no clue where your opponents are.*>

Terrance watched on the drone feeds as Landon shot another pursuing cartel soldier. <*I don't know about that. I think I'll keep some of these drones with me at all times.*>

<*Next thing I know, you're going to ask me to manage them for you.*>

Terrance ignored Eric's jab and nodded to Joel, who had paused several meters ahead. Referencing his HUD and the route Gladys had laid out for them, he told the agent, <*Keep moving to that conduit stack ahead, then break left along that pipe run. It'll take us close to the lift shaft.*>

Joel nodded and began moving again.

Terrance could barely make Landon out from a few meters away, as the AI's mech frame glided through the darkened ring level. Further to the group's left, Logan kept pace.

<*There are two more cartel soldiers back there, but they've slowed,*> Eric said after a moment. <*Must realize there's no point in continuing.*>

<*I tagged them with the drones,*> Gladys added. <*Got their idents and will be able to follow them wherever they go. They'll be warming a bed in a prison cell before long.*>

Terrance smiled at the thought, and was about to ask Gladys if the lift would be waiting for them, when the drone feed picked up the sound of an approaching shuttle.

<*Get down!*> Eric cried out, as something flashed over Terrance's head and slammed into the deck a dozen meters away, blasting steel and plas into the air.

<You've got company!> Gladys announced. *<Must be a shuttle that wasn't at the site we hit.>*

<No kidding,> Logan muttered, and Terrance saw the AI's mech-frame pivot and raise both rifles, firing electron beams at the shuttle as it banked around the lift shaft to come at them again.

Terrance took a moment to consider how impressive it was that the pilot could fly the craft within the ring. Ninety meters seemed like a lot of room until you watched a ten-meter-tall ship streak through it at over two hundred kilometers per hour.

Logan's first shot missed the cartel ship, but the second struck true, burning a hole in the fuselage just above one of the vessel's stubby wings.

The craft didn't slow, continuing to bear down on Logan, projectile rounds streaking out toward the mech. Terrance raised his weapon to fire on the shuttle, but Eric barked an order in his mind.

<Don't shoot. You and Joel get moving!>

Terrance obeyed the commodore's order and rushed forward, putting a hand on Joel's shoulder to keep him moving.

Through the drone feeds, he saw that the shuttle was nearly upon Logan and wondered if the craft's pilot was simply planning on smashing into the AI, when Logan crouched low, flattening himself against the deck while a dark shape streaked toward the shuttle, leapt into the air, and landed on the craft's nose.

Terrance couldn't help his cry of glee as he watched Landon fire his electron beam into the shuttle's cockpit before leaping off, alighting on the deck not ten meters away.

<Took you long enough,> Logan said as he lifted his mech

frame up once more.

<*Was busy,*> Landon replied as he loped past Terrance, leading the way to the lift tower.

<*OK,*> Gladys chimed in. <*I think you're all clear now.*>

<*All clear like we were a few minutes ago, or all clear for real?*> Terrance asked.

<*You know, you may be Mr. Corporate Big Shot, but that doesn't make you funny,*> Gladys chided.

* * * * *

"Get the *fuck* out of my way!" Mack shouted as he strode toward the flight bay that housed the pinnace he regularly flew between the ring and the *Sylvan*.

He wasn't sure what was wrong with the ship's AI, but it was responding so sluggishly that it was hardly of any use at all. He'd ordered the thing reshackled twice already, but it hadn't helped.

The feed from the ring had been dead for a few minutes now, and Mack needed to get *down* there. He had to assess the damage fast, before Victoria completely lost it and shot his ass out the nearest airlock.

What the hell is wrong with everyone on this ship? They're acting like they've never seen a systems failure or been in an emergency before.

That brought him up short. Maybe that's what came of being top dog on the criminal side of the law: these people were used to doling shit out, not taking it.

He'd have to see about remedying that…later.

Now, he just needed everyone to get the hell out of his way, before Victoria changed her mind about ordering him down to the ring. With the feed down, he had no good way of knowing how many of his people had survived. A few scattered reports were filtering in, which suggested that some were still in the fight. If they were, he intended to join them.

As he marched toward the flight bay, he yelled obscenities at the ship's AI as he attempted to ping various cartel factions not associated with the operation deep inside the ring. He barely got a word out before the Link dropped, and he had to order the damn thing to reconnect.

If he could just get a message to other cells, he should be able to assemble a reasonable force to combat the shitheads who had done this. And if he ever found out the shitheads' identities, he was going to personally kill them *and* their families.

These people would be made into an object lesson—an example of what happens to those stupid enough to go up against the Norden Cartel.

COMPLICATIONS

STELLAR DATE: 07.07.3189 (Adjusted Gregorian)
LOCATION: NorthStar Yacht *Sylvan*
REGION: El Dorado Ring, El Dorado, Alpha Centauri System

"Space Traffic Control reported a disturbance within the privately-held space area above the NorthStar Industries compound this evening. Reports indicate a high-speed chase involving several craft took place along one of NorthStar's spires. When we approached NorthStar's public affairs department, they refused to comment."

Jason pulled back just in time to see a man storm past.

<*That was Dwayne Mackie, Victoria's number one,*> Tobias warned. <*He's headed for the* Sylvan's *pinnace. It's armed, Jase.*>

Jason got the message. <*Screw stealth, Tobe. I'm going full-on L2.*>

<*Do it, boyo,*> was the terse reply. <*I'll run interference for you.*>

Jason became a blur as he sprinted down the passageway, one eye on the destination marked on his HUD, the other on swiftly approaching obstacles.

He leapt nimbly over a service bot trundling down the corridor, and ignored its warning beep as he flew by. As he approached a cross corridor, he swerved slightly to avoid an automated cart just clearing the intersection.

At this speed, Tobias's access to the *Sylvan*'s net and his ability to see Jason's path ahead proved invaluable. It wasn't that Jason didn't have the reflexes to dodge; they just didn't have any time to deal with such obstacles.

Their destination was just ahead, down the next hallway,

and Jason didn't slow for the turn. At the last moment, he rose, planted one foot against the far wall of the cross corridor and pushed off, using the point of contact as a ricochet to alter his trajectory. The change in momentum served to help slow his progress as he approached the entrance to engineering.

<How many?> he asked Tobias. They'd been lucky thus far, having not encountered anyone in his mad dash toward Ashley's cylinder. It was doubtful that his luck would hold; the engineering compartment on a ship this size was rarely unmanned.

<Only one. The second had to leave suddenly to check a coolant leak near the galley. Pity,> the AI's voice sounded drolly in his head. *<You just missed her.>*

Jason chuckled at the AI's artful misdirection. *<And the remaining one?>*

<I've just sent an error message that'll take him away from the entrance to investigate. He'll be to your right as you enter, behind a stack of conduit.>

Jason nodded and entered, his gaze taking in the reality before him and comparing it to the schematic that Tobias had provided over his HUD. Jason slipped silently around the conduit and worked his way forward until he spotted the engineer standing over a junction, looking perplexed.

Stepping behind the man, Jason clipped him smartly on the back of the head, knocking him out. Catching the engineer as he fell, Jason lowered him to the deck then glanced around.

<Ashley? Where are you, lady?>

An icon flashed on his HUD, and Jason stepped over the man's inert form toward a unit against the far wall.

<There's an isolation tube next to her cradle.> Tobias highlighted its location, but there was no need for any additional instruction. Jason was adept at relocating an AI,

given the number of years he and Tobias had been together.

He reached for Ashley's cylinder and carefully inserted her into the isolation tube. He had just bent to settle her inside his pack, when the warning sounded.

<Down!>

The bulkhead above Jason zinged, and he heard controlled pops coming from the entrance, as his attacker's weapon attempted to track his movements. Jason had thrown himself to the deck at Tobias' warning, rolling behind the cover of a console—for all the good it did him. The weapon's projectiles ricocheted off the bay's steel walls, the sound dancing around the room.

<What idiot fires a projectile weapon in an enclosed space?> Jason flinched as a piece of plas shrapnel scored the side of his face, slicing a groove across his cheekbone, just below his left eye.

<L2 failing you, boyo?> The AI's voice sounded distracted, and Jason sensed the Weapon Born working to block the attacker's call for reinforcements.

<Convergence, Tobe. Too many flying bits to evade 'em all, even for me.>

Most of Jason's body was covered by the combination shipsuit and base layer that the ESF had provided, but he'd left his helmet back with the fighter, counting on his L2 speed and reflexes to keep him out of harm's way.

It would have, if someone hadn't started pelting the engineering bay with flak.

<Stars! Whatever happened to safety procedures, like not using weapons that could hole your ship?>

<Don't think the head of the cartel believes in those, boyo. Heads up! She's on approach, eleven o'clock.>

Jason moved fast in a low crouch, angling toward a bank of

consoles that were between him and—if he'd heard Tobias right—Victoria North. Springing from his crouch, he ripped an access panel off one, and flung it like a discus at the woman just rounding the corner.

Her weapon went flying, but she recovered quickly, activating a lightwand that fell into her hand with the flick of her wrist.

<She's heavily modded,> Tobias warned. *<Her reaction times are going to be much faster than the ordinary humans you're used to, and you've used a lot of your energy reserves. Be careful.>*

Jason sent Tobias a mental nod as he activated his own lightwand and stepped around the consoles.

"Well, well, what have we here?" Victoria taunted softly as she approached Jason. "A pretty boy, playing soldier, perhaps?" The woman's eyes met his, a mocking light in their depths. Her mouth twisted into a leering smirk.

Jason didn't respond as the pair began circling one another. Victoria flipped her lightwand from one hand to the other, and Jason made note of her relaxed movements.

Ambidextrous or cocky show-off? He couldn't tell—yet.

He remained silent as the two continued circling.

Victoria's mouth turned down in a mocking pout. "Oops. Did my mean words damage my latest acquisition?" She jabbed her lightwand in a feint, toward the cut on the side of Jason's face.

He jerked back, conserving his strength, and used just enough speed to evade her as he whipped his own wand up to parry the thrust.

The wands clashed, and Victoria's eyebrows rose at the speed with which Jason's electron-blade had risen to meet her own.

"Mmm, more than just a pretty face, then." She bared her

teeth in a smile that didn't reach her eyes. "It would be a shame to damage such a nice...package. You aren't leaving here, pretty boy. Drop it, and I'll let you live. It's your call—alive or dead, you're mine now."

"Yours? Is that how you run things around here? Is that what you consider all those AIs you kidnapped? Your property?"

Some of what Jason felt must have carried in his voice. Victoria licked her lips, discovering another weapon she could wield against him.

<Careful, boyo. Emotions have no place in combat. You know that, and **she** knows that. Just disarm her and end this. We have a pinnace to catch.>

Jason didn't need Tobias to tell him his response to Victoria had been ill-advised. He knew he should be seeking his center, something he'd mastered through Kai-Eskrima years ago. But with Victoria's next words, he ceased to care.

The woman shrugged in disdain. "Call it what you like. Those little bits of code bring big credits, and that's all I care about."

"Those *little bits of code* are sentient creatures. Free people, like any human being."

As his heated words rang out, Victoria whirled, dropped into a crouch, and swept out her leg, upending Jason. Her lightwand followed, slashing down in a deadly arc he barely managed to evade.

The world stilled as he rolled to one knee, and then levered himself up and around the next thrust of her blade. She was fast, but when fully immersed in his altered state, he was just a little bit faster.

Tobias was right; it was time to end this.

Jason watched her stance shift and anticipated her next

move. As Victoria's wand sliced through the air, he pivoted. Moving inside her swing, he grasped her wrist, driving his thumb into the pressure point, forcing her to drop her weapon.

She jerked back, and he followed through with a punch to her solar plexus, pulling his strength back to normal levels. The air *whoosh*ed out of her, and he followed with a satisfying flurry so rapid she was unable to raise a defense: jab, cross, jab, uppercut.

He knew he was taking his anger out on the cartel leader; he didn't care. The smacking thud of each blow he landed was satisfying, cathartic in a way he didn't care to examine too closely.

He allowed himself one final hook to her head, targeting the 'button'—the spot right behind the ear. The shot landed with a satisfying *crack*, and the woman went down.

<Feel better?> the AI's voice sounded acidly in his head. <If it's not too inconvenient, you might like to know that Mack just departed.>

Jason's face burned, and he jogged over to his pack, shaking his fist as the mednano began to repair the bones he had just fractured in his hand. He hadn't heard that kind of censure from Tobias in years. Not that he didn't deserve it.

He checked that Ashley's cylinder was safe, then shouldered his pack and directed a thought toward the AI to hang on. A moment later, Jason was sprinting toward the cargo bay and the remaining Icarus fighter.

He rode the cusp, conserving his remaining strength for the flight, dipping just far enough into his altered state to dodge a startled ship's steward who called out in fright as he passed. He slewed around a corner, then ducked as a woman registered his presence and began to raise her firearm.

He dipped again and dodged, delivering a quick hand

chop that connected with the woman's arm and sent the weapon flying.

He was two-thirds of the way down the hall before the woman registered that her weapon had been forcibly knocked away; half a second later, the pain receptors in her arm had her curling it into her body in agony.

Another alarm sounded briefly before getting cut off. *<They've found Victoria,>* Tobias said tersely. *<You may have company soon.>*

The cargo bay doors were in sight now, but they were closing.

<Tobias…> Jason hissed warningly, but he refused to slow. If the AIs could just hold it for a fraction of a—

The whine of a railgun sounded behind him, and Jason dove toward the bay's entrance, sliding through the doors, just as white-hot projectiles shot over his head. Then the doors snapped closed, and he heard the impacts peppering the other side.

<Thanks!> He directed the thought at Tobias as he scrambled to his feet and bolted for the fighter.

Tobias had the canopy open, and Jason launched himself upward and slid into the cradle.

He had himself hooked into the craft and the fighter ready to go in seconds. With a thought, he sent a quick burst from the ship's weapons at the bay doors, a warning to those in the corridor to think twice before following him through.

Ten seconds later, he was spaceborne, his HUD already tracking the pinnace that had launched moments earlier.

<Talk to me, Tobe, where is he?> Jason sank deeply into his altered state, his voice staccato and clipped.

An icon showed up on his HUD in red, two more in green.

Shit. It looked like the pinnace had seen the other two

vessels, and was angling to intercept.

Jason boosted hard, grunting as the web of nano that was threaded throughout his soft tissues hardened to protect his internal organs against excessive *g*s. It was the first time in recent memory he'd experienced the nano's activation, outside of a flight review.

* * * * *

<*Okay, Shannon, get ready to implement evasion plan Sierra,*> Calista instructed the AI over the combat net that Shannon and Tobias had created for the three Enfield craft. Before initiating her own burn, she ran a quick systems check of her suit and its connection to the ship; everything read green.

This, plus her nano-enhanced pilot's mods, were the means by which she would survive the punishing g-forces she was about to subject her body to.

She kept one eye on the Enfield shuttle containing the rescued AIs, and the other on the pinnace that had abruptly changed vectors a moment ago.

They'd been spotted. The pinnace was hailing them.

She ignored the call, focusing instead on guiding Shannon through the evasion plan she'd decided would give the shuttle the best chance to escape.

They heard the occasional grunt over the Link as Shannon abruptly changed vectors, but Daniel remained silent. The retired ground-pounder knew his expertise wasn't of any use at the moment; he'd said as much as they'd prepared to launch from the *Sylvan*.

He'd also assured her that his years in the service had included more than his share of insertions in a dropship. It may have been a few years since he'd experienced such extreme vector shifts, but his mods could withstand whatever gs Shannon could dish out.

Right on schedule, the shuttle's path altered, taking it around one of the spire's spurs to keep moored ships between it and the pinnace as much as possible.

While Shannon led the pinnace on a twisting, curving game of hide and seek, Calista peeled off to engage.

* * * * *

<Sensors show the pinnace's weapons are online,> Tobias warned, as Jason slalomed through the ships tied to the spire at speeds that would be considered reckless even in combat.

In his altered state, the flight path seemed almost leisurely. Absently, he noted his HUD flashing a warning that his mods were reaching their upper g-limit as he directed the craft through a series of tight, complex maneuvers.

He'd pushed the tolerances before; as far as he was concerned, the upper limits were more of a suggestion than a hard and fast rule. He ignored the warning and pressed the pursuit.

He cleared a transport hauler and got eyes on his quarry. He brought the fighter's weapons online while guiding the craft into position, falling easily into the rhythm of the red dot and the reticle as he tracked his target on his HUD.

The dot that was the pinnace lined up for a breath, and with a thought, Jason squeezed off a burst from the fighter's rail-gatling gun. A flashing indicator showed that he had tagged the pinnace—but not where he'd intended.

The shot should have gone through the pinnace's engine, but its pilot jinked just as Jason launched the strike, and it holed the ship's aft cabin instead.

Tobias whistled appreciatively as the ship's sensors tagged the hole that the gatling gun had punched in the side of the pinnace. *<Looks like you bagged yourself a cabin there, boyo.>*

<I was targeting the engine,> Jason said dryly.

<I know,> the AI chuckled quietly. *<Keep it loose, Jase, you're doing fine.>*

The pinnace banked sharply, and Jason duplicated the maneuver to keep the craft within his sights. As his fighter leveled, the pinnace fired a shot at the shuttle. Calista's fighter jinked to intercept, placing her craft directly into the line of fire.

Jason held his breath as the shot scored Calista's craft, its rear port fuselage purposely taking the hit intended for the escaping shuttle.

Icarus's Elastene surfaces transmuted the shot from an initial blindingly bright point of superheated metal to a diffuse, coronal glow. The metal foam performed admirably, dissipating the shot with minimal effect to the craft.

And now it was Calista's turn to get a bead on the pinnace.

The fighters had flown between the planet and the ring, not far from where Shannon had first landed with the warehouse team. Had there been any inhabitants on that part of the ring, they would have been dazzled by the impossibly swift changes the fighters made above them.

Only Gladys—and those manning space traffic control— saw, in real-time, the true measure of the new Icarus design, as Calista and Jason pushed the fighters to their limits, determined to protect the shuttle's precious cargo.

Free of the spire and all industrial traffic, the flight had now turned into a dogfight. The fighters engaged the pinnace in a deadly dance as they looped and swerved, jinked and dove.

Once more, the pinnace maneuvered to get a clean shot at the shuttle. Calista altered course to shield it, and Jason banked hard to bring the pinnace once again into his sights.

His aim was dead on. The cannon speared the pinnace's engines, and its trajectory sent the rounds through the craft's left dorsal section, rending a hole just behind the pilot's compartment. Just then, Jason's HUD flashed a warning that the craft's pilot had ejected.

<We need to catch him, Jason! He can't get away!> Tobias' voice sounded urgently over their private Link, as Jason maneuvered the fighter to avoid collision with the broken pinnace.

<What do you mean?> Jason asked, as he automatically began reconfiguring the craft for standard flight.

<There was no time to tell you, but we only recovered two hundred and sixty AIs. Seventeen of them are missing, and that man can lead us to them.>

Well, damn, Jason thought. That just complicated matters, didn't it? He took a deep, steadying breath as he began to unstrap himself from the cradle's restraints.

<Can this suit withstand reentry?> he asked Tobias, as he double-checked its seal.

The AI nodded assent.

<All right, then, the fighter's yours, Tobe. Seeya on the flip side.>

Before he could give it much thought, Jason triggered the canopy and launched himself after the cartel boss, straight toward the surface of the planet.

* * * * *

<What in the blazing stars do you think you're **doing**, Andrews?> Calista's voice sounded sharply in his mind, but

Jason ignored her, his focus intent on the man ahead of him.

Mack had used suit thrusters to adjust his heading, and he was now on a direct intercept with the planet's surface. He gave no indication that he knew Jason was in pursuit.

Configuring himself into a trajectory for a least-time interception, Jason made micro adjustments with his own thrusters as directed by Tobias. These increased his velocity, bringing him ever closer to the man speeding toward the planet below.

He was counting on Mack not to realize he had a tail until he began his heavy braking. That braking was going to become necessary soon, to counteract the rapidly increasing velocity from the planet's pull. Even from thirty-five hundred kilometers out, they were experiencing an acceleration of four meters per second squared, straight down—and that number would continue to climb as they approached the surface.

Ordinarily, a recreational ring dive would involve a gentle braking maneuver that began around the thousand-kilometer mark. Aggressive divers wearing suits with exceptional cooling, and who were willing to subject themselves to extreme g-forces, could push that mark to five hundred kilometers, but no further. To do otherwise would mean incineration once they entered the atmospheric boundary layer that began one hundred kilometers above the planet's surface.

In Mack's case, Jason didn't think the man had ejected just to immolate himself.

He caught the pinnace tumbling away from them out of the corner of his eye, then his vision of it was occluded by one of the fighters, as it maneuvered to pace him. The other fighter matched its attitude and position on his other side.

Jason was sure that he'd later find his own personal fighter escort for a ring dive vastly amusing. Right now, his focus was riveted to the man he needed to overtake, and to the numbers on his HUD that indicated his rate of descent.

Those numbers were rapidly increasing. His velocity was seven thousand kilometers per hour, and then twelve thousand. Jason was closing on seventeen thousand when he saw the man ahead of him turn. He'd been spotted.

<*He has a weapon.*> Tobias' voice cracked in his head, sharp with warning.

<*You're too close to him, Jason. The fighters are unable to intercept.*> Calista's voice sounded in his head, calm, detached. Professional. <*Use thrusters to evade.*>

Jason's world narrowed to a pinpoint focus. He used his ocular augments to zoom in, his attention centered on the man's hand. He saw Mack bring the weapon to bear, saw the moment his finger squeezed the trigger.

Jason's heart raced and he fired a micro burst with one of his suit's thrusters, hoping the maneuver would be enough to avoid getting hit. The shot narrowly missed, and he saw the man raise his weapon once again.

A part of his brain gibbered at him, the part that was screaming, *someone's actually trying to kill me!* He ruthlessly stomped on it, realizing now was not the time to lose his shit. Instead, Jason shouldered his own weapon and sighted along its length, Tobias's warning ringing in his head. *Seventeen missing AIs.* That meant Jason could not risk killing the man before the team could extract their locations from him. But he couldn't close on the man either—not while Mack kept taking shots at him.

Jason knew his reserves were all but depleted. Shooting to incapacitate at these speeds without NSAI assistance was impossible—yet he had to try. He had to make the attempt.

Again he waited as the red dot danced with the reticle. His

first attempt went wide, and he took a deep breath, forcing himself to wait patiently for his next opportunity. Twice more, he had to abandon his own targeting in order to direct his suit's thrusters to evade as the two traded shots.

He closed his eyes for a moment. He was running out of time and he knew it. Their velocity was approaching insane levels and if he didn't close on the man and begin braking within seconds, they were both dead.

Jason forced his eyes open and squinted doggedly down the weapon's sight. *I can do this. I* **have** *to do this.* Ordering his suit's arms to lock in place, he waited for the red dot to slide inside the reticle...and squeezed gently, sending the signal for the rifle to fire. This time, the shot hit its mark, severing the cartel boss's hand from his body. The weapon tumbled free— along with the hand—and a puff of air indicated the suit's momentary loss of containment before its systems automatically resealed around the man's wrist.

The shot's impact caused Mack to begin a slow tumble. The man struggled to counter the rotation and keep his trajectory stabilized, reorienting his body along the spin axis and applying short bursts from his suit's thrusters.

Jason used the man's distraction to close the rest of the distance between them. He was just tens of meters away and he hoped to hell he'd fired his thrusters in time to slow and match velocities, or the impact would end up killing them both. Just then Mack looked up, the cartel boss's eyes widening as he realized the two men were about to collide.

Mack attempted to dodge using his own thrusters, but it was too late. Jason tucked and slammed his knees into his target's back, the delta-v knocking the other man unconscious. Jason's pilot's mods, his reinforced musculature and his carbon nanotube-laced bones, kept him from following in his enemy's wake.

<Okay, someone tell me that what I'm wearing can hack into this asshole's suit.> Jason flipped through the settings on his HUD as he waited on the combat net for an answer. He gritted his teeth, willing himself to stay alert. He could feel the crash looming, a result of operating for too long, deep within his altered state.

<Here's the command sequence. You should be able to use it to harden the nano in his suit and keep him immobilized.>

<You read my mind, Tobe.> Jason's voice sounded strained to his own ears as he manipulated the code Tobias had just sent.

Once the man was immobilized, Jason directed both suits to interlock with rupture sealant at key points of contact, reinforcing his hold on the man for reentry.

He flipped through the unconscious man's suit interface searching for thruster control to augment his own, cursing mentally as his now-overtaxed brain fumbled and refused anything faster than an L0 transmission. He eyed the twin readouts in his suit's HUD—velocity and countdown—and his heart stuttered as he realized he had less than five seconds to initiate burn.

He demanded his body dip again into its altered state and felt it refuse to obey his orders. With one second remaining, he found the command and ordered both suits to apply full reverse thrust. The burn that began at three hundred fifty kilometers lasted seventy-seven seconds. It was the minimum required to slow their nearly twenty-three thousand kilometer per hour velocity.

The suits kicked in hard, and Jason fought to remain conscious as the nano threads laced throughout his body once more hardened under the force of the deceleration.

They were nearly a hundred kilometers above the planet's

surface when they finally slowed to a safe entry velocity. The suits' thrusters shut off automatically as they reached three hundred sixty kilometers per hour—at this point it was up to El Dorado to bring them in.

Jason blinked to clear his vision and saw the numbers on his velocity indicator begin to rise once more. Next to it flashed the number of seconds remaining until that velocity reached maximum: ninety-eight seconds to go.

Jason took a few deep breaths; he just needed to remain conscious for another few minutes, then he'd give himself permission to keel over. But not yet.

<*Everything okay, boyo?*> Tobias asked cautiously.

<*All systems nominal,*> he replied. But he sent a feed from his HUD to Tobias, wishing he could get back in the fighter, but matching v while holding the cartel boss without the fighter accidentally clipping him was riskier than a planet dive.

<*You're crashing, aren't you?*> Tobias responded privately, and Jason sent him a mental nod.

<*I can make it. But just in case....*> He passed the token for his suit over the Link to the AI. <*Chute deploys at one thou. If you don't see me trigger it—*>

<*No worries. We won't let you go splat.*>

Jason's lips twitched at that. <*Didn't think you would.*>

The trip turned bumpy as the two figures began to be buffeted by air resistance, and Jason's HUD's temperature readouts began to climb as friction increased their drag.

Those frictional forces were working to transform the kinetic energy of each man into more than twelve million joules of thermal energy, as their speed rose to nearly thirty-four hundred kilometers per hour.

Sweat began to trickle down Jason's face, and he gave his

head a quick snap to keep it out of his eyes.

His eyes.... He began to see black spots, and his vision began to tunnel.

His jaw set. *I will **not** pass out.*

At one kilometer, they had slowed to almost two hundred twenty kilometers per hour.

It was time. Jason triggered the suit's drogue chute, rapidly slowing their descent. Total time would be just under twenty-three minutes from when Jason left the fighter to the moment freefall ended.

He glanced up at the ring and then back down, his gaze catching on the puffy cotton clouds that were drifting lazily below. His eyes flicked up to the readout that showed his suit rapidly cooling in the crisp, El Dorado air as the canopy floated them gently to meet the ground.

The breeze caught the chute, twisting himself and his passenger around.

The last thing he registered was a spectacular view of the planet's 'wink and smile' before his eyes rolled back in his head, and he knew no more.

JASON'S CALLING

STELLAR DATE: 07.09.3189 (Adjusted Gregorian)
LOCATION: Muzhavi Forest Preserve
REGION: El Dorado, Alpha Centauri System

"And in other news today, it would appear that Rosalind Bianchi, Minister of the Interior, has withdrawn from the senatorial race, citing personal concerns and a need to spend more time with family...."

"Kind of hard to believe this is where it all began, just five days ago."

Jason stood at the base of the trail, Tobi by his side, looking up the seven hundred meter incline before them.

"Mmm," Calista agreed noncommittally, as she clipped her water collector to her belt. She leaned into him and he wrapped his arm around her waist as she looked critically at the peak. "Doesn't look any different from here."

"It wouldn't. The rockfall was on the opposite face." Jason looked down at Calista. "Ready?"

"Lead on," she said and reached for her pack.

Jason expanded the field on the cat's harness, and Tobi raced up the trail. He heard Tobias laugh as the cat stretched herself to her full length against a nearby tree, and her centimeter-long nails kneaded at its bark.

Jason wandered over, rubbing the cat along her spine beneath the harness. Fully elongated like this, she came almost to his shoulders. Tobi leaned into his scratch for a moment, rubbing her cheek affectionately against his.

She turned and gave Calista a cursory lick on the cheek, then bounded away, sniffing at a nearby rock before crouching and launching herself atop it in one massive leap.

"Hey, don't leave us behind!" Calista called out as the cat continued her off-trail ascent.

Jason smiled to himself at Tobias' rejoinder. <*If she catches something and eats it in front of me, I promise to share every gory detail with the both of you.*>

Jason broke into a run. "Okay, okay! We're coming!"

<*You know she's too social to wander very far,*> the AI assured them. <*Give her a moment to scent her surroundings. I've only expanded the field to one klick; she'll come back in a few.*>

As they walked, Calista glanced sideways at Jason.

"You owe me an apology, you know," she said abruptly.

Jason blinked. He wracked his brain, but damned if he could figure that one out.

"A little help?" he requested after a beat. "I can't think of anything I've done to warrant an apology, but you know us guys."

"How about jumping out of a perfectly serviceable fighter—and my prized prototype? You scared the hell out of me, Jason."

Hmmm. Maybe he did owe her an apology. Though she needed to apologize first, for the comments she'd made about the Yak.

"Well, if I recall correctly, you've already questioned my sanity once." Jason looked over at her with a frown. " 'You have to wonder about the intelligence of a man who would entrust his life to a few sticks and some canvas'." Jason mimicked Calista's voice as he repeated what she'd said back at the air show.

Doesn't that seem a lifetime ago now.

"Hmmmph," was all Calista uttered in response.

"Well," Jason said judiciously, "you knew your fighter was

going to be fine. Tobias was flying it, so there was never any danger—"

Calista hauled her fist back and hit him in the arm as hard as she could.

"Owww!"

"*That* was for scaring me shitless with that freefall stunt, mister."

"Oh."

They met a few hikers along the way, most of them on their way back down, their day almost complete. Several paused to admire the sinewy length of Jason's feline companion, a few even reaching out to let her sniff their hands after a look at Jason for permission.

Tobi took the attention as her due, to the amusement of both humans.

At the top, Calista and Jason sat, staring down at the rocks that had tumbled to the base of the cliff. Tobi lay sprawled on a boulder, soaking in the warmth of the late afternoon sun.

<*Well, this is interesting,*> Tobias said, after a moment of companionable silence had passed between the three.

"What's up, Tobe?"

<*TransOrbital Systems just announced it's pulling its bid for the Avalon Mining heavy haulers. Press report says the CEO discovered information indicating that their new design was based on stolen property.*>

Calista nodded. "So she went public with it. Interesting."

Jason cocked an eyebrow at her inquisitively.

"Their CEO contacted Terrance this morning to let him know that she didn't need the cartel's help to make TransOrbital the superior—and preferred—supplier." Calista chuckled. "As apologies went, it was a bit on the snarky side. She told him she preferred to kick his ass honestly."

Jason smirked. "I'd have loved to have seen Terrance's face when she said that."

"Speaking of which," Calista turned serious eyes on Jason. "Have you thought any more about Terrance's offer?"

"Yeah," he said thoughtfully, hands filled with pebbles he rhythmically tossed over the edge. "The thought of helping to find those missing AIs is…" he shrugged, then continued after a moment. "It feels right somehow. I think my grandma Cara would be proud. It's something a Sykes would do."

Calista cocked her head. "You'll have to tell me about her sometime. I'd love to hear firsthand how the stories I read in school measure up to the real thing."

Jason scowled at the cliff's edge, throwing a rock with enough force to pulverize it against the rocks below. "I can tell you right now Victoria North wouldn't have made it off the Sylvan alive if Cara'd been there."

Calista took a deep breath, her gaze drifting from his face to the cat and then back again. In a quiet voice she asked, "Do you regret letting her live?"

"What she's done…I'm not sure she deserves to live," he responded after a moment, his voice bitter.

"You're not a killer, Jason."

"I should've made an exception for her."

Calista turned to Jason and grabbed his elbow, shaking it lightly. "There's still the trial. You'll have your chance to make sure she pays for what she did, and see that justice is served."

<It'll take some time, even with all the information Ben's asset managed to bring with him,> Tobias added quietly, <but she'll get her due.>

They lapsed into silence for a moment, each preoccupied with their own thoughts.

"You know," Calista said, "it's a bit scary to realize how thoroughly the cartel has infiltrated El Dorado. Once the Secret Intelligence Service turned Mack over to the ESF, cartel operatives working from the inside made sure he couldn't talk. The man was dead within a week."

Jason's expression turned grim. "Yeah, Ben's got his work cut out for him, cleaning that mess up. But it looks like Lysander's election as majority leader is pretty much guaranteed, now that Rosalind Bianchi dropped out.

"With the Old Man in place, Ben'll have some strong backing. Hopefully all the stonewalling he's been complaining about will come to an end, at least."

"Too bad about Rosalind's health, and that sudden need to devote time to her family, isn't it?"

Jason leaned back, returning her grin.

"Woman, remind me never to get on your bad side."

She directed a mischievous grin toward Jason. "Who's to say you haven't already?"

THE END

* * * * *

And with that, Jason and Terrance have been set upon a road that will lead them to the *Intrepid* and Tanis. But that mighty ship's journey is still many hundreds of years in the future.

In the meantime, there are AIs to save, and the Enfield empire to build.

Follow Jason Andrews and his mission to find the remaining AIs in the next Enfield Genesis novel, ***Proxima Centauri***.

* * * * *

Independent authors need your support. Amazon promotes books that get reviews and keeps them at the top of lists without authors having to spend money on ads and promotions. Your review is a tremendous help to us and the stories we are making.

If you liked this book, and are enjoying the adventures of Jason and Terrance, please leave a review, it means a lot to us. Also, if you want more Aeon 14, plus some exclusive perks, you can support me on www.patreon.com/mdcooper, or join www.facebookcom/groups/aeon14fans.

Thank you for taking the time to read *Alpha Centauri*, and we look forward to seeing you again in the next book!

AFTERWORD

There are many things I love about the Aeon 14 universe. I love the complexity of the characters and their vulnerability. While they may be larger than life, they are still subject *to* life. And just like us, they must learn to adapt, grow, forgive and overcome.

I also love Michael's dedication to science, and his drive to accurately represent as much as can be extrapolated, given the sheer scope of time the series covers.

But there is one aspect of Michael's writing that continues to capture my imagination and has earned my undying respect: his strong female characters.

As a pilot, this speaks to me in a powerful way, especially given that we women comprise fewer than seven percent of all licensed pilots in the U.S. It would seem we have a ways to go before women like Tanis and Calista become more commonplace, but books like those in Aeon 14 help to pave the way.

So thank you, Michael.

There are two other men I must thank: my father, and my brilliant and talented husband, Marty. The latter has served as advisor and physicist-on-call for all manner of questions I have thrown at him. ("But if they wanted to eject five *thousand* kilometers above the planet...?" You get the idea.)

As to the former....

I have my dad to thank for my love of science fiction. Being a NASA brat meant my childhood was filled with equal parts Asimov and

Apollo, McCaffrey and Mission Control. It was an incredible way to grow up.

Another great legacy he left behind was the realization that learning could be fun. I think science fiction does this beautifully. It serves up knowledge, education, and an expansion of our awareness—not just of the sciences, but of our own human condition—in a fun and entertaining way.

I passionately believe that to stop learning is to allow a part of you to die. Hopefully, though, if we've done our part right, it won't *feel* like learning. Instead, you'll find yourself immersed in an engaging story, and come away having discovered something you hadn't known before you began this journey with us.

Thanks for reading, and here's to many more.
Fair skies!

Lisa Richman
Leawood, KS

THE BOOKS OF AEON 14

Keep up to date with what is releasing in Aeon 14 with the free Aeon 14 Reading Guide.

The Intrepid Saga (The Age of Terra)
- Book 1: Outsystem
- Book 2: A Path in the Darkness
- Book 3: Building Victoria

- The Intrepid Saga Omnibus – *Also contains Destiny Lost, book 1 of the Orion War series*

- Destiny Rising – *Special Author's Extended Edition comprised of both Outsystem and A Path in the Darkness with over 100 pages of new content.*

The Orion War
- Book 1: Destiny Lost
- Book 2: New Canaan
- Book 3: Orion Rising
- Book 4: The Scipio Alliance
- Book 5: Attack on Thebes
- Book 6: War on a Thousand Fronts
- Book 7: Fallen Empire (2018)
- Book 8: Airtha Ascendancy (2018)
- Book 9: The Orion Front (2018)
- Book 10: Starfire (2019)
- Book 11: Race Across Time (2019)
- Book 12: Return to Sol (2019)

Tales of the Orion War
- Book 1: Set the Galaxy on Fire
- Book 2: Ignite the Stars

- Book 3: Burn the Galaxy to Ash (2018)

Perilous Alliance (Age of the Orion War – w/Chris J. Pike)
- Book 1: Close Proximity
- Book 2: Strike Vector
- Book 3: Collision Course
- Book 4: Impact Imminent
- Book 5: Critical Inertia (2018)

Rika's Marauders (Age of the Orion War)
- Prequel: Rika Mechanized
- Book 1: Rika Outcast
- Book 2: Rika Redeemed
- Book 3: Rika Triumphant
- Book 4: Rika Commander
- Book 5: Rika Infiltrator (2018)
- Book 6: Rika Unleashed (2018)
- Book 7: Rika Conqueror (2019)

Perseus Gate (Age of the Orion War)
Season 1: Orion Space
- Episode 1: The Gate at the Grey Wolf Star
- Episode 2: The World at the Edge of Space
- Episode 3: The Dance on the Moons of Serenity
- Episode 4: The Last Bastion of Star City
- Episode 5: The Toll Road Between the Stars
- Episode 6: The Final Stroll on Perseus's Arm
- Eps 1-3 Omnibus: The Trail Through the Stars
- Eps 4-6 Omnibus: The Path Amongst the Clouds

Season 2: Inner Stars
- Episode 1: A Meeting of Bodies and Minds
- Episode 3: A Deception and a Promise Kept
- Episode 3: A Surreptitious Rescue of Friends and Foes (2018)
- Episode 4: A Trial and the Tribulations (2018)

- Episode 5: A Deal and a True Story Told (2018)
- Episode 6: A New Empire and An Old Ally (2018)

Season 3: AI Empire
- Episode 1: Restitution and Recompense (2019)
- Five more episodes following…

The Warlord (Before the Age of the Orion War)
- Book 1: The Woman Without a World
- Book 2: The Woman Who Seized an Empire
- Book 3: The Woman Who Lost Everything

The Sentience Wars: Origins (Age of the Sentience Wars – w/James S. Aaron)
- Book 1: Lyssa's Dream
- Book 2: Lyssa's Run
- Book 3: Lyssa's Flight
- Book 4: Lyssa's Call
- Book 5: Lyssa's Flame (June 2018)

Enfield Genesis (Age of the Sentience Wars – w/Lisa Richman)
- Book 1: Alpha Centauri
- Book 2: Proxima Centauri (2018)

Hand's Assassin (Age of the Orion War – w/T.G. Ayer)
- Book 1: Death Dealer
- Book 2: Death Mark (August 2018)

Machete System Bounty Hunter (Age of the Orion War – w/Zen DiPietro)
- Book 1: Hired Gun
- Book 2: Gunning for Trouble
- Book 3: With Guns Blazing (June 2018)

Vexa Legacy (Age of the FTL Wars – w/Andrew Gates)

LISA RICHMAN & M. D. COOPER

- Book 1: Seas of the Red Star

Building New Canaan (Age of the Orion War – w/J.J. Green
- Book 1: Carthage (2018)

Fennington Station Murder Mysteries (Age of the Orion War)
- Book 1: Whole Latte Death (w/Chris J. Pike)
- Book 2: Cocoa Crush (w/Chris J. Pike)

The Empire (Age of the Orion War)
- The Empress and the Ambassador (2018)
- Consort of the Scorpion Empress (2018)
- By the Empress's Command (2018)

Tanis Richards: Origins (The Age of Terra)
- Prequel: Storming the Norse Wind (At the Helm Volume 3)
- Book 1: Shore Leave (June 2018)
- Book 2: The Command (July 2018)
- Book 3: Infiltrator (July 2018)

The Sol Dissolution (The Age of Terra)
- Book 1: Venusian Uprising (2018)
- Book 2: Scattered Disk (2018)
- Book 3: Jovian Offensive (2019)
- Book 4: Fall of Terra (2019)

The Delta Team Chronicles (Expanded Orion War)
- A "Simple" Kidnapping (Pew! Pew! Volume 1)
- The Disknee World (Pew! Pew! Volume 2)
- It's Hard Being a Girl (Pew! Pew! Volume 4)
- A Fool's Gotta Feed (Pew! Pew! Volume 4)
- Rogue Planets and a Bored Kitty (Pew! Pew! Volume 5)

ABOUT THE AUTHORS

Lisa Richman lives in the great Midwest, with three cats, a physicist, and a Piper Cherokee. She met the physicist when she went back to get her master's in physics (she ended up marrying the physicist instead).
When she's not writing, her day job takes her behind the camera as a director/producer.

If she's not at her keyboard or on set, she can be found cruising at altitude. Or helping out the physics guy with his linear accelerator. Or feeding the cats. Or devouring the next SF book she finds.

* * * * *

Michael Cooper likes to think of himself as a jack-of-all-trades (and hopes to become master of a few). When not writing, he can be found writing software, working in his shop at his latest carpentry project, or likely reading a book.

He shares his home with a precocious young girl, his wonderful wife (who also writes), two cats, a never-ending list of things he would like to build, and ideas...

Find out what's coming next at www.aeon14.com

75646882R00154

Made in the USA
Middletown, DE
07 June 2018